UniformsEx

Erotic Stories of Women in Service

Edited by Linnea Due

alyson books

los angeles | new york

MANUFACTURED IN THE UNITED STATES OF AMERICA.

THIS TRADE PAPERBACK ORIGINAL IS PUBLISHED BY ALYSON PUBLICATIONS,
P.O. BOX 4371, LOS ANGELES, CA 90078-4371.
DISTRIBUTION IN THE UNITED KINGDOM BY TURNAROUND PUBLISHER SERVICES LTD.,
UNIT 3, OLYMPIA TRADING ESTATE, COBURG ROAD, WOOD GREEN,
LONDON N22 6TZ ENGLAND.

FIRST EDITION: SEPTEMBER 2000

00 01 02 03 04 🅰 10 9 8 7 6 5 4 3 2 1

ISBN 1-55583-545-7

LIBRARY OF CONGRESS CATALOGING-IN-PUBLICATION DATA
  UNIFORM SEX : EROTIC STORIES OF WOMEN IN SERVICE / EDITED BY
  LINNEA DUE.—1ST ED.
    ISBN 1-55583-545-7
    1. LESBIANS—FICTION. 2. EROTIC STORIES, AMERICAN. 3. LESBIANS' WRITINGS,
  AMERICAN. 4. UNIFORMS—FICTION. I. TITLE: UNIFORM SEX. II. DUE, LINNEA A.
  PS648.L47 U55 2000
  813'.540803538—DC21   00-032772

CREDITS
COVER PHOTOGRAPHY BY PHYLLIS CHRISTOPHER.
COVER DESIGN BY PHILIP PIROLO.

Contents

Introduction

When I was a kid, my favorite outfit was a white sailor's suit, which I wore everywhere I could, and certainly every time we played war. When I wore that uniform I was someone else—not a girl, not a child, but a young man with a mission. That this last persona more closely described my growing sense of myself had a lot to do with my never wanting to take off that sailor suit.

Uniforms are the embodiment of paradox. They hide and reveal at once; they are an absence of individuality and a potent statement of individual truth. And as the wonderful stories in this volume prove, they—and their swirling contradictions—are damned sexy.

Navy SEALS in the swamp? Catholic school girls? Candy stripers dispensing massages? That whoa-handsome park ranger? Find your fetish and feast.

But don't forget the yin and yang of it. A uniform that holds great personal truth for the wearer can also serve to conceal that wearer from an admirer blinded by the cloth. Not sure what I mean? Read J.M. Redmann's "Naked."

In "High Pressure," a firefighter comes home to sleep, but her girlfriend has other ideas. In J.L. Belrose's "House Arrest," the uniform takes on a life—and an authority—of its own. Food service employees get toasted in "Fries With That?" and "The Cafeteria Lady." Cecilia Tan takes us into the world of high school marching bands in "Drumbeat."

Although opening up opportunities, uniforms can also symbolize limitations. Putting on a uniform coincides with circumstances that force the protagonists apart in Jane Futcher's wistful "Betty and Veronica." And in Yolanda Wallace's "Full Service," a gas station attendant confronts the poverty of her world when she meets a uniform-lover who is as much an icon as the mechanic herself; the mechanic is coaxed to see herself in a way she'd been too hemmed in to glimpse.

Each story in this collection has similar complexities; places where the individual and the collective, the iconic and the down-to-earth, bump into each other—sometimes painfully, sometimes ecstatically. What's certain is that when those edges meet, sparks fly.

Linnea Due
August 2000

Drumbeat Cecilia Tan

*I met her at the—ha!—*hot dog stand behind the bleachers in West River Stadium. The woman who taught me the thing I didn't know. I'll get to that in a minute. There I was, standing in line for a Coke, served flat in a waxy cup with a cracked translucent plastic lid crunched down on top of it, when I noticed her in the next line over, with a couple of other Wildcats. The sound of drums thundered off the concrete walls of the stadium as another corps took its place on the field. I inched closer to the front of the line.

Miles of leg. That's what I was thinking as I looked her over. She wore spotless white over-the-calf boots; they must have been custom jobs given how they fit. Not a stupid Dallas Cowgirl-type fringe boot or anything but a genuine up-to-the-knee majorette boot, laced tight, without a grass stain or smudge. Her tights were something skin-tone but spangly, which made her thighs look as long as a summer day, topped by the perfect white at the bottom of her leotard. Her jacket was white, double-breasted, two rows of brass buttons marching over the hills of her chest in front, long seams of gold running down satin-lined tails in the back, hiding the curve of her ass like a stage curtain. Hung on one arm was her hat, a smart, pseu-do-military affair, and tucked under that same arm was her baton. Not a twirling baton, mind you—a majorette baton. She tossed her shoulder-length blonde hair back from her gold epaulettes, and my breath caught in my throat. This woman was born to lead.

I'd seen her the day before at the hotel where several of the drum and bugle corps were staying. Out in the parking lot, she'd been supervising the loading of the Wildcat flags and banners into a rental truck. She'd been wearing a pair of running shorts and a T-shirt tied at the waist into a sexy knot; I'd kind of tucked the image of her into the back of my mind.

But seeing her there by the hot dog stand in her full regalia…well, let's just say if I'd been in the Union army and she'd been in the Confederacy, I'd have switched from blue to gray in an instant. As it was, I was standing there in the uniform of the Atlanta Zephyrs, which did have a sort of faux Civil War look to them. I liked the Zephyr uniform, which squared my shoulders and had copious pockets inside, although the black pants were hell during the summer parade season. I had buzzed my hair short, and under the plastic lining of my hat I could feel sweat prickling. What was I going to say to her? I knew I had to say something. It's not every day you see a girl in the concession line who makes your throat go dry.

She turned around and saw me looking and smiled like she rec-ognized me from the hotel lobby. Heck, maybe we had even met before—the Wildcats and Zephyrs had both done the parade on the Fourth of July in Wilmington, Virginia. I smiled back and waved, the white gloves tucked in my sleeve peeking out to wave too.

Then she was at the front of her line and I was at the front of mine, and I lost track of her for a minute, until she found me stand-ing next to the condiment table gnawing on my straw. She bit into a hot pretzel, wrinkled her nose, then dropped its corpse into an empty waste barrel where it hit bottom with a gong-like clang.

"When do you go on?" she asked casually, saving me the need to invent an opening line.

"Second to last, I think," I said. "And you're last, right?"

She smiled a pretty, pretending-to-be modest smile. The Wildcats had won the Mayor's Cup the year before, and thus had the privilege of going last in this year's competition. "That's right," she answered. She had one manicured hand wrapped around the ball end of the baton, and the white finger tips of her gloves were sprouting from inside her hat, hung on her arm like a sand pail. "What do you play?"

The question caught me off guard—I was too busy looking at how the gold-trimmed collar on her jacket accentuated her long, graceful neck.

"Tuba," I blurted.

"Aha," she nodded. Most of my cohorts were wandering around with trumpets or coronets in hand, but the tuba just wasn't practical to carry around. We had piled our sousaphones and drums at the edge of the field, waiting for our turn.

Suddenly her hand was reaching toward me like she was going to brush some lint off my jacket, but instead she brushed her fingers against my lips and said, in a low voice so I almost could not hear her against the blare of brass echoing off the walls, "I hear tuba players have the softest lips."

Well, I wasn't about to turn down an invitation like that, not with her spangly thighs all a-beckoning and her white gloves a-peeking.... We adjourned to the Wildcats' equipment truck.

The clasp of her collar came undone, and I slid my hands along her jaws, cradling her head as I kissed her. I don't know about other tuba players, but I do have damn soft lips. Hers quivered, and I made my way down her body, parting the starchy wool of her jacket to find the satin lining underneath. My hands cupped spandex-encased breasts inside their satin outer wrap, my thumbs ranging over her hardening nipples. Then I buried my face there, in the sweet smell of parade sweat, dry-cleaned satin and wool, and the tang of her skin. My hands slid around to her buttocks, and she sucked in her breath.

Suddenly there was one white boot against my shoulder as she leaned back against the driver's side door and pushed me down. I gladly buried my face between those sparkly nylon thighs, my tongue lapping at the perfect 50%-polyester white triangle that was her most tender place.

But a tongue isn't enough to penetrate lycra. She had a wicked gleam in her eye as she picked her baton off the dashboard. One end was round, the bulb handle, but the other was pointed—not sharp, but pointed, tapering to a point slightly blunter than a knitting needle. She ran the tip down her crotch and over the spot where I guessed her clit was. She drew tight circles with it on the taut cloth, then slid down farther in the seat, bringing both booted feet up and spreading her legs as wide as the seat would allow.

I saw it then, the one imperfection in her uniform, where the seam had given up the ghost, where the spangle met the white in the crook of her leg…and she handed me the baton.

I eased the tip into the hole in the fabric, widening it and letting it slide up and down her cunt. When I pulled it out, the tip was wet, and I tasted the honey I found there. Then I slid my finger into the hole, and into her.

Her eyes closed, and her whole body relaxed as I sent my finger probing into her wet cleft. It was she who taught me what that hole was for. I'd always been more of clit girl myself, and my last girlfriend hadn't liked penetration all that much. But there, with my finger snug deep inside her, I learned at last there's no more intimate thing. She had, literally, opened up and let me in.

I let a second finger follow the first, holding my hand in bang-bang-you're-dead pistol position, my thumb planted firmly on her clit, my hand rocking to the rhythm of another band leaving the field, and thinking to myself, when she high-steps she'll feel this juice between her lips; when she goes down to one knee in her salute, she'll feel the empty place where my fingers were. She was just starting to pant hard when I pulled my fingers away.

"Hey..." she said as I sat back.

I pursed my tuba-playing lips. "Consider that a down payment. You can collect the rest tonight. If the Wildcats win, I'll do whatever you want."

She wrinkled her nose and threw back that perfect blonde hair. "And if the Zephyrs win?"

I told her I'd expect the same. But that was all talk, because in the end, the Garfield Cadets won, and she and I spent the night as intimately as we could anyway.

2

Fries With That? Lauren Dockett

One out of every eight Americans has worked at McDonald's.

You've done it to me again. I'm speeding down 295 in the middle of the day with hot tears streaming down my cheeks and my car speakers so angrily amped, they're shaking. The fall wind is blowing my ears cold, but I'm keeping the window rolled down for punishment. I can't get our fight out of my mind.

Twenty minutes ago we were fucking. I was coming and you were coming and all was wet and good between us. Then a joke I made in the afterglow got shot down. The edge that took over your voice turned into an incredulous stare, and a moment later we were both screaming.

When I walked out, you were yelling at me from the bedroom like a crazy person, your naked body red with rage. When I turned back to glare at you, you had gotten up onto your knees, your neck veins pushing purple and your tight lips pinched and white and pulling off your gums like a dog's. All the want that was in me half an hour before evaporated at the sight.

That's the image I can't shake as I pull off the highway to pee.

There's a McD's at this exit. I remember it from high school road trips. Without you with me, I'm just going to march right in there and use the bathroom. No buying anything. Now that would surely piss you off. "The poor kids who work there," you'd lecture me, "make next to nothing, and they're made to enforce the customer to pee-er ratio." It never fails to amaze me how you can muster solidarity for absolute strangers and make no effort to try to understand me.

There's a line of mud-stained soccer girls inside at the women's bathroom, and that yellow crime-scene tape is cordoning off the men's. The longer I stand in line, the more conspicuous I feel, and the madder that makes me. You and your hypocrisy. Open relationship, you said. Monogamy is an opiate. You preached to me about how incidental fucking around can be and encouraged me to find out for myself. So I did it. I slept with the guy who dances at Cheri's bar. But when I joked about how much easier it is getting you off than it was trying to please his prima donna self, you started to lose it.

"Jesus, I can't believe you fucked him," you said, rolling away from me under the sheets.

My skin grew warm with anger, but I held back to let you dig yourself a little deeper. "How…do…you…know…he's…clean?" And you exploded it. That festering blister of truth you'd been denying. It's always fine when the polyfidelitous dyke wants to have her fun, but let a bisexual try it out with the boys and the game's going to get nasty.

"Wake up!" I screamed. "You knew what was at stake when you asked for this. This is what you get for not being able to love me. This is all your doing!"

The McDonald's kids are darting about the back tables. They're sliding little hills of salt and ketchup packets into dustpans, and their drone presence is making me nervous. I finally make it into the john and sidestep one of the soccer girls at the sink. She's left a sweaty ring on the toilet seat, which brings your pissed face back to mind. The room smells like grease and bleach, and when I get out I think

I'll get food after all. Who knows how long I'll be driving, now that you've made me run away like this.

I step up to the counter and order a fish sandwich. You'd be rolling your eyes at me right about now, but the pimply kid behind the register doesn't care that I'm eating real meat. She's searching the touch pad for the right colored square when I notice how completely different her uniform is. Gone is the cardboard brown polyester from my youth. She's got on a polo shirt and a baseball cap. She looks sporty, like she could just as easily be coming off a morning run as pushing french fries. Sure enough, she says it: "Fries with that?"

I've told you about the boy I did in the back of McDonald's the summer before college. You didn't seem to mind him. In fact, you've asked me to tell that story again and again. It gets you all hot, and then we laugh afterward about what might've gotten into the special sauce.

You've never slept with a boy. I know how much "butcher" you were than me as a youngster, how much butcher you still are, but I started in on girls earlier than you. My high school girlfriend's fist had long since cracked me wide when I had this guy. He was my first boy ever. The first dick I'd seen, first tender balls I'd ever touched. And when he unzipped those stiff polyblend supercreased pants for me, I remember being filled with awe.

I still felt outright admiration when I was 18 for anyone who would expose their stuff to me. I was so Catholic. So embarrassed about the way I smelled and how I used my pussy for peeing. When my girlfriend would give it to me, I'd take her cunt into my hands and mouth with a mix of shame and pride. It must mean something, I used to think. Something like she loves me or is so hot for me that she can't help giving in to the urge to do this. I always played with her for long stretches, lingering in her tart new scent, holding my tongue strong when she came. When she'd let go like that, of so much teenage modesty, it felt like a small miracle. I started believing sex was the secret promise of life, what the world was all about.

The anger in your face today makes me think maybe I wasn't so far off the mark.

I knew the McDonald's guy from school. Bobby something or other. He'd graduated like me and was still in town waiting to go to music school. He played the tenor sax in the marching band and had fingers so long they'd wrap around his instrument when the band would swing and dip on the playing field. He also had a head of wiry hair, funky and pushy enough to work its way under those purple band berets. That night he was mopping the floors, diddling the mop handle like it was his sax. His puff of black hair had edged the papery uniform cap into a jaunty, precarious crown on top of his head.

I was drunk. I'd just spent another pretend dinner in Carol's basement, doing her and drinking her dad's J&B. I had to bike home with a bellyful of postsex pee. The promise of a toilet was calling to me as soon as I spotted those golden arches through the late-night mist. When I got to the side entrance it must have been close to midnight, and the big glass door stuck when I pulled. I pounded at Bobby through the glass, tried smiling big and doing the universal got-to-pee dance. He let me in.

Bobby was a good-looking boy, and it felt to me like one more teenager's curse, having that kind of beauty boxed in by a doofy uniform. He had a nice big mouth, enormous girlish eyes, and a sexy could-have-been-broken kind of a nose. He went to lean his mop against the kitchen door to unlock the bathroom, and I saw, on the middle finger of his right hand, a thick scar that snaked past his knuckle. The sight of it then, rising like a vein over stretched skin, made my drunken head a little dizzier. When he caught me looking, he said, "Dog bite," smiled, and reached past me with the keys.

A toughie, I thought, who'd survived a vicious canine attack. The idea of it, man against beast, man definitely wearing something hotter than this, gave me a swooner's moment, and I closed my eyes to the intense nerdiness of his uniform, trying to savor the dense foot of space between us.

When I came out of the bathroom he was still standing there, leaning slack-shouldered against the men's room door and spinning the keys. I swayed up and pressed into him with a thank-you hug. He smelled like Tide and Pert shampoo under all that grease, and the polyester of his shirt scratched against my bare summer arms.

The hug was where it all started. When I slid down to pull away, his cock had risen against my hip. I stepped back to stare, like the drunken schoolgirl I was, and when I looked from the crotch-strain to his face he flushed with embarrassment. We smiled at each other, and I, operating under some drunken force, watched as my tanned right hand lifted from my side to land on the rock in his pants. I remember thinking, justifying, that I reached toward the bulge more to comfort him than anything else. But my action had the opposite effect. He stood there frozen, getting, I knew, dangerously close to feeling ridiculous. The discomfort made me hot, and I grabbed his scarred hand and pushed a finger past my lips. I sucked, spreading warmth between us, taking one long finger after another. All of them tasted like too many fries, with a hint, a top scent, of bleach.

His breathing got higher the longer I sucked, and when I looked up his beautiful lashes had closed, the hat was somehow gone, and his free hair peaked in its absent shape. *What am I doing here?* I was thinking between fingers. *My girlfriend will kill me.*

But by then my body had gone automatic, and I reached to pull him in, my free hand grabbing a fistful of polyester at his chest. He took a step toward me, and the fry smell whooshed in. I walked my hand under his shirt, and the feel of his hot stomach skin brought an ache back to my pussy. *Aw, Carol*, I thought. *Shit.*

Bobby's fingers were filling my mouth like thick salted candy, and my ears had started to ring with his low moans. Flashing on my girlfriend wasn't enough to make me stop. We stayed that way for a heated second, his arm coming around my back to press us together harder, the air between us a noxious blend of whiskey breath and a shift's worth of grease. I pulled his fingers out of my mouth and reached up for his mouth instead. His larger lips sealed off mine, and his tongue pushed through, filling me better than his fingers, pressing into tissue and tongue and watering glands.

With my free hand I tugged at the bottom of his shirt. He backed off to raise the scratchy pullover away from the soft muscle of his belly. A sweet line of thin black curls trailed from his navel to his waistband's straining metal clip. I wanted in there.

Bobby crossed his arms in front of his naked chest, making a show of his modesty, and we both started to giggle. He tugged at my shirt with a frown, and as I pulled it off he whistled in air. "God," he said in a whisper, and I looked down. No bra. *Shit*, I thought again. *Carol*. My girlfriend had ripped the bra off hours ago, and it was now scrunched somewhere in the bottom of my backpack. Before I could think, Bobby's hands went right to my breasts, and he splayed his fingers for a gentle feel. My giggling came back, and he smiled big, his eyes fastening on my nipples as they grew. "It's cold," I said. "Uh-huh," he answered. I liked this boy.

My hands went to his arms, and he pushed against my breasts, walking us backward toward the booths. When my ass bumped a table top he reached down to lift me up, but I stopped him, emboldened, and slid around to get in front of him, pushing his own ass against the plastic table, reaching again for his cock.

Going down on Bobby was like touching some outer edge. The stale smell of his wet balls and the tricky seam of his cock's head were so strange to me, but pulling him into my mouth, like Carol and I had groggily watched countless women do on late-night Showtime, felt just right. In a flash I was sure of the adept power of my mouth and the easy slack in my jaw. I closed my eyes and took his tiny ass in my hands, pushing him against the back of my throat and stretching my tongue to the fuzzy base of his shaft. He moaned above me, unsteadily placing his hands in my hair.

"Your change," said the girl behind the counter, and I blinked her sporty self back into view.

"Right," I mumbled, uncurling my hot palm and reaching toward the money, my face growing warm from the sin of my thoughts. I pushed Bobby out of my mind and worked up the courage to ask, "When did you get those new uniforms?"

Back in the car with the fish and fries on my lap, I think about how fast he came. How I didn't know enough to catch his come and spit it onto the shiny floor, and how when he was done the drunken spell broke. I was sober as soon as I was off my knees, and I thought I'd be cheating a little less if I got out of there right then. I kissed him and stepped away, grabbing my shirt and giggling. "Wait," he said. But I wouldn't stop. I smiled at him one last time and ran for my bike.

When I first told you this story, you gave me shit for that. For not getting my own. But I had just been with Carol and needed nothing more from Bobby. Since then I've gotten all of what I need from all sorts of people. A fact you say impresses you. But after today, I don't know that I believe you.

I want to hear it from you. What you think of your plan now. Whether the pain of what I've done with this latest boy is calling all this nonmonogamy into question. I want a promise to look at me anew. An effort to understand what it might be like to lose me to another lover. This is no longer high school, I want you to know. This is true love. So I go back.

You're in the garage, hammering at that new chair for your baby niece, your tattooed arms brown and flexing, your ex's name in black-green cursive getting longer, then fatter on your bicep with every strike. Your short showered hair glistens in the late-day sun, and I know that you've gone and tried to wash off the pain. Your face is soap-dry and intense until you see me pulling into the driveway. Then the tautness lets loose, and you start to crumple. You lay down the hammer and turn toward the car. You're not going to come to me, but you have to keep one hand on the worktable for balance. I know you're going dizzy with emotion, and I walk to you quickly, taking your weak-kneed weight into my arms.

"Baby, I'm so sorry..." you start.

"Shhh," I tell you, and neither of us can stop from crying. Your strong face is a wet pillow on my neck, and I pull you as tight as I can, whispering your name while you sob. Your thick fingers pull and smooth my hair while I tell you I love you: "More than anyone, I love you." I say it again and again, and you choke on your sobs, coughing and catching your breath and finally raising your slick wet face to kiss me. Your lips are a sop of salty tears, and I kiss you hard to stop their flow. I want you to breathe into my kiss, to transfer all the hurt to our hungry mouths and let it go completely. The moment comes when you push back at me with hot lips and tongue. Your strength is returning, and your desire slices through my leftover anger until all I can feel is your want. "Baby," I cry, and my hands reach up to pull at that solid place in your upper back, the place that convinces me of what I have. I dig in hard with my nails.

"What am I doing to us?" you want to know between kisses.

"You're making it too hard," I tell you. Your hands drop onto my shoulders, quieting us both. I start to open my mouth again, ready to launch into an explanation of how unloved I'm feeling, how creepy things get when I do sleep around. But your voice beats mine. "I don't want us to have to be everything to each other," you say.

I can't help it; it just comes out. "You already are everything to me."

"Jesus, Jane," you say, and it sounds an awful lot like forgiveness and realization and regret. You step up to me, taking my smaller face in your hands; your workwoman's palms a sandy caress on my cheeks. There's a confused half-smile on your face as you back me up to the table's edge.

I bend back in front of you, arching, until my pelvis tilts to yours, until my shoulders touch the table. You lean into me, your full chest weighing me down with a force I've been longing for. When you pull off, you press your hands onto my breasts, smearing downward over my ribs and belly, as if you're smoothing me in preparation. You linger over my hips. I'm beginning to have trouble breathing, caught up in the thought that this may be the one act of sex that consummates our new togetherness. Feeling like a virgin with a whole lot to gain.

I close my eyes to concentrate. *Lord, grant me the power to make this the best fuck she's ever had.* I raise my legs to wrap around you. You reach down to my thighs and trail with your nails the contours of soft muscle and skin that are bared from my shorts to my boots. I'm still shut-eyed. "What do you see in the dark?" you whisper, and I open my eyes to that same distant smile. I need more of you and sit up, springloaded, for a full-on hug. You squeeze me, then scoop the hair off my neck, running a quivering tongue from my collarbone to my ear, then resting to blow hot and soft above the lobe. You do know what gets me started.

I want to play too, and run my tongue in circles along the little channels of ear cartilage, forcing a moan out of you, and then another, until you're whimpering at that place between bad and good and trying to pull away. I grab at your head and stay steadfast on the other ear. You tear at my shirt, too worked up to unbutton me, yanking it free and diving your hands under the cup of my bra. You pull my breasts out over the underwire, and the rush of air and nakedness makes me squirm. I let go of your head, and you crush my breasts upward, your hot mouth seizing on me like a deprived child. Your teeth graze and then bite down on my nipple with a building force that takes me almost to a scream. I push at you, and you fasten on the other nipple. The moment's relief brings my need into view, and I tighten my ass to grind my thinly covered cunt into the hard rolls of your jeans. As you chomp at my nipples, I work to pump into you as best I can, raising up to your steely belt buckle, hoping to angle the edge to nick my clit.

Your hands go to my ass and knead my cheeks while your teeth let loose my breasts and fasten onto my neck. You scratch at the backs of my thighs, then get hold of my bare calves to unwrap my legs and stretch them high.

I feel suddenly like I'm in a hardware ad, pinned back on the table like that, breasts bare, shorts falling into my crotch like underwear. I see the far-gone look in your eye and stifle the observation.

I barely feel my shorts come off but sit with your hands on my ass as you lay me lovingly back down. I scoot back until the length of my body is solidly on the slab, knees bent to steady my feet on the edge.

You waste no time pushing my knees apart and fastening your hands onto my open thighs. Your head bends to my cunt, and you pull with your thumbs at the sides of my encased clit, popping it free. You're talking and moaning over the lapping you've started, but I can barely hear you. I grab your head to signal my response, pushing into your face until everything in me is there, at the slow-motion pinnacle of my clit. We're both holding strong at the best spot, and I wriggle back to make it last. An orgasm crashes despite me; I'm tearing up and screaming your name and bucking so hard that you have to let go your hands and brace the table.

When I stop, the come and saliva puddle on the wood beneath me and you scoot away. "Right back," you groan, and I sit up to watch your fevered self go, the wetness I'm oozing staining your precious table.

I stare at the incredible sight of you coming back in, your shirt wet and muscles gleaming, your wood-dusted jeans undone, and the black dildo you've strapped on shining seal-slick with lube. I want to make a crack about hardware but see that alpha look in your eyes and think better of it. You look past me as you climb on, silent and gone, and crash your cock into my cunt, all the way in, to the nervous point of penetration pain. I want to fucking hit you. Your breath is short and hard, barely audible. "Fuck!" I scream. It's indignance, but all you hear is the cry. You let go a litany: "God, baby, what a good little fuck you are. Do you love this? Is this what you've been trying for? You want this from me, baby? You want this?

Well, you've fuckin' got it, take it bitch, take my cock all the way down into your whack pussy...." and I'm thinking, this woman hates me, and the tears are close, but the pounding is getting good, and I won't stop you, despite the hurt that's back in me, "You...fucking...slut." It comes out dirty and hateful, and I think this is it, the absolute last time I let her.... "I fucking love you!"

And you've done it, we're finally free, and I'm screaming for real, bucking your awesome cock, rising to smash into all of your body that I can, ratcheting my nails into your back. You are my god. My man, my woman, my very best fuck. And it's out of my mouth, all of it, how much I want you, how every thought of you, every day we've been together, has me spinning.

And you've stopped calling me a slut, and now it's my own name in my ears as we pound each other, my flesh to your soaked clothes, your cries layered over mine. I start to come from somewhere out-side myself, somewhere at the base of the dildo, from somewhere inside you. You ride me through it, matching my screams, growing louder than I've ever heard, shivering in delayed response to my aftershocks.

When it ends we fall together into the softest heap. Silent and bal-anced above the ground, we're floating in a moist cloud of new love.

"And now?" you ask.

I answer for both of us. "Ice cream."

Affairs are for kids, I've decided. And I will make you talk it out with me after we've both swallowed our treats. You roll off gently and hand me my clothes, tucking the dildo into your pants, quickly zipping yourself up. We climb, both of us wobbly, into the car. We're caked in drying juices and tears, and as I settle against the seat, I get the first real feel of splinters in my ass. "What's that smell?" you ask. *Jesus*, I think, and start giggling.

"Leftover fries," I snort. "Want some?"

3

Full Service Yolanda Wallace

Jo slid under the car to check for leaks. Finding none, she wiped her hands on a rag and slammed the hood. She grabbed a pen to fill out the "Next Service Due" slip but couldn't find the little plastic stickers. She always kept them in the same spot, while Lonnie dropped them wherever he happened to be at the time. There they were, on top of the battery tester.

Sitting in the front seat, she wrote down the current mileage and the date, attached the sticker to the windshield, and backed the car out of the garage. A battered primer-covered pickup blaring Garth Brooks's "Friends in Low Places" barreled through the parking lot and nearly hit her. Lonnie. Parking the car, she shook her head at him and walked around to the office. "Your car's ready, Mrs. Parker."

Mrs. Parker looked up from her book. "Oh, thank you, dear," she said, taking the keys. "I'll see you in another three months."

The retired English teacher drove an average of eight miles a week—four miles round trip to the grocery store every Saturday, plus daily trips to the post office—but she had the oil changed in her '72 Impala every three months like clockwork because she'd read somewhere that responsible drivers were supposed to do that.

"Lonnie's back, Uncle Ray," Jo said. "I'm going to lunch now, OK?"

The portly man in the CAT hat spat a stream of tobacco juice into a bucket under the counter. "Don't go too far. You know Lonnie don't know jack shit about that car he's working on."

Jo unzipped her coveralls and let the top half fall to her waist. She liked the way the sleeves flapped as she walked. "I'm heading over to Sonic," she said, watching Lonnie fumble with the Grand Prix he'd been working on the past two days. She knew he was nowhere near fixing it, so she thought she'd stay late and fix it herself. The owner was probably tired of driving around in the dented Rabbit Uncle Ray had loaned him.

Then she crossed over to Lonnie. "You want anything?"

Lonnie slung his stringy brown hair out of his face. He thought he looked like Tom Cruise in *All the Right Moves*. Jo thought he looked more like the "other brother Darryl" from *Newhart*. "Not unless that redheaded carhop with the big tits is on the menu."

Jo pulled her coveralls over her work boots and slipped them off, hanging them on the hook by the tire rack. "Then I guess I won't be bringing you anything."

She walked across the street to the fast food restaurant. Tammy, the redheaded carhop with the big tits, saw her coming. "One brown bag special and a large sweet tea, right?" she asked with a wink as she delivered a tray of hot fudge sundaes to the van at window six.

"That's right," Jo said. "Am I that predictable?"

"Most of my regulars are. Grab some bench, honey, and I'll be right back."

Jo sat down and drummed her fingers on the table while she waited for her order.

"You've got really nice hands," Tammy said, appearing out of nowhere.

"You think so?" Jo asked with a start. She was ashamed of her nails. She cleaned them constantly, but they never stayed that way for long. She slid her hands off the table and into her lap before Tammy could see the grease under her nails.

But Tammy picked up Jo's right hand out of her lap and inspected it. "Have you tried some of that Lava soap? It's real good."

"Uncle Ray has some kind of grease-cutting goo in the shop. I use it all the time, but it's probably bad for my skin, huh?"

Tammy stroked Jo's palm. "Feels soft to me."

Jo gently pulled her hand away and wiped it on her dark green pants. "Yeah, well, I'll try some of that Lava you were talkin' about."

"Glad to help," Tammy said with a twinkle. "Let me see if your order's ready. Sometimes Gene can whip it up in a heartbeat, and sometimes he takes forever. We'll see what kind of mood he's in today."

Jo watched Tammy's round hips sway from side to side as she walked away. Tammy had always been surrounded by boys back in high school, but Jo couldn't remember her ever getting serious with one then or in the years since. Sure, she flirted with all the customers—even Lonnie—but she never went home with anybody.

"Just for a change, I got you a lemonberry slush instead of a sweet tea," Tammy said, bringing out the food. "Thought the ice might cool you off. Tell me tomorrow how you like it. I gotta warn you, though. It's kind of tart once you get to the bottom where the lemon is. It turns most people's mouths inside out, but I kinda like the way it makes me feel."

Jo paid for lunch and headed back. She ate sitting on the canopy-covered gas island so she could watch Lonnie and look out for customers at the same time.

Ray's Service Station had been a constant in Jo's life since she was 16. In the beginning, the job was a way to make extra money over the summer. But when she finished school, it became a way to make a living. That was ten years ago. Ray Johnson liked to say his station was the only full-service gas station left in America. Jo thought there had to be another place out there somewhere where they pumped your gas and could fix your radiator too, but Ray's did feel like a throwback to an earlier age.

She tapped her work boot against the concrete as Bruce Springsteen's "Dancing in the Dark" blasted out of the shop radio. *Born in the USA* was one of her favorite albums. In the video for "I'm on Fire," the Boss had captured the fantasy of every mechanic and blue-collar worker alive: that a rich, beautiful woman would drive up one day and ask for more than a lube job. Lonnie talked about it every time he saw an expensive car pull up, but Jo didn't foresee that happening. Not in her part of the world. Maybe someplace else. Someplace more exotic—like Savannah or San Francisco. Any expensive car that showed up around here, she thought, usually belonged to befuddled tourists who had gotten lost and were grateful for directions to the interstate—but not that grateful.

Jo polished off her burger and fries and tossed the bag into the trash. She was just finishing the lemonberry slush when a silver BMW with out-of-state plates drove over the cable next to the gas pump. A bell rang inside, and Lonnie stuck his head out of the shop. He whistled when a beautiful brunette with long legs and a short skirt stepped out of the car.

"Unleaded," the woman said to Jo. She was tall. Impossibly tall. As she turned to study the embroidered patches on Jo's olive green uniform shirt, she seemed to block out the sun. Jo used the opportunity to examine the woman's eyes, which seemed to change color depending on the light. Or maybe it was her mood. Jo had never seen eyes that color. "Fill it up," she continued.

"Hey, Jo!" Lonnie called, running over. "You need some help?"

"No, I got this." Jo stood up and polished off her drink. The tart fruity liquid hit her taste buds and made them explode. She ran her tongue around the inside of her mouth as she picked up the hose.

"No, I'll do it," Lonnie insisted, taking the hose. "You're still at lunch, anyway, ain't ya?" He winked at her. "Why don't you take a look at that Grand Prix? I can't figure out what's wrong with the dang thing. Maybe you can."

Jo let him have his way. What was the point in arguing? A woman like that wouldn't be interested in someone like Lonnie anyway. Looking over her shoulder, she saw herself being proven right.

Lonnie slung his stringy hair out of his face and flashed his cockiest Tom Cruise *Color of Money* grin. "Check under your hood?"

The woman laughed and walked away. She crossed the lot with long, purposeful strides and headed for the office. She sure didn't look like a lost tourist. She looked like someone who always knew where she was going.

Jo thought the woman must be some kind of executive. Shaking her head, she told herself it was pointless to dwell. No way a woman like that would be interested in her either. She stepped into her coveralls and went to work on the Grand Prix. "The problem is the motor's not getting any fire," she said, feeling someone behind her. "This battery cable here is a little frayed. Looks like it might have a short."

"Really?"

Jo whirled around. "I thought you were Lonnie," she said, nearly dropping the wrench.

The woman smiled. "Apparently." She spoke with an accent that Jo couldn't place; it seemed to have a combination of influences. Like Audrey Hepburn's or the fake ones Kathleen Turner used. Tina Turner too—must be a Turner thing. What was she thinking? The woman tapped a pack of sugarless gum against her right leg. "Jo," she said, watching Jo check out her legs. "Is that short for Josephine?"

Caught, Jo blushed and cleared her throat. "No, it's Jo-Joanna." Despite the cold drink, she was sweating in the sweltering south Georgia heat. The woman, on the other hand, looked cool and comfortable, even though she was wearing a dark business suit and a long-sleeved blouse.

"I think I prefer Joanna," the woman said, her mood-ring eyes slowly traveling up and down Jo's body, examining it through the coveralls. "What time do you get off, Joanna?"

"The instant you touch me," Jo said, then blushed furiously. "Did I say that out loud?"

The woman smiled. "Yes, you did."

"What would Lonnie say?" Jo mumbled, then cursed herself for an idiot.

"Who cares?" the woman asked. Leaning forward, she continued in a conspiratorial whisper, "For the record, though, he'd probably say, 'Can I watch?' "

Catching a whiff of spearmint Trident, Jo breathed in the woman's scent. It was light and crisp. She even smelled cool.

The woman glanced back over her shoulder at him. "I'd better go before he comes running over here to rescue you again. I don't think you need a knight in shining armor, do you? You don't look like a damsel in distress."

Jo didn't feel like one either. Awake after a long sleep, she felt like Snow White being kissed by Princess Charming. "I get off at 5," she said in a rush, as Lonnie, of course, ran over to them.

"That'll be 18 even," he said, grinning wildly.

The woman handed him a twenty and told him to keep the change. "I'll see you at 5," she said to Jo.

Jo and Lonnie watched the woman stride to the car, get in, and drive off. "What's happ'nin' at 5?" he asked, scratching his balls.

"I have no idea," Jo said.

She was no good for the rest of the day, checking the clock every ten minutes to see what time it was. At 4:45 she started looking for the BMW, craning her neck every time she heard a car approach. By 5:15, the woman still hadn't shown.

"I'm headin' out now," Ray said, locking the office door. He and Jo were the only ones left at the station. The last customer had left right at 5, and Lonnie had taken off shortly after. "How much longer you plannin' on stayin'?"

Jo popped the hood on the '57 Chevy she was rebuilding. "Not much longer. I'm going to work on this for a while and shove off about 6."

"What are you gonna do about dinner?"

"I'll grab something on the way home."

"Sonic again?"

She looked at him out of the corner of her eye. "I thought I might. Why?"

"Just askin'." Ray peered at the Chevy's engine. "Once you get the rest of the parts, beat the dents out, and slap some paint on her, she's gonna be a beaut. Damn fine car." He patted the dented front bumper. "Well, I'd better scoot off. You know how much your Aunt Barbara hates it when I'm late for supper. Lock up when you leave."

"Sure thing," Jo said as she turned back to the car. When he did- n't leave right away, she asked, "Forget something?"

"That Tammy likes you, you know," he said, jangling the change in his pocket and flushing extra-red. "If you ask me, she's got some pretty good taste."

"Thanks, Uncle Ray," Jo replied with an equally embarrassed smile.

After he left, she looked around again for the BMW. Why'd she ever think the woman would come back? She was probably two states away by now. Jo peered under the Chevy's hood and decided to call the parts supplier to see what the holdup was. While she searched for the number, she heard a car pull in. Past being disap- pointed, she didn't bother to see who it was. The driver would probably see the CLOSED sign and turn around anyway. Sure enough, the car pulled off.

She found the number she wanted and sat on top of the desk, her knees bouncing to the beat of "Little Sister." The numbers on the shop phone were obscured by layers of grease, but the act of punch- ing the digits was so automatic that Jo didn't even bother to look at them. "Hey, Randy, it's Jo. I'm calling to check on my order." She heard another car pull up but ignored it too. "It's order number 742681. Yeah, I'll hold."

She spun around and faced the wall. Lonnie's *Playboy* calendar hung behind the desk. He liked the February Bunny so much he photocopied her picture and taped them over the models on the other 11 months. Jo was concentrating so hard on the calendar that she only dimly registered a car door slamming. "Another two weeks? I was really counting on having that this week." She sighed. "No, I understand. If there's nothing you can do, there's nothing you can do. All right. I'll talk to you in another couple of weeks."

She turned and hung up the phone. When she looked up, the woman was silhouetted in the doorway. "Hello, Joanna." The woman reached up and grabbed a strap that dangled from the end of the door. She gave it a tug and the sliding door came down. "Sorry I'm late."

"You came."

"I told you I would." The woman walked over to the desk. Spreading Jo's legs, she stood between them. "Didn't you believe me?" She unzipped Jo's coveralls and slid them off.

"Things like this don't happen to me," Jo explained. On the radio "It Only Hurts When I Cry" ended and "The Heart That You Own" began.

The woman leaned forward. "They're happening tonight," she said.

Indicating the grease that covered her face, hands, and clothes, Jo backed away. "I don't want to get you dirty."

"I like it dirty." The woman unbuttoned her jacket and placed Jo's hands on her white silk blouse. "Kiss me, Joanna."

Jo did as she was told. If the woman didn't mind the handprints, why should she? It wasn't her cleaning bill. The woman's body was firm beneath the silk, as if her trips to the gym were frequent and prolonged. Yet her hands were delicate, the fingers long and expressive like a pianist's.

"Very good," the woman said, shrugging off her jacket. "Is this your car?" She trailed her fingers across the hood of the Chevy.

"Yeah, it's my baby," Jo replied proudly.

The woman walked around the car and held one door open like a valet. "I don't think she'll mind. Do you?"

Jo climbed into the backseat. "No," she said, playing along. "She's not the jealous type." When the woman climbed in and closed the door behind her, Jo grew uneasy. She'd had experiences before, so she knew what to do, but none of them had adequately prepared her for this. "I feel like I'm at the drive-in," she said nervously.

The woman removed Jo's sweat-stained Atlanta Braves hat and tossed it into the front seat. "I don't have any popcorn," she said, running her fingers through Jo's hair, "but shall we steam up the windows?"

"I don't even know your name," Jo said as the woman unbuttoned her work shirt and pulled it off.

"I'm whoever you want me to be, Joanna." She went to work on the dark green pants.

Before Jo could protest, her underwear was around her ankles, the woman's mouth was on her, and she couldn't speak. *Man, she has an aggressive tongue*, Jo thought. But before she could give in completely and enjoy, she was seized by a sudden worry. The woman had closed the door, but had she locked it? There was no easy way to explain the scene a visitor would find: Jo with her feet in the air, Hanes Her Ways blowing in the breeze, a goddess between her legs. Then an even bigger worry came flooding in: She especially hoped Tammy wouldn't waltz on over, wondering where she was for dinner. She hadn't noticed Tammy all that much, but now, with this stranger's head between her legs, she realized that Tammy was plenty noticing her. *I've been too shy and too certain nothing would ever happen to see what* was *happening*, Jo thought.

Jo held onto the seats for support, her skin sticky against the leather seats. She wanted to grab the woman's head and hold it in place so she wouldn't go anywhere, but she hated when someone did that to her. She thought the woman probably felt the same way, so she resisted. "I'm going to come in your mouth," she warned.

"Mmm," the woman murmured, clutching Jo's pistoning hips to ensure she would.

When it was over, Jo walked the woman to her car on unsteady legs. "A Thousand Miles From Nowhere" softly played in the background.

"You'll tell Lonnie good-bye for me, won't you?" the woman asked, fastening her seat belt.

Jo smiled. "Sure thing."

"Kiss me, Joanna."

Leaning into the window of the silver BMW, Jo did as she was told. She could taste her own juices on the woman's tongue.

Jo watched the woman speed away. Ray pulled up in his Cadillac when the BMW was no more than a silver speck in the distance. "Hey, Jo. Your Aunt Barbara says I'm workin' ya too hard. She told me to come over here and get you before you pass out. Why don't you come over to our house for supper? Hop in and I'll run you over."

"Sure thing." Jo closed the shop and climbed into the passenger seat of the Cadillac. "Uncle Ray," she said, closing the door, "call me Joanna."

4

RecuperationSuzanne Corson

"What're you sleeping for?" Gabe's aunt Liz barked at her.

Gabe woke with a start and slid her chair over to her aunt's hospital bed. "Ah, *zietta*, it just makes me so tired, trying to keep up with you! Besides, I was up all night studying." Gabe gently picked up one of her aunt's hands and kissed it. "How are you?"

"All this fuss for a broken leg, Gabriella." Liz scooted herself backward, trying to sit upright.

"Here, let me. Broken leg, nothing—compound fracture, plus a sprained wrist. You're lucky you didn't get a concussion too!" Gabe helped her sit up. "Can I get you anything?"

"Cherries jubilee. Flambé, of course."

"Very funny," Gabe mock-scolded as she patted her aunt's arm. "How about some water?"

"How boring. But OK, thanks...." Aunt Liz closed her eyes briefly and cleared her throat. "Or ice?"

Gabe stood and reached for the plastic pitcher on the side table. "Will do. Don't try to get up or anything, OK?" she said with a grin as she kissed her aunt on the forehead and left the room.

Gabe smoothed her black jeans as she walked toward the nurses' station, where a woman was talking on the phone. Gabe put the pitcher on the counter and smiled as the woman held up the it'll-just-be-a-minute finger. Gabe nodded and leaned on the chest-high counter.

It appeared to be a busy time at the hospital, at least on this floor. Gabe was glad her aunt had the room to herself. Most of the other rooms were full, and the last time Liz shared a room with someone, she and her roommate had fought constantly.

At the far end of the nurses' station, a doctor was talking on the phone and reviewing some paperwork. Another nurse was on a third phone, waving his hands emphatically as he spoke.

Down the hall toward the lounge Gabe noticed a couple of candy stripers, one rolling a cart with some vases of flowers, another holding a stack of magazines. In the opposite direction, toward the elevators, a man in a robe and slippers walked with a younger man's arm around his waist for support. A candy striper approached them from one of the rooms along the hallway, put her hand on the patient's shoulder, and spoke with them for a bit. Gabe was startled to catch herself admiring the young woman's figure. *Great,* she thought, *it's been so long, I'm scoping out teenagers.* Gabe shook her head and glanced down at the nurse in front of her. The nurse caught her eye, mouthed, "Sorry," and shrugged. Gabe smiled, then looked back down the hall.

The candy striper's blonde French braid reached down her back, ending just above the pink-and-white striped waist tie, shaped in a bow at the back of the pinafore. The tails from the tie lay in the middle of her well-rounded behind. Her skirt hem landed above the back of her knees, exposing muscular-looking calves in white nylons, which continued down to her white shoes. Gabe blinked and turned toward the counter again.

"OK, then—you want ice, right?"

Gabe nodded and handed the nurse the pitcher. "My aunt woke up, and in lieu of cherries jubilee, she'll take ice."

The nurse chuckled as she scooped ice from the small freezer behind her. "She's quite a character. Skateboarding at her age. She's in her 60s, right? Any pain?"

The blonde with the braid came up to the far side of the nurses' station and reached over for a phone. She looked older than the other candy stripers. She glanced up as she waited for an answer, caught Gabe's glance, and smiled. Gabe grinned back and looked down at the now-familiar counter.

"Your aunt—is she in any pain?" the nurse asked again, setting the full pitcher in front of Gabe.

"Oh, uh," Gabe sputtered. "I'm not sure—she didn't mention it, but she still seems kind of groggy." She quickly looked past the nurse to see the blonde again. The woman's free hand was inside the V of her blouse, rubbing her neck. Gabe couldn't see her face very well, as it was obscured by the phone. She did notice that the uniform was snug on the woman; her breasts strained against the stripes.

"Well, I'll look in on her in a few minutes." The nurse sat down and reached for a folder at the top of a tall stack.

Gabe looked up as she picked up the pitcher; the candy striper was unabashedly staring at her. Gabe held the stranger's gaze. She wanted to hear this woman's voice; only 15 feet or so stood between them, but with the other people around, Gabe couldn't distinguish which voice was the blonde's. Gabe felt the beginning of a blush on her cheeks. She pushed her fingers through her short black hair and grinned sheepishly at the nurse in front of her. "Thanks," she said, raising the pitcher of ice. "See you later."

"Sorry I took so long, Aunt Liz." Gabe poured some ice into a mustard-colored cup and brought it to her aunt's mouth.

The older woman took the cup from her niece. "I still have one good hand, you know."

Gabe backed away and sat down next to the window. "Yeah, I know. How'd you manage to keep that one intact?"

Her aunt stopped sucking on the ice and looked sidelong at Gabe. "Don't be fresh, young lady," she garbled around the ice, then discreetly spat the cube back into the cup. "Besides, Jesse was there. She grabbed this hand when I fell," she said, holding up the unbandaged hand that curled around the cup.

"Ah, your savior! She's a sweet kid."

Liz nodded emphatically. "And a baby butch if I ever saw one! Just like you were."

"*Zia!*"

"Well, you were. You know that, I knew that, everyone knew, no one talked. But then you talked when you were ready...." Liz leaned back and closed her eyes. "So you'll be leaving soon, eh? Hot date tonight, Gabriella?"

"No, no...."

Liz opened her eyes and looked over at Gabe questioningly. "So how long are you going to pine for her, eh?" her aunt asked gently.

Gabe sighed, walked to the bed, and gave her aunt a careful hug and a kiss on her cheek. "Please don't worry about me so much, OK? I'm just going to sit and read a bit. It's nice and quiet here anyway."

"Sure, sure," her aunt said sleepily, squeezing Gabe's cheek. "But you do need to get out more. Not just sitting with your old *zia*."

"I like being here with you, that's all." Gabe leaned in again and kissed her aunt's forehead.

"Uh-huh," her aunt replied groggily, closing her eyes.

Gabe sat down and watched her aunt settle into sleep. Carefully, Gabe slipped her feet onto one of the rails of the bed and stretched her long legs.

Liz had been her usual supportive self the year since Bev and Gabe had broken up, and she was especially patient with Gabe those first few months. Gabe knew Liz had never really liked Bev and was disappointed that Gabe had postponed grad school to support Bev while she went, but Liz mostly held her tongue during the five years the two were together. She continued to be silent about Bev, knowing Gabe had been quite attached to her, but Liz had recently begun urging her niece to date.

Gabe watched her aunt sleep. Outside it was getting darker, though she had no idea of the time. She turned around and closed the blinds, noting the light traffic on the highway. Definitely after rush hour, she thought. She angled the lamp away from her aunt, grabbed her book from her backpack, and began to read.

Gabe glanced up at the door when she heard it squeak open. "Hi," Gabe whispered. She leaned over to slip her book into her bag, thinking *Oh, my god, it's her.*

"Hello," the blonde with the braid replied in a deep, quiet voice. "How's she feeling?" She walked toward Aunt Liz's bed.

"I'm awake," croaked the patient with eyes still closed. She cleared her throat and tried to sit up. Both Gabe and the candy striper came to the bedside to assist her. Liz opened her eyes and first smiled at Gabe, then at the blonde. "My, my, such attention for an old woman. This will go to my head, I'm sure."

The candy striper laughed and patted Liz's shoulder. "I'm Leigh Austin. I just wanted to see how you're feeling, Ms. Mezzullo."

"Thirsty. And bored." Liz winked at Gabe before turning back to Leigh. She cocked her head toward Gabe. "This one sleeps more than I do! And she forgot to bring cards!"

"Aunt Liz…" Gabe started, a blush creeping up her neck from her chest. She poured some water for her aunt, then sat back down in the chair. Her eyes downcast, she stole a glance at Leigh's shapely legs.

"Oh, hush, you know I'm kidding. So Leigh, aren't you a little old to be a candy striper?"

"*Zia!*" Gabe exclaimed.

Leigh just laughed. "That's OK. I get that all the time. I'm only, what, five years older than most of them?" She sat on the other bed and crossed her legs. "My mother's the volunteer coordinator. During semester breaks I help out here, kind of acting as a big sister to the others. And for morale, I wear one of these too," she said, indicating the uniform with a flourish of her arm.

Gabe heard her aunt and Leigh laughing, and she joined in. She felt a bit lightheaded and warm, so she reached over to the table and took a sip from her aunt's cup. She caught Leigh watching her from the corner of her eye. Gabe looked down again and sat back in the chair.

"So what do you do when you're not a big sister?" Liz asked.

Gabe knew Leigh was speaking, could see her lips move, but she was now drawn to Leigh's eyes. They were a bright dark blue, almost purplish. When Leigh moved her arm, Gabe's attention was drawn to the side of Leigh's pink-and-white striped pinafore, her ample breast showing its curves. Gabe imagined touching the shoulder strap of that uniform, slowly moving her fingers down to the bib portion, teasing the side of Leigh's breast....

"Gabriella?"

"Um?" Gabe managed, turning to her aunt.

"Aren't you hungry yet?" Liz winked at Gabe. "She's been studying all afternoon. She's in graduate school, at Tufts, you know," she informed Leigh. "As I was saying, Gabe, since Leigh's shift is over, you could walk her to her car and then go for dinner, right?" She smiled at Leigh. "I've been telling her she doesn't have to stay here."

"Well, it would be nice to have an escort to my car. We have to park in this lot about two blocks away." Leigh got off the bed and stretched. "But I could ask one of the guys downstairs."

Gabe stood up. "No, it's fine—"

"Don't be silly. Gabe can go." Liz patted the side of her bed. "Come say good night."

Gabe watched Leigh walk to the door as she reached her aunt's bed. Leigh turned back to them. "I'll meet you at the elevator. Good night, Ms. Mezzullo."

"Good night." Liz grabbed Gabe's hand. "Now you go have a good time."

"You are a menace, you know that, *zietta?*" Gabe said, leaning over to kiss her aunt's cheek.

"I love you, Gabriella—now go, be happy, come see me tomorrow."

Leigh was leaning against the wall of elevators as Gabe approached. "I really do appreciate this," she said.

Gabe pushed the down button. "Of course. I hope she didn't..." She let her sentence fade, unsure of how to describe her aunt.

"She's terrific," Leigh said as she placed her hand on Gabe's forearm.

"Yeah, she is," Gabe replied, feeling the heat from Leigh's touch. "She's just a bit overprotective sometimes. But I do know it's not the safest around here at night."

The elevator arrived and they stepped inside, squeezing in next to an orderly with a man in a wheelchair. "Hey, Ted," Leigh said, "press two for me, would you?"

Gabe looked sideways at Leigh, who just smiled in reply. Gabe turned away and stared at the indicator lights until they arrived at the second floor. "Here?" she asked.

"Good night, Ted." Leigh took Gabe's elbow, prompting her to walk out. "See ya tomorrow."

"You two stay outta trouble now," the orderly teased as the doors closed.

"So where to?" Gabe asked.

Leigh moved her arm down and around Gabe's waist. "I need to grab my bag. Are you in a hurry? We could grab a soda or something here."

"OK." Gabe's heartbeat accelerated.

They walked quickly, Gabe's strides matching Leigh's. Gabe's boots clacked on the shiny floor, and various machines hummed as they passed, but Gabe was most aware of the swish of Leigh's panty hose. As they turned a corner, Gabe looked around her, noticing a few signs in the hallway: PHYSICAL THERAPY, HYDROTHERAPY, OUTPATIENT REGIS-TRATION. They turned another corner: ULTRASOUND, MAMMOGRAPHY, RADIOLOGY.

Leigh pointed to a corridor on their left. "The volunteer office is down that way." She squeezed Gabe's waist. "I know I'm too old for this uniform, but it's a lot better than what the older volunteers wear. Chartreuse, please...."

"No, um, yes, this, well, you look terrific." Gabe rolled her eyes. *Real smooth*, she thought.

Leigh reached for Gabe's hand. "Why, thank you," she said, moving into an exaggerated curtsy.

Gabe willed her hands not to sweat as she helped Leigh up, not failing to notice Leigh's cleavage before she stood. "Now where are we—"

"You *are* in a hurry, aren't you?" Leigh teased. Gabe blushed and looked down. Leigh cupped her palm around Gabe's chin and moved it upward. "Hey," she whispered. "I like a woman who's direct." She leaned in and kissed Gabe, her hand moving around to the back of Gabe's head.

Holy shit, Gabe thought as their lips touched. The heat coming from Leigh's hand traveled across Gabe's back and chest. She reached for Leigh's waist.

Leigh pushed back and took Gabe's hand, laughing softly. "Come here, you," she said, leading Gabe up the hallway.

Gabe looked around, suddenly aware of where they were during the kiss. She drew her free hand nervously through her hair, then shook out her arm while they walked. The hallway was empty; Leigh was obviously familiar with the surroundings and confident about where she was heading.

"Doctors' Lounge?" Gabe read as Leigh unlocked the door.

"My friend Renee's a resident. They only use this place during the day." Leigh pushed the door open and flipped a light switch. "Would you like something to drink?"

"Sure." Gabe sat on the sofa near the door, glancing around the lounge. There were lockers and cabinets on one wall, and a cluttered counter stood along another, covered with magazines, mugs, sweaters, and stacks of paper. Several round tables with molded plastic chairs surrounded the two women. Leigh stood at a vending machine in the corner, the back of her skirt hiking up a bit as she rummaged in a front pocket for change. Gabe imagined running her hands up Leigh's exposed leg, reaching her ass, leaning in to bite....

"Coke, Diet Coke, Sprite, root beer, ginger ale—what's your pleasure?"

"Why don't you come over here?" Gabe asked quietly. She kept her hands together, resisting the urge to pocket them.

Smiling, Leigh slowly walked to the table where she had left her bag, felt around in it, then continued toward the sofa and sat next to Gabe. She crossed her legs and rubbed her left ankle.

Eyes fixated on Leigh's legs, Gabe cleared her throat. "I could rub your feet if you'd like."

"I'd like," Leigh replied, and quickly unlaced her shoes. She scooted herself back to the edge of the couch, shifted sideways, and stretched her legs out in front of her, toward Gabe. Gabe picked up both of Leigh's ankles and gently placed them in her lap. She began by cupping a hand around each ankle then slid her hands down the top of Leigh's feet to her toes. Leigh leaned her head back and sighed. "You're hired."

Gabe chuckled as she ran her hands back up to Leigh's ankles. The white panty hose felt warm beneath Gabe's hands. She kneaded Leigh's left foot down to the toes, then pulled each toe gently. Soft, guttural sounds came from Leigh's throat. Gabe kept her eyes on Leigh's feet but felt Leigh slide down on the couch, moving her feet farther across Gabe's lap. Gabe took Leigh's ankle in her hands and carefully rotated it back and forth. She flexed Leigh's foot, then extended it, and rubbed her fingers along the base of the foot, placing extra pressure on the ball area.

A slight swish of nylon alerted Gabe to Leigh's movement before she felt her toes on her abdomen. Gabe paused and her back tensed up. Leigh cupped her foot across one of Gabe's breasts, causing a sharp intake of breath. Gabe looked over at Leigh, who was grinning. "Oh, please don't stop—you're terrific."

"You're a bit distracting." Gabe resumed the foot rub.

"Just a bit? Well, I'll have to do something about that!" Leigh sat up, pulling her feet away from Gabe, then leaned back on her elbows. "Here you go." She extended one foot to Gabe.

Gabe sandwiched Leigh's foot in her hands, pressing them together, then moved her hands up a bit and pressed again, moving across the foot. Leigh's other foot slid over and ran across Gabe's belt. Her toes tipped over Gabe's waistband and beneath, returning to the bottom of Gabe's shirt. She pulled the front of the shirt out and placed her foot on Gabe's stomach. Gabe quickened the pace with which she rubbed Leigh's other foot, pleased to hear her contented noises.

Gabe's fingers moved above the ankle, reaching Leigh's calf. Leigh suddenly pulled her feet back and sat up. Gabe looked at her quizzically. "That wasn't my foot," she said, shaking a finger at Gabe with a smile. Gabe caught Leigh's finger and brought it to her lips for a kiss. "Neither is that. Someone needs a basic anatomy lesson." Leigh leaned forward and pushed Gabe down on the couch. "It'll have to wait 'til tomorrow, though. I'm starving."

Leigh swiveled her legs behind her and leaned into Gabe. Their lips, then tongues, met and collided. Leigh placed her hands on Gabe's face as they kissed hungrily. Gabe moved her arms behind Leigh and pulled her in closer. She rubbed Leigh's back, then reached down and tugged at one of her ties.

"No," Leigh gasped, sitting back slightly. She reached behind her and adjusted her ties. Gabe started to reach for the jutting breasts beneath Leigh's pinafore. "No," Leigh repeated, grabbing Gabe's hands. She kissed Gabe quickly on the mouth. She firmly moved Gabe's arms to her side. "I didn't say you could touch anything except my feet."

Gabe laughed. "No, really——" she said, reaching for Leigh.

"I mean it, Gabe," Leigh said, pushing Gabe's arms back down. "My hospital, my rules." She grinned, holding Gabe's hands to the couch.

"Your hospital?" Gabe asked, leaning forward to kiss Leigh.

"Uh-huh," Leigh murmured beneath Gabe's lips. She broke off the kiss and moved her hands down Gabe's neck, over her chest, roughly massaging Gabe's breasts over her bra and T-shirt. Gabe emitted a low groan as Leigh leaned forward to kiss and nibble her neck. Gabe squirmed and shifted her weight on the couch but managed to keep her hands at her sides. She opened her eyes and watched Leigh's hands travel underneath her shirt. Gabe gasped as Leigh reached under the sports bra and pinched her nipples. Then Leigh's fingers began kneading Gabe's breasts as she pushed the bra out of the way. Her teeth skidded across one breast toward the nipple. Gabe jumped at the sharp tug. Leigh's fingers explored Gabe's other breast before sliding down her abdomen.

Gabe watched Leigh unbuckle her belt. "I can——" she started.

"I got it," Leigh said breathily while snaking the belt through the loops. She tugged it out and dropped it to the floor. The button fly was next, quickly undone by Leigh's nimble fingers. She reached up and grabbed at the waist of Gabe's jeans, pulling downward. Gabe wiggled side to side as Leigh pulled off her jeans.

"A basic black day, I see," Leigh remarked before removing Gabe's jockeys. They joined the jeans on the floor.

Gabe's breathing was uneven and heavy. A quick shiver went through her as Leigh touched her legs. Her initial touch, feathery and light, barely made contact with Gabe's large thighs. She then started stroking them, up and down, firmly over her skin. Gabe's legs tensed when Leigh parted them. She knelt on the couch, between Gabe's legs, spreading her hands in continuous motion over Gabe's thighs, calves, back up and then over the abdomen, brushing against her pubic hair, along the side of her waist, and over Gabe's breasts again. Gabe leaned her face forward, and Leigh obliged her with a quick kiss. "You've got a luscious body," she purred.

"You," Gabe gasped, "I want to touch you."

Leigh moved her hands down Gabe's torso. "No, remember? My rules." Leigh slid her own body between Gabe's legs. She leaned forward and licked a line up the inside of Gabe's thigh, blew hot breaths across her mound, then licked a line back down the other thigh to the inside of the knee.

Gabe felt hot, confused, wet, and slightly nervous. She looked down at Leigh: stiff, short white sleeves covered the tops of long arms attached to amazing fingers. Blonde strands escaped from the braid, wispy at the sides of Leigh's head. Gabe closed her eyes again and leaned back.

Leigh's index fingers swam through Gabe's labia, parting the way for her tongue. Gabe gasped again and looked at Leigh; all she could see was a blonde head with a long braid, and pink-and-white straps on the shoulders of a woman who was stroking and licking her way into Gabe's pussy.

One of her hands made an arch, holding Gabe's lower lips open. Leigh licked up and down the slit, inserted her tongue, and then slid up and down. Gabe's breathing came quicker. "Please," she rasped.

Leigh went to Gabe's clit and licked figure eights around it, teasing the edges and occasionally gliding her tongue over the top before licking the underside of the hood. She adjusted her hands and pushed her face in closer, sucking the growing clit. Gabe squirmed beneath her, moaning loudly.

Gabe reached up and grabbed the back of the sofa's armrest, then pushed her pelvis into Leigh's face. "Oh, god, yes," she gasped as Leigh grabbed her buttocks and dug her fingers into them, scratching as she mashed her mouth on and around Gabe's clit.

Gabe felt something unusual, cold and wet, then the tip of Leigh's finger slipped into her ass. "What—"

Leigh stopped for a breath and gasped, "Relax, just relax." She lifted her head up and rested it on Gabe's stomach briefly, placing one hand on Gabe's shoulder. Slowly she moved her finger in small circles, pushing slightly deeper. She could feel the muscles relax a bit, so she moved back down to Gabe's cunt.

So much was happening that Gabe felt lightheaded. She doubted she'd be able to come; she was feeling so many different sensations, she couldn't concentrate, so she just swam with the rhythm. She took a deep breath and felt Leigh's finger stop moving. The fullness, new and different, was intoxicating.

Leigh slid her tongue up and down and around Gabe's clit. She fell into a rhythm there, then moved her finger deeper into Gabe's ass. As Gabe moaned loudly, Leigh flattened her tongue against the clit and quickened the ass-fucking. She opened her mouth and gently bit. Gabe gasped, "Oh, god, yes, yes!"

Gabe pushed herself into Leigh's face as Leigh pulled the clit into her mouth and ground her tongue all around, fucking her ass, biting her clit, licking all over. Gabe's legs stiffened, then her body shuddered for several seconds. Leigh stilled her finger but kept the pressure on her tongue.

During the last waves of orgasm, Gabe brought her arms down and hugged herself, surprised to find herself sobbing. She quickly wiped her eyes.

Leigh moved her finger slightly to break the suction and gently withdrew from Gabe's ass. She pushed her face into Gabe's cunt, thoroughly wetting her cheeks, generating a chuckle from Gabe. Then she pulled herself up and lay partly on Gabe's abdomen.

"You're incredible," Leigh said. "Thank you." She rubbed Gabe's arms and face with soothing strokes.

"Thank *you*," Gabe said softly. "Jeez, that was amazing. *You* are amazing." She surreptitiously wiped her eyes again.

Leigh looked up at Gabe and caressed her cheek. "Completely my pleasure."

Gabe put her arms around Leigh, and they lay there quietly, the hum of the vending machine and the clock ticking on the wall the only sounds in the room.

Finally, Leigh said, "So…how long will your aunt be cooped up in here, anyway?"

❊   ❊   ❊

"Great morning, isn't it? How is she?" Gabe asked at the nurses' station.

"Feisty. Definitely feisty," a nurse replied.

Gabe laughed and continued down the busy hallway. She heard her aunt from inside her room as she approached.

"You have the hands of an angel," Liz said.

"You still have to stay another night," came an unknown woman's voice.

"But I'm fine, really, I'm fine."

Gabe walked into her aunt's room. "Hi, there." She went to the bedside and kissed Liz's forehead. "Are you giving this nice woman trouble?" The woman was just finishing rewrapping Liz's ankle.

"Gabriella, you tell her, I'm fine."

"I know you are, Ms. Mezzullo—"

"Call me Liz, please."

"—Liz, but you heard the doctor. Your wrist needs more time to heal before you can use crutches, and she also wants to keep an eye on you for a bit longer." She gently patted the large bandaged ankle. "I'll see you later."

"All this fuss...." Liz pushed herself back upright.

"Aunt Liz—"

"Gabe, sit down, how are you, tell me everything, how are you?"

Gabe pulled the chair over and took her aunt's uninjured hand. "I'm fine. How are you, besides causing trouble?"

"Fresh mouth," Liz muttered, then smiled at her niece. "That lady was wonderful. She gave me a good foot bath, nice warm water. And then she rubbed lotion on my hands. They're very nice here."

"Yes, they are," Gabe nodded.

Liz looked inquisitively at Gabe. "Yes, they are?"

Gabe felt a blush coming on. "*Zietta*, you're something else, you know that?"

Liz shook her head emphatically. "Of course. So you want to talk?"

Gabe glanced out the window. "Um, not just yet. OK?"

Liz patted her hand. "OK." Gabe turned back to face her aunt. Liz squeezed her hand. "Yes, this is a very nice place. Lots of nice people. Healing hands, warm foot baths. It's not so bad. I guess I can stay another night."

Gabe laughed. "I'm sure they'll be glad to hear that." She reached behind her for her backpack. "So, you want to play gin?"

5

Venus in Uniform Thomas S. Roche

Vanessa sits uncomfortably in her chair, waiting. She feels the tingling throughout her body; her entire being is focused, as it is every morning, on this single, overwhelmingly important event. It's as if everything she has ever cared about has become centered on the instant that Perfection walks through that door: Venus in uniform.

Vanessa wonders if Perfection will be wearing shorts today. Shorts and combat boots, so much hipper than the Eddie Bauer or Timberland hiking boots most FedEx people wear. But this FedEx lady, Vanessa's FedEx lady, wears adorable little combat boots that frame her glorious, muscled calves beautifully. Well, *little* is a misnomer—they're big and butch and shiny and leather and tough as nails, which is what Vanessa likes about them. They're fastened with a zipper, just like paratroopers wear. That's so they can jump into them in a second, right from their bunks. Vanessa fleetingly pictures the FedEx lady jumping out of an airplane wearing those boots and nothing else. Ooh la la.

After the boring weekend she has had, if Perfection is wearing shorts and those combat boots today, Vanessa's afraid she just might spontaneously combust.

Since she took this temp assignment at Maclaren Industries a month ago, Vanessa's work life has resolved itself into two segments: 1) 8 A.M. to roughly 10:30, waiting for the FedEx lady. 2) 10:30 A.M. to 5 P.M., fantasizing about the FedEx lady. But then again, things get mixed up: Sometimes she indulges in a fantasy while making coffee in the morning or sitting there wishing the phone would ring.

If only they'd let me bring a book, Vanessa thinks, *I wouldn't be so obsessed.* But part of her knows that's not true—after all, this is Perfection we're talking about here. Vanessa licks her lips as she remembers the sleek bulge of the FedEx lady's calves—smooth-shaved liquid power poured into human form. But Vanessa vacillates between lust and worry when she thinks about those calves—I mean, the chick can't be a dyke if she shaves her legs, right? Dykes don't shave their legs; everyone knows that. Except Vanessa shaves her legs, but she's only been a dyke since senior year at Santa Cruz—less than 18 months ago, after all. She's not sure if at some magical point she'll just stop shaving her legs or what, but in the meantime she kind of likes the attention it gets her—out of the office, we're talking. I mean, like she even bothers to *notice* that foul Mr. Waters and his lascivious leers while he makes endless numbers of no-doubt unnecessary copies at the Canon next to Vanessa's desk. Vanessa fucked that son of a bitch up good, asking Janette, the HR woman, about the company's sexual harassment policy while Mr. Waters was eavesdropping. Vanessa had been unable to suppress a smile as she watched the guy blanch and make himself scarce. Not a leer since.

Of course, the attention that Vanessa does like is fairly frequent, but she's found that liking the attention and liking the woman are two very different things. Take Susan, for example. Wait, Susan? Or was it Suzanne? Sue?

Oh, shit, I can't remember her name. Vanessa stares wide-eyed into space as she ransacks her memory. *Suzette? No, it can't be Suzette, I'd remember a name like that. God, that's really scary, I can't even remember her name.* Susanna or whatever had been a shameless flirt on the dance floor, raw and kind of sexy, over 30 but wearing an Ani DiFranco T-shirt, butch in that not-trying-too-hard way Vanessa likes. But there were other ways in which What's-Her-Name didn't try too hard, which had become all too evident by the time the sun came up on Sunday morning. "I'll call you," Suewhatever had said nervously, and Vanessa responded with a somewhat snarky "Right," knowing Whatever wouldn't bother and wouldn't be missed.

Am I just a bitch? she wonders. Frigid or something? That was the fourth woman she'd picked up since moving to San Francisco in June; actually the fourth woman she'd picked up *ever*, her other feminine love interests being entirely driven by dorm-room keggers and personal ads, those love potions of modern life.

It wasn't that she hadn't been attracted to the women she'd picked up. They always seemed so interesting at first, out on the dance floor or pamphleting or whatever, but get them home and it was "Whatever turns you on turns me on" or "What I want is to see you have a good time" or even worse, "I don't know, what do you like?" How much fun is it to make love to a woman who just wants to make you happy? Booorrriiinnnggg.

What I wouldn't give for a selfish, heartless bitch, Vanessa thinks. All this sensitive, considerate lesbian crap is getting her down. *Give me a real woman, one who doesn't give a shit.* Vanessa knows she's being too harsh, but if she has to answer the question "What turns you on?" one more time, she's going to put whoever asks it in a headlock and force-feed the bitch her copy of *The Motherpeace Tarot*.

The FedEx lady wouldn't be like that. No way. She'd be the one putting me in a headlock. She'd just throw me down on the bed and do me. "What turns you on, Vanessa? Wait, don't answer that, because I don't give a fucking shit. Now on your back, bitch!" Vanessa shifts uncomfortably. She shouldn't be thinking things like this at work. But what else is there to do? Mrs. Fitzwater—"Missus" Fitzwater, Vanessa was emphatically corrected the one time she referred to her by the assumed-proper "Ms." (what the fuck was wrong with these corporate people, anyway?)—told her at the outset of this job that company policy decreed that receptionists not read personal materials during work hours. "No problem," said Vanessa, the eager-to-please temp, thrilled to be getting $10.50 an hour no matter what she was doing. "I'll be happy to help out with secretarial work if there is any."

"There certainly will be," said *Mrs.* Fitzwater.

There wasn't. Isn't. Won't be, Vanessa is quite sure. Consider, furthermore, that Maclaren recently upgraded to a new phone system that allows callers to dial their party's extension into the recorded voice of a receptionist about a hundred times more friendly-sounding than Vanessa's. Add that to the fact that most of Maclaren's clients are in Chicago, New York, and Los Angeles. Then top it with the fact that everyone has E-mail nowadays.

"You must remain at the front desk at all times in case someone dials zero while in the automated voice mail system," Mrs. Fitzwater told Vanessa on that first day. And, to be fair, Vanessa does get a call roughly once every other hour, usually consisting of three sentences: "Maclaren Industries, this is Vanessa speaking, how may I help you?" "Extension 123, please." "Thank you very much, one moment and I'll connect you."

Not quite as exciting as, say, underwater welding or flying an F-15, the two careers she considered when she was in high school. Vanessa has read the Maclaren Industries employee manual a dozen times, and it wasn't all that interesting the first time. She's sorted the paper clips by texture—no mean feat when you consider that they're all pretty much the same. She's sorted the memos in the top drawer by date, something that will be of dubious use considering that they're all from 1994 and written by someone named "Cyril LeGrange," who, as far as Vanessa can tell, doesn't work there and may never have.

One day a couple of weeks ago Vanessa did smuggle in a copy of *The Stern Governess*, a nasty little Victorian novel she picked up for a quarter in that thrift store on Valencia—but that caused its own problems, since Vanessa only gets a bathroom break once every two hours. She wasn't about to put herself in that position again, dammit.

"Please, God, please, let there be a bomb threat," she whispers softly, massaging her throbbing eyes.

"Good morning," comes the familiar voice, and Vanessa jumps.

"Oh," she says, smiling cheerfully at the FedEx lady with what she hopes are not painfully obvious goo-goo eyes. "Um, how's it going?"

"Just great," she says, handing Vanessa a flat package addressed to Mrs. Rhonda Fitzwater. "Just a letter-size today," the FedEx lady says. Vanessa squints to get a glimpse at the woman's name badge, but her glasses are still in her bag, and she's not about to grab them and put them on now. I mean, how obvious would *that* be?

"Thanks," smiles Vanessa, doing her best to be coy. She can't see the lady's face, but she's just sure she's getting a response. "You don't usually wear your name badge."

The FedEx lady shrugs. "I always forget."

Vanessa laughs, as charmingly as she can manage. Smiling, she just goes and says it: "Unfortunately, I'm nearsighted, and I forgot my glasses today." She stands up, leans over the big pressboard desk, and reaches out for the name badge, her fingertips tingling as she touches the warm polo shirt—it's hot out there today. Vanessa puts her face close to the woman's breast.

"Jill," she says. "That's a nice name." She could kick herself—she sounds like a state trooper trying to pick someone up while he writes her a ticket. "I'm Vanessa." She puts out her hand, and the two of them shake hands in an uncomfortable, limp way. Vanessa's dad once insisted that she learn to shake hands like a man, real firm— probably explains a lot, that—but of course she has never gotten the hang of it and still shakes hands like a girl, which usually isn't a problem, but she really hates the fact right now.

"Nice to meet you," says Jill, her eyes lingering perhaps an instant longer than they ought to. "Funny you should introduce yourself today. This is my last day on this route—I'm going on vacation starting tomorrow, and then when I get back they're moving me up a block to California Street."

Vanessa's ears ring. She prays that Jill the FedEx lady can't see her face going white as a sheet. She wrings her hands under the desk.

"Really," mumbles Vanessa uncomfortably. "Really. Humm. Hmmmm. Mmmmm. Really." She feels about ready to cry.

"Well, see you around," says Jill, and turns to go.

"Um, you know, I'm kind of, I'm kind of, um—" Vanessa wishes she had a brick to pound against her head right about now.

"Yes?" says Jill politely as she turns back toward Vanessa.

"I'm kind of new to the city…you know, just starting to meet people. I was wondering…" Her voice trails off.

"Yes?" says Jill, even more politely.

"Well, you're going on vacation. You're probably pretty busy."

Jill shrugs noncommittally. "Actually, I'm already packed. I'm an inveterate planner."

Oh, shit, thinks Vanessa.

"I was wondering if you'd want to go get coffee or something," blurts Vanessa, consciously aware of the faint spray of saliva her drooling mouth must be making. "Say, tonight?"

"Um," says Jill, and Vanessa is about to spew forth an excuse and a retraction—*I suffered brain damage this morning, I've been smoking crack at work again, I left my IQ in my other skirt*—when Jill shrugs again and says, "I'd love to."

"Wow," says Vanessa, unable to suppress the expression of awe that crosses her face. She feels sick to her stomach. "You're sure?" As soon as she says that, she curses herself inwardly, but manages to smile as if it's a joke.

Jill laughs nervously. "Of course I'm sure. After work or something?"

"I'm off at 5," says Vanessa, permitting herself one last shameless glance over the FedEx lady's unbelievable calves as they descend, elegant and strong, into the shiny black combat boots.

"Five it is," says Jill. "I'll meet you here. See you then." She turns and is gone. Vanessa suppresses a sudden need to jump up and down, screaming.

Five o'clock sharp and Jill turns up not one minute late. Vanessa almost passes out when she sees that Jill's still wearing her FedEx uniform—blue shorts, blue polo shirt—and those combat boots.

Vanessa says she has to freshen up, a hopelessly retro phrase that has made more than one fetching dyke assume heterosexuality. She races down the corridor to the bathroom, realizes she's forgotten the key, races back, stops outside the office door, ambles in casually, removes the Snoopy key ring from its hook while Jill looks on, sitting in the waiting area—Jill being the only person who has waited there since Vanessa started at Maclaren. Vanessa leaves again, runs down the corridor to the rest room, breathes easier—her last bathroom break was at 1 P.M.—and checks to make sure she doesn't look hideous.

Then she reflects for the hundredth time that day on her luck—she was wearing her favorite skirt, the vintage ankle-length black satin with a slit up to the knee, kind of hot in a peekaboo sort of way. And her lucky blouse, the off-white one she was wearing at the Lexington that time, though Vanessa supposes she couldn't really call it lucky since it resulted in going home with that holistic practitioner—what was her name again, Mona, Monica, Monique. Yech. *Gee, it's almost 4 A.M. Let's talk about patriarchal body politics some more instead of having sex, shall we, Mina?* Vanessa touches up her lipstick, feeling unforgivably femme—women in uniform can do that to a girl—unbuttons another button on her blouse, making it now two buttons lower than office propriety dictates, and feels a rush of pride. "I am one hot fucking tamale," she says out loud, and then, with a little gasp and a whimper of dismay, checks each stall to make sure she's alone.

Vanessa runs back down the corridor, stops outside the Maclaren door, takes a deep breath. Enters. "Sorry to keep you waiting," she smiles at Jill. "Ready for a cup of coffee?"

"Yeah," says Jill. "You know anywhere you'd like to go?"

"I'm new in town," Vanessa replies. "Surprise me."

"Well, everything sort of shuts down in the financial district at 5," says Jill. "Probably best to go to another neighborhood—say, the Mission?"

"Wherever," says Vanessa. "Whatever you think." She feels like kicking herself again.

"All right, then," says Jill. "Let's catch the BART to 16th Street and go to Muddy's."

"Oh, great," says Vanessa, too quickly. "I live right by there." And then, in response to the puzzled glance from Jill, "I, uh, won't have to walk too far to get home after, um, after we have coffee."

"Yeah," says Jill. "I live by there too."

"Really," says Vanessa, again too quickly. "Fascinating. Just fascinating. Where people live, I mean. It just fascinates me where people live." *I am going to hang myself if I say one more stupid thing.* They step onto the escalator down to the train.

Vanessa regards Jill over the scattered remnants of their falafel plate, surveying the information mined from the preceding four hours. Coffee has turned into dinner, and now it's almost 9 on a school night.

Friendly conversation about love affairs (a nonmonogamous lesbian marriage that ended in tears three years ago, when Jill was

27), graduate school (just a dissertation and a statistics class away from a Ph.D. in Women's Studies when she said "fuck it" and became a FedEx lady), vegetarianism (strictly on political grounds, and no tofu), vacations (Jill leaving for a week's worth of hiking in Hawaii in less than 12 hours), and long-distance cycling (Berkeley to Santa Cruz every other weekend for a year now, holy fucking shit, no wonder her calves are so hot) has yielded the nuggets of information Vanessa so desperately needs. She's mined the precious metals of the covert agenda, the coppers, silvers, and platinums of the impromptu courting ritual. And with Jill she's apparently struck gold: Jill is 1) a dyke; 2) currently unattached; 3) kind of slutty; and 4) still the biggest hottie Vanessa has caught a glimpse of since moving to SF. But the diamond—or, perhaps more accurately, the Uranium 238—still eludes Vanessa: Is Jill hot for her?

The conversation turns to such things as leg shaving: "Strictly for the aerodynamics," Jill says with a smirk. "I don't go in for that femme crap."

The wry smile tells Vanessa that Jill's busting her femme chops.

"With me it's strictly for the femme crap," Vanessa smiles back, nudging the slit of her long black satin skirt aside as if in venomous sexual challenge. "I don't go in for aerodynamics."

Jill, with a nod and a faint reddening of her cheeks as she looks at Vanessa's pretty legs, offers her a regretless touché.

It's over their third shared Turkish coffee, lipstick on Vanessa's side of the little cup, electricity flowing through Vanessa's veins as she realizes she's not going to be able to sleep tonight if she drinks any more Turkish coffee, that she finally blurts it out like the idiot she surely is.

"So you probably have to get up early in the morning," she says. "You probably want to get to bed early. I mean, get to sleep early. But, you know, I was thinking if you were still up for a drink...."

"Afraid I don't do bars," Jill breaks in smoothly. "The smoke's bad for the lungs. But if you'd like a nightcap, I'd like one too. As long as we can have it at my place."

Damn, thinks Vanessa. *That was easy. I guess she's sluttier than I thought.*

They go back to Jill's apartment—an attic studio near Castro and 20th, so tiny it's not even legal, perched so high atop the ancient but revitalized Victorian that you have to climb a ladder at about a 75-degree angle to get there.

"How the hell do you get furniture up here?" Vanessa calls up after Jill, admiring the view of those smooth calves as she climbs.

Then Vanessa's head pokes up through the little hatch, and she mutters "Oh" as she looks around at the frameless futon mattress sprawled on the floor and the stacks of books on windowsills.

"Airlift," says Jill, stretching as she makes for the tiny kitchen. "It was a bitch finding a helicopter big enough to lift that mattress. And getting it through the skylight was next to impossible."

With that, Vanessa notices the skylight for the first time—high up on the slanted ceiling, wide open to the night air and the encroaching fog of the city as it raced by overhead. Vanessa adores the way the fog comes in every evening, rushing down from Twin Peaks as if past the windows of an airliner. She wraps her vintage lace shawl around her shoulders, catching a bit of a chill, and draws a deep breath of the night air, loving its sharp foggy scent.

"Sorry if it's a little cold," says Jill, handing her a tumbler filled with ice and booze. "Bourbon on the rocks OK?"

"Jesus Christ," says Vanessa. "Glad to see my shaved legs didn't prejudice you."

Jill grins. "Strong drink for strong women."

"I'll say." Vanessa takes a drink, the warmth spreading through her mouth and throat.

"Is it too cold? I can shut the skylight and turn on the heater."

Vanessa glances down at her nipples, but they're not erect. She reddens, hoping Jill hasn't noticed the absurdity of the gesture. Vanessa is momentarily tempted to say, "We can make our own heat, baby," or something else suitably laughable, but all she manages is, "Please don't. I like it."

"Me too," says Jill. She gestures toward the futon mattress. "I'm afraid the only place to sit is the futon."

Vanessa kicks off her low-heeled pumps, sits down on the well-made bed, stretches out her legs, and makes sure the slit in her vintage skirt is pointed toward Jill.

"I don't think that'll be a problem," she says huskily, running one foot up her calf. She feels a quiver of embarrassment as soon as she says it, but the response she gets from Jill is worth it.

"Now you're talking," Jill says, and sits down next to Vanessa, putting her arms around her, their lips meeting smoothly, easily, as if it is preordained that they should kiss hungrily at this very moment, with bourbon-bite and the warm mingling of tongues. Vanessa turns her head and kisses Jill back, her shawl sliding off as her arms go around the FedEx lady. That polo shirt feels deliciously rough against Vanessa's forearms.

Everything is perfect for a time—probably, in the real world, just 15 minutes or so, but it feels like a delicious eternity. Their kisses grow in tension as they recline on the futon, the drinks forgotten on the low windowsill beside the bed. Their hands rove hungrily but respectfully, beginning tentative explorations as if to establish territory—as if to say "I'll get back to you." Vanessa feels Jill's fingertips brushing her ass through the thin silken skirt, as she coils her legs up between Jill's calves and nuzzles her small breast, biting the hard nipple through the polo shirt. Those calves feel divine up close, and it's as if Vanessa can't stop running her own calves up and down against them, feeling the place where Jill's muscled legs, tough and strong and butch but shaved smooth like the nelliest femme, meet the thick, zippered leather of her combat boots. When Jill goes to unzip those boots, Vanessa gently touches her wrist.

"Please don't," she whispers. "I like them."

"Really," says Jill, pretending to be scandalized. "A leather fan? A thing for women in uniform?"

Vanessa giggles. "No, I just like *you* in uniform."

"Fair enough," says Jill, who goes back to kissing Vanessa, all the excuse Vanessa needs to reach down and touch the tops of those boots, feeling the place where leather becomes flesh. Then, as Jill nuzzles Vanessa's ear, Vanessa hears the question she's been dreading without even knowing she was dreading it.

"What do you like?" Jill asks, and Vanessa's spine stiffens.

No. No. Not her. Not this hot, sexy woman in uniform, not this in-control jock, this Fed Ex Aphrodite, this polo-shirted and combat-booted dreamboat! Vanessa's throat seizes up as she runs the question through her mind over and over again. *What do you like?* Remembering all the unsatisfying trysts, all the times she couldn't say what she liked because she didn't know, or didn't have anything to draw on. *What do you like?* What a stupid question. Try me. Try anything. But don't ask me about it.

But Vanessa's fear and desperation passes as quickly as it came, as she feels the smoothness of those leather boots under her fingertips. She throws it to the wind.

"I'll show you what I like," says Vanessa wickedly, and disappears between Jill's legs.

"Oh, my God," says Jill, wide-eyed in the darkness.

Vanessa starts by running her tongue around the tops of those boots, her tongue tip flickering from flesh to leather and back again. Jill is wearing low socks, so there's no pesky cotton to get between the two fetish-fabrics of Vanessa's choice, skin and flesh. Then, as her excitement mounts, Vanessa licks her way down the side of those well-polished boots, one hand snaking slowly up Jill's leg as the other caresses the upper.

Vanessa is shocked at herself—she's never taken control like this, although is she really taking control by licking this girl's boots? But then again, this is exactly what she's fantasized about, a hundred or a thousand times while sitting at her desk at Maclaren, the memory of these glorious calves filling her mind. Licking these boots, fondling those calves. How odd that she would have to be so commanding to enjoy this gesture of submission—or *is* it a gesture of submission? Vanessa doesn't give a fuck anymore. Now she's licking the upper, surprised at how rough the well-polished leather feels under her tongue. Her fingertips trail up Jill's leg, caressing the gorgeous calves, but each time inching higher, farther up Jill's body, as Jill sighs and moans softly with each caress o f Vanessa's fingertips on her inner thighs. God, Vanessa can't even believe she's doing it—but there she is. Her hand's sliding up Jill's pant leg, disappearing into those mysterious, hallowed shorts. Exploring the curves of Jill's upper thigh, and delving deeper—

Vanessa almost curses. Jill is wearing biking shorts! *What did I expect?* Vanessa wonders. *A G-string? Hardly workaday wear....* Then Vanessa remembers that she, in fact, is wearing a G-string under the silk skirt, so maybe it wouldn't have been that out of the ordinary. Not really Jill's idiom, though.

Vanessa manages to do what she does almost without missing a beat. She has to, because if she pauses, Jill will notice that her hands are shaking. She reaches up to Jill's belt and unfastens it with one hand.

Jill just watches—doesn't move to help, the way Vanessa's recent lovers have. Doesn't interfere with the magic to be had, the succulent feeling of undressing your lover. Vanessa's tongue is still resting against the leather of Jill's boot as she reaches up and draws the zipper of her shorts down, grabs hold of the belt and of the waistband of Jill's bike shorts and, with one movement smoother than Vanessa would have dreamed possible, she pulls off the whole mess in a single gesture.

Vanessa's fingertips rest lazily against Jill's pubic hair as she licks her way one last time around those gorgeous calves in their black-leather sheath, and then licks her way up Jill's legs—passing the sharp scent of her sex, saving that for later—and wriggles fully atop Jill, hands sliding up under the polo shirt.

Then the kisses again, fiercer and harder than before, like Jill is trying to eat Vanessa in one bite. Vanessa goes wet to the knees.

With minimal struggle they get Jill's polo shirt off and discard it atop the growing pile of clothes next to the bed. Then comes the tiny little sports bra—Double-A—and lucky Vanessa, she's always had a thing for women with small tits. Then it's Vanessa's turn, Jill's hands surer than they were before, confidence gained from the taste of leather on her lover's tongue. Vanessa's lucky blouse, then her skirt, mingling with Jill's shorts and polo shirt and bra on the floor. Then off comes Vanessa's little half-slip, her bra, her little G-string before Vanessa even knows what's happening. She can feel the lustful tension in Jill's impressive muscles, feel the demands pulsing through that taut, athletic body. There will be no more "What do you like" tonight, Vanessa knows, but she's hardly prepared for the tangling passion in Jill's limbs as she pushes Vanessa onto her back and then, a quick slug of bourbon for a purpose Vanessa doesn't realize until she feels that ice-cold tongue on her clit and shrieks. She shudders and moans as the tongue traces a path from clit to cunt, then tenderly around her labia, the ice cooling her but quickly melting as Vanessa's heat rises.

Vanessa looks down to see Jill hunched hands-and-knees over her, face buried in her thighs, pillow wedged under Vanessa's ass—how the hell did that pillow get there?—and Jill's gorgeous calves taut with muscle, framed, as before, in those lovely, sexy combat boots. But even as Vanessa climaxes, it's not the combat boots she sees, though that's what she's looking at—it's the concentration in Jill's eyes, about all Vanessa can see of the FedEx Lady's face, the passionate intensity in those sparkling baby-blues as Jill's mouth wrestles and plays with cunt and clit. The top of Jill's tongue finally drives Vanessa over the top, making her whole body shudder and squirm with orgasm as the talented tongue returns to her clit and pushes her past the brink.

It's a long time later—almost dawn, in fact—when Vanessa awakes after an hour-long nap to see the FedEx lady dressed again. Jill's face is scrubbed and pink from a hot shower in this pre-dawn chill. She's no longer wearing a polo shirt or walking shorts—she's got on an AIDS Ride T-shirt with the sleeves cut off, black spandex biking shorts—and Timberland hiking boots. Her backpack is next to the "door"—really more of a hatch.

"Sleep as long as you want," Jill tells Vanessa, leaning down as Vanessa rolls over, the damp white sheet clinging to her naked body. Jill kisses Vanessa on the mouth, and Vanessa just stares, smiling, unable to believe she just made it with this vision of perfection, with Venus in uniform. "Just close the garage door downstairs when you leave. It locks automatically."

"Thanks," says Vanessa. "I have to get to work soon anyway. When do you get back?"

"A week from tomorrow," says Jill.

"You going to call me?" Vanessa's almost holding her breath as she asks that one.

"Maybe," says Jill with a mischievous smirk, and Vanessa breathes more easily. A "sure, of course" would have meant a definite no. And a "maybe" meant "maybe," which Vanessa could deal with. "Maybe I'll just drop by one afternoon," Jill adds with a wicked look, and Vanessa smiles.

"I'd like that," she says.

Then there's one more kiss, and Jill is gone, down the hatch that leads to the garage that leads to the street. And Vanessa is rolling over, twined in Jill's sheets, deeply inhaling the FedEx lady's scent. She has to masturbate three times to get herself to leave, and she's 20 minutes late to work.

There must be some sort of lesson here, Vanessa thinks as she hands the single outgoing FedEx to the buffed-up guy who replaced Jill on the route. Except Vanessa can't figure out, even with her hours and hours of empty time to think about it, what the lesson is supposed to be. Something about asking for what she wants or, more likely, something about shorts and leather combat boots? Vanessa can't see how it really matters.

She never does confirm it—how could she, really?—but Vanessa is pretty sure *Mrs.* Fitzwater decided to get rid of her that very day because of the doodling thing. Fitzwater just happens to walk up when Vanessa is doodling absently on the desk blotter—drawing a woman in a FedEx uniform, a suspiciously tight FedEx uniform, with walking shorts and knee-high combat boots. Vanessa reddens at the time, but later she takes a certain pleasure at having freaked the old bitch out enough to get herself fired. I mean, grow up, right? Vanessa gets her call from the temp agency that afternoon: *Maclaren Industries no longer needs a receptionist.*

But Vanessa must have someone looking out for her—Venus, maybe, nestled comfortably at 35,000 feet between here and Hawaii, wearing hiking boots and a pair of too tight biking shorts, casting spells of love down upon San Francisco's mortals. Because, wouldn't you know it, the temp agency has just gotten a call for another position, this one in the mail room of a nonprofit, where it will be Vanessa's duty to handle all outgoing shipments through all couriers—including UPS and FedEx. The job doesn't pay that well, but on the other hand, it's located on California Street. Vanessa thinks she probably says yes too fast, sounding desperate. But she doesn't want some cruel twist of fate to sever the phone line or otherwise take away the job before she can accept.

She doesn't mind the cut in pay. Besides, now she can wear jeans to work. Or shorts.

Vanessa carefully folds her drawing, tucks it into her purse, and with a cheerful "See you, *Mizzzz* Fitzwater," bids the biddy good-bye.

6

One Sexy Scout Cara Bruce

She came walking out of the forest like a grown-up Girl Scout not yet gone wrong. Her dark-brown button-up forest ranger shirt hugged her ample chest tightly, and her olive-green shorts landed just above her knees. Behind her came a small team of sightseers, watching with intense admiration as she lifted her sculpted arm and pointed out various specimens of leaves and trees. I wondered if she knew about nuts and cones and things like that or if she was a woman more into juicy berries and pretty flowers.

Her tour was ending, and the group was fast approaching the visitor's center. I rose from the bolted-down park bench and headed toward the tiny hut.

She was answering the last few questions outside the visitor's center, pointing convincingly to the laminated map. I stood there in awe as the sunlight played upon her auburn hair. She was pretty in that authentic sort of way, but what really got me was the state-issued kneesocks that traveled down rounded calves and ended in those clumsy mud-covered hiking boots. All at once rugged, sexy, and innocent.

"Did you have a question?" she asked me.

"I was just wondering when the next tour was." Of course I didn't really care about the foliage of Northern California, but if she would give me a private lesson about the birds and the bees, then that was something else entirely.

"There are no more tours this afternoon." She looked sad, as if she were personally responsible for my lack of woodsy education.

I kicked a few leaves and looked down at the ground, pouting my lips and saying, "Damn, I was really hoping to get a tour. I have to go back home tomorrow, and this is my last chance." It was a lie. I felt guilty. But it worked.

She looked up at the sky, the majestic redwoods towering above us. She appeared concerned, upset, unsure what to do. She was conscientious and caring, and she wanted me to know exactly what sort of tree loomed overhead and exactly what it did for the entire ecosystem. I thought of telling her what she did for *my* ecosystem, but decided I ought to wait to make sure she was actually part of the same species.

"I guess I could take you," she decided. I smiled like a bear in a honey pot. I wanted to take her hand and clasp it tight; I began having flashbacks to my Brownie days. The shit-brown tunics with sashes that cut through the space of not-yet-existent breasts, and of course, the kneesocks. I smiled at her and caught her eye. She looked back at me and hesitated, suddenly wary of disappearing into the woods with this crazed, cunt-hungry tourist.

We went anyway. I admired her for that. A fearless leader.

She began her spiel about the woods, about old growth and the necessity of fires that burn away life-choking underbrush. I tried to listen, really I did, but when she began talking about bushes and petals, my attention wandered to more natural concerns.

I think she could feel my thoughts, and we meandered along in silence for a while. Our arms brushed lightly against one another, and I stopped to tie my shoe. She waited, patiently.

"Look at this," she said, bending down and gently fingering a small violet.

"It's beautiful, like you," I said. She blushed crimson, and I took full advantage of the opportunity. I leaned over and kissed her, probing every nook and cranny of her mouth with my tongue as she stood rooted in place, suddenly shy. But my trail ride wasn't over. I had just begun to explore the paths I was most interested in, and I wasn't letting her go. Her breath quickened, and I gently pushed her against a tree. The cheap buttons of her California Forestry shirt looked about to pop, and I thanked the heavens for government spending. I pulled, not too hard, and the nylon shirt split wide open.

She gasped.

"My uniform," she said. I thought about answering her, but my mouth was busy on her tit. Her concerns about the shirt gave way to concentration on her shorts, which were rapidly being unbuttoned. I was sure I was going against every single regulation, but I didn't care. This ranger was going to get her own private tour of the intricacies of all five of my fingers. I parted her big hiking boots with one push of my foot and lodged my knee into the crevice of her canyon.

The shorts came down, and I was on my knees in a bed of pine needles, my face framed by those ever-present brown socks. Her pussy smelled like fresh air, and I knew I wanted to be the troop leader. I decided to let my tongue do the talking. I dove in, making smaller and smaller circles until I was practically biting her clit, fucking her with my face. She arched against the peeling pine, thrusting her crotch deeper into my mouth. I went for it, giving her my right hand one finger at a time. Her hot cunt clenched around my hand, my fingers enveloped in her wetness. She moaned and quivered, searching for a branch, some bark, anything to hold onto. My face was soaked, and she was spouting out the names of all the trees in the forest. I felt her tense, clench, and relax. She slumped down onto me, and I held her, my sexy scout, all fucked and pretty in the most natural way possible.

7

Butch Talk Nicole Foster

Slate buried her head in her hands, exasperated. "A lot of times they spray this glossy crap on the engine to make it look like it's brand spankin' new." She looked straight into the TV camera now, her kohl eyes nearly piercing the lens. "You gotta act like you know your shit when you're buying a used car, Tinkerbell. You can't let some dickweed guy pull the wool over your eyes. Show that bastard what you're made of. Got it, princess?"

"Got it. Thanks a lot. You're always there when I need you."

"Anytime, C.J. OK, next caller, you're on *Butch Talk*...."

When are these girls going to get it together? Slate said to herself as she held her head in both hands and made a loud "pop" in her neck. *If it weren't for me, they'd be dead in the dyke water.* As the next caller spoke, Slate tuned out, going over the ten or 11 calls she'd received that night—*What's the best hair gel? I've got this rattle in my engine. How come the chicks don't dig me?*—on her cable access show, *Butch Talk*. The program, which she'd been hosting for the past five months, had become the talk of the Madison, WI, dyke community where so many sisters knew each other biblically, you'd think it was freaking Jerusalem.

"Slate?"

Slate came back to earth with a jolt. *Jesus F. Christ*, she thought, *what's this bitch droning on about?*

"Yeah, honey, I'm here…we were just having a little technical difficulty. Lost your signal for a second. Can you repeat the question?"

"I said," the caller's voice turned petulant, "my girlfriend wants me to ride with her in the parade, but I'm afraid people from work will see me."

"So you're wondering if you should ride with her?"

"Yes," the caller dragged the word out into three syllables, then heaved a sigh the size of Hurricane Irene.

"Now listen here, sugar cube. Don't take that fuckin' attitude with me." Slate pointed directly at the TV camera, looking for all the world like a dyked-out Uncle Sam. "Watch your tongue and listen up, 'cuz Daddy's gonna answer you: You should be honored to be asked to ride with your woman. What kind of princess are you to even think about saying no? You should be proud to ride behind her, and you should be proud to let the whole world know this is your woman. If you can't handle it, maybe you should find some J. Crew bitch up in Maple Bluff and let a real woman have a shot. Got it?"

Slate, brow furrowed, felt herself getting hot. These little bitches who wanted to dabble in the wild side with a real woman—but only as long as they didn't get their hands dirty—really bugged the shit out of her. And she wasn't about to sweeten her wisdom with honey; she saved that for the flies.

There was silence on the other end.

"Are you listening to me?"

"Yes." The caller's voice was far more subdued now.

"I know it seems like I'm being hard on you, but it's for the best. You want your woman to know you love her, right?"

"Yes."

"And you want her to know you're a strong, proud butch?"

"Yes."

"Then get on that hog, hold your head up high, and scream it to the world, OK?"

"I'll try."

"You do that."

"But what if—"

Slate punched a button to cut the caller off. She ran her fingers through her dark, bristly crew cut, then looked to Cara, her stage manager, who cued Slate for the next segment: a parody commercial her pals Pam and Deb had put together for "Save the Butches," followed by their ad for Labia Lager, the beer of choice for dykes on the prowl.

"And now, a word from our sponsors," Slate said with a wide, toothy grin into the camera, then held up two fingers on each hand. "Peace out!"

As the commercials ran, Slate looked over at Cara. Damn, that was a fine piece of 20-somethin' ass, all cradled in those tight-fitting black vinyl pants, the crotch riding up into her pussy, showing every line and nuance, her navel peeking out to reveal a small silver hoop. She knew she could fuck that doll good and hard, way better than Cara's tired-ass girlfriend Melissa could. That wannabe butch had been washed up ever since that day two years ago when Cara had pussy-whipped her into settling down. Melissa was even *cooking* for her girlfriend now—and we're not just talking steaks on the grill.

Slate licked her own chops, then ran her fingers through her buzz cut again. "Hey, Cara, sure you won't drop Melissa for a real butch like me?"

Cara looked up from her clipboard, where she'd been jotting down segment times for next week's show, and swept a few luscious red curls off her forehead. "Yeah, whatever, Slate. Mel's got more 'butch' in her monkey wrench than you've got in your entire body." She snapped a rubber band at Slate's Levi-covered leg. "Gotcha."

Cara had endured Slate's monotonous flirting and lame-ass come-ons ever since she'd started interning on the program three months before. But she needed an easy two credits to complete her communications degree at UW, and if her cohort Diana hadn't helped her finagle college credit for this two-bit show, she'd have been gone from day one. Still, Cara kind of liked putting Slate in her place every once in a while; she enjoyed topping the top. And she did think Slate was kind of cute—charismatic too—even if she did act like she'd cornered the Rico Suavé market, even if she *was* pushing 35.

Slate knew she didn't have a butch's chance in Bloomingdale's with Cara; in fact, she wondered if she'd ever screw another woman again. It'd been ten months, five days, and four hours since Lucy had up and left her to move in with that lousy FedEx piece of snatch in Whitewater, one of those girls who drives down for Madison ass on the weekends then scurries back for five days of their piddly towns and lackluster jobs; "bush burglars," Slate called them.

Lucy always did go for babes in uniform—cops, meter maids, garbage collectors, hell, even those girls in the goofy get-ups at Hot Dog on a Stick. Slate herself was proof of that. So many nights she had come home from her 12-hour physical therapy shift all sweaty and Lucy would almost fall to the floor at the sight of Slate's strong, toned runner's body clinging to her hospital blues.

Well, Slate thought for the millionth time, that glorified delivery girl could have Lucy; she could push whatever she wanted up her mail slot. Didn't bother Slate a bit—or so she bragged to all the butches at the Connection on Friday nights. Of course, they knew better. They each had their own Lucy. Still, Slate never let on to anyone that she hadn't had any in nearly a year. Imagine what that would do to her rep. And even though she was tough as nails on *Butch Talk*, she'd never even come out to her coworkers at the hospital, didn't want word leaking out to her patients that she was a dyke, afraid they'd run out screaming "Pervert!" under her touch. Slate had issues.

As the words "The foam is the best part" rang out from one of the monitors, Slate realized the Labia Lager commercial was coming to a close and that she'd have to take another whiny call. Where were all the tough butches? The no-nonsense, hard-ass bitch butches? The Martinas, the k.d.s, the *Fonzes*? The dishrag butches in this lousy town were giving her breed a bad name. Real butches were a dying species, Slate thought, the T-Rexes of sapphic civilization. But she knew it was her job to whip these lasses into shape, her calling from above.

With a long sigh—almost a moan, really—she looked up at Diana, her bald-headed, baby-butch camerawoman, who flashed a knowing grin.

"Hey, buddy, it could be worse," Diana said, cracking her knuckles. "We could have a bunch of clueless *femmes* calling in."

"Wanna be my relief pitcher?" Slate chuckled.

"And top your butch expertise? Kinda like Bonzo the Chimp takin' over for King Kong, doncha think?"

"Ten seconds, girls," Cara piped in.

"Exactly how long Mel takes in bed," Slate tossed back.

Cara stuck her tongue out, which of course, only made Slate hornier. "And four, three, two…"

And right before Cara pronounced "one," a stroke of brilliance flashed through Slate's mind. She looked into the camera, one eyebrow raised. "OK, little ones, a few lines are lighting up, but I'm not going to take any of these calls. You heard me right." Cara gazed inquisitively at Diana, who just shrugged. "It seems our lesbian community is ill, diseased almost. Where are the real butches—hiding in caves? Have they all fled to higher ground to avoid the flood of wimpy placebo studs invading our quaint hamlet?" Slate looked like she was about to cry in front of the camera, although that would have been as likely as the Terminator asking for his mommy.

"I'm issuing a challenge," Slate continued, "to every dyke stud east of the Mississippi. Well, every stud who's watching now. If you're a hard-core butch, if you've got the *cojones* to speak your mind, to not take shit from nobody, then I'd like to invite you on our show for a guest spot. That way, we can show all the beautiful femmes in this town that there are some rough 'n' ready, in-the-know gentledykes left in Butch Land. So, unless you're anything but top-grade sirloin, you might as well flip the channel to *The View* right now."

Slate looked down at the phone lines, which were lighting up like crazy, then faced the camera with her infamous grin. "Looks like we might just have a few good butches left around here." She punched one of the phone lines. "First caller, you're on *Butch Talk*."

"Top of the evening to you, Slate."

Slate cut the caller off. "What the hell was that? What do you think this is, a Lucky Charms commercial?"

"Next caller, you're on *Butch Talk*."

"Hey, Slate."

"So you think you're a real butch, eh?"

"I sure am. I've even got a bike to prove it."

"Oh, yeah? What kind?"

"A Honda."

"A Honda what?" Slate prompted.

The caller paused. "Umm…"

"A Honda what?" Slate was getting annoyed.

"A Honda Spree." The caller hung up before Slate could even start in on her.

"I guess I'm the last decent butch in town. I better clear my social calendar, 'cuz it'll be babes-a-million for me." Slate roared a hoarse, cackling laugh, the laugh that sounded a bit like Mr. Ed and had scared off more than a few girls. She punched another phone line, ending with a grand flourish of her hand.

"Next caller, you're on *Butch Talk*."

"Listen, you bitch," a deep, resonant voice came through the line. "I've been watching you. I see you swaggering around, hands deep inside your pockets, probably feeling around for your balls, 'cuz, Shirley Temple, you ain't got none."

A chill ran down Slate's backbone at the mention of her real name, Shirley. How did the woman know? Maybe it was just a coincidence. But maybe not. Slate gathered her courage. "Oh, you've seen me around, huh, Mabel? Lots of girls have seen me around. That's why they call me Slate—'cuz I'm always chalking up another one."

Diana, shaking her head, laughed out loud at that.

"Well, I've seen you at your worst," the caller growled. "All cowering, desperate for anyone's attention. You're a wuss at heart."

Slate decided to take the direct approach. "Cut the shit. Who are you?"

"Let's just say I'm a lady in uniform who could hang you—and yours—out to dry." As the caller spoke, Slate thought she heard some glasses clinking in the background, the strains of Melissa Etheridge's "Come to My Window" playing softly.

Well, Slate pieced together, *maybe she's just one of those nitwit softball players from the Connection calling in to razz me.* But what if it was Lucy's FedEx fuck getting back at her for all the crank calls and late-night pizza deliveries she'd phoned in under the bitch's name and address? Or worse, it could be that hospital cafeteria bulldagger she ripped a new asshole into last week for not wearing a hair net. Slate did love pushing her weight around that place. But what if that woman was spreading rumors about her at the hospital? Slate never really thought anyone from work would be watching her show. Didn't they have better things to do? And, besides, she never saw any *real* butches around that place anyway. Not much ruffled Slate's feathers, but now she was really starting to freak out.

Silence, thick and heavy, hung in the studio air. Slate took a quick sip of water from a bottle on the table next to her, then mustered her strength. "So, Chatty Cathy, you think you can top me?"

"Oh, I know I can. In fact, I think you deserve a good, hard butch fuck; a long slow, excrutiating, *blinding* screw," the caller crooned. "Slatey's got a big ol' empty space longing to be filled. She's an itty bitty chocolate bunny with a hollow center that leaked out the butch in her long ago."

What was it about that voice? Had she heard it before? Slate tried to get it together for one final assault, but the warm, wet sensation between her legs startled her, and she lost her bearings. She had to do something—and fast. Slate disconnected the call before anyone else figured out she'd been whipped.

"I'm sorry, but my lovely stage manager is saying we're out of time. So, until next Thursday, ladies and gents-in-training, keep the peace and, above all, keep your cool." Slate flashed her usual good-night grin, but anyone within six feet of a TV set could see her upper lip quiver as it hadn't since that night in '98 when the Packers had won the Super Bowl and she'd finally let Lucy go down on her after months of pleading.

"What was that all about? Looks like you've met your match," Cara chuckled.

"Or your secret admirer," Diana said with a devilish grin. Even though she was still a baby butch, she'd enjoyed enough nights of splendor with leather daddies to catch onto the chemistry between Slate and her new rival.

"Leave it alone, girls." And without a good-bye or sassy comeback for Cara, Slate slung her backpack over her shoulder and headed out.

Who the hell is she? Slate wondered as she gunned her Dakota Sport through a yellow light on University Avenue on her way back to her apartment. *That voice sounded so familiar.* She was just about to take a left onto Park Street when she had a quick change of heart and roared her truck in the direction of the Connection. She looked at her watch. Ten o'clock. Maybe some of those softball girls would still be around after their Thursday-night game. And wasn't it league night at Westside Bowl? Yes sir, she could put a stop to this right now and show that wannabe butch up. Slate *knew* this woman couldn't undo her again. Tonight was just a fluke, right? A one-in-a-trillion mutation, like a two-headed calf or a femme mechanic. But then those words *long, slow, excrutiating, blinding screw* began to play in her head, and Slate went wet and limp as a noodle.

A pair of giant neon lips flashed from a sign ahead, and Slate pulled into the parking lot of the Connection. She killed the engine, then slid her hand between her legs—damn, still wet. She took a look in her rearview mirror and ran her fingers through her hair. Her complexion was rosy; she almost looked freshly fucked. At least the ladies would think she'd already gotten some that night.

As she entered the Connection, Slate looked up to the television above the bar, where Bobby Oaks, the wiry local conspiracy theorist was going on about the Freemasons and Kennedy. Shit, everyone had to have seen her show tonight; Bobby's program always came on right after *Butch Talk*. It wasn't as crowded inside as it was on Friday nights, but Slate spotted a few red-and-white Hawks uniforms and a smattering of girls from the bowling alley.

As if Slate had been wearing a cowbell, a group of women at the bar turned in unison and applause filled the bar. Riffs of "Hey, hey!" "Someone's been topped!" and "Long live the new king!" shot across the room, burning Slate's ears.

Slate approached them. Most of those girls—Rita, Janice, Lori, Kate, Brenda—were old pals. She knew they were just having fun. "It's sweeps week for cable access, m'ladies," Slate grinned. "Just a ratings ploy. Never fear! Slate will not be toppled from her throne." Still, Slate listened closely to their voices. Maybe one of them *had* called tonight.

Rita, a brawny butch with closely cropped bleach-blonde hair, sidled up next to Slate. "Well, pussycat," she cooed in her best Greta Garbo, "if I'd known you liked the tough ones, I'd have bedded you years ago." Slate slapped Rita's hand away before she could get it up Slate's T-shirt.

"Oh, yeah, daffodil," echoed Janice, an even beefier version of Rita, "maybe you could help me out with this banana bread recipe I've been working on. I could use a lady's touch around the house."

"Look in the mirror, then, sweetheart." Slate knew that was her lamest comeback in eons, but these girls—her friends, even!— were rattling her nerves.

"Whoa! Take it easy, pal." Janice wrapped her muscular arm around Slate's broad back. "Lemme get you a beer."

Slate scanned the room, looking for any butches, especially those in uniform, who might be the woman who'd phoned earlier tonight. In the corner a clutch of tough girls sat playing euchre, fingering their cards like it was group sex. There was Toni, the ESL teacher. Linda, the sociology grad student. And Perry, the...cop! Oh, man, that had to be her. She was always slyly putting Slate down, always threatening to cuff her and haul her into jail for "impersonating a good butch," as she put it. Well, Slate would show her who was boss. She grabbed her Heineken from Janice and strutted up to their table, the keys on her belt loop jangling against her blue-jeaned hip.

"Hey, there, Officer Odorous. How's it hangin'?"

Perry grinned, her blue eyes setting off her salt-and-pepper hair, then in a gravelly whisper of a voice said, "Not great, Slate. Gettin' over the flu. But wouldn't miss euchre night for all the femmes in China." Her laugh turned into a cough from deep in her chest, and Linda slapped her hard on the back.

"Feel better. Later, Perry." Slate turned away. *Damn!* thought Slate. She'd really thought she'd found her too. Then a lightbulb flashed over her head, and she followed the chords of the Rolling Stones' "Satisfaction" to the jukebox in the corner. Slate slowly browsed through the discs in the glass case, feeling like she was in some tired-ass episode of *Diagnosis: Murder*. Is this what she'd been reduced to? Still, she pressed on. There inside was Melissa's *Brave and Crazy, Never Enough, Your Little Secret*...crap, no *Yes I Am*. What kind of excuse for a dyke bar was this? There was no way the call could have come from the Connection, not without "Come to My Window" in the jukebox. Slate slammed her fist on top of the juke, then took a long draw from her Heineken. "Goddamn women," she said loud enough for everyone to hear, then placed her bottle on a nearby table and stormed out.

Back at her apartment, 20 minutes later, Slate had just undressed. Standing in the bathroom, she took a good, hard look at herself. Nice firm pecs. Taut legs. Boxer's arms. She had a few lines around her eyes, but damn it, she was in the best shape of her life. No wonder that woman had called her tonight. She was just envious of what she couldn't have. Yeah, that was it. And who wouldn't be? Slate ran her fingers over her breasts, down to her firm abs, then slipped a finger inside her pussy. She was wetter than she could remember being in a long time—and she was damn horny. Slate shut off the lights and went into her bedroom.

She walked over to the TV/VCR combination perched on top of a couple of milk crates by her dresser, thumbed through a stack of videos—*30-Minute Butt Workout*, *VH1 Behind the Music: The Spice Girls*, and an A&E *Biography* on Amelia Earhart—then found her favorite: the bootleg Indigo Girls tape she and Lucy had made a few summers ago. Slate slid the tape in—that act of insertion alone was enough to bring her over the edge—and climbed under her down comforter.

She always fast-forwarded the first few minutes: Lucy in the driver's seat on the way to the Madison Coliseum, popping PEZ from an Incredible Hulk dispenser into her luscious mouth; teasing Slate about how she was going to sleep with Amy and Emily after the concert; saying "Surely, Shirley" over and over until Slate yelled, "For fuck's sake, cut it out!" Too many memories.

She stopped scanning until she could see Amy approach the mike to start Slate's anthem, "Romeo and Juliet." The words "A lovestruck Romeo sings the streets a serenade..." spurred an all-too-familiar but glorious ache in Slate's loins. She slid her hand between her legs, circled her clit with her index and middle fingers. Her left hand traveled up to her small, taut breasts, the pinkish-brown nipple perking under her touch. She looked up at Amy mouthing the words to her favorite song. Damn if that bitch wasn't playing to *her* that night. And God, just look at Emily, that devious smile on her lips, her blonde locks falling over her gorgeous eyes, taunting Slate. This was Slate's secret indulgence, pining over these two unbelievably sexy, capable butches. She was gushing, in her heart and cunt, her slick juices rushing out with the splendor of the Girls' guitar chords, their sweet harmonies pulling heat out of her from deep within. With her fingers still circling her growing clit, Slate licked the fingers of her left hand and moistened her breast, building into a rhythm that matched that of Amy and Emily.

Just when she thought she could take no more, she reached into the oak night stand next to her bed and pulled out a dildo she'd kept ever since Lucy left, hoping she might have the opportunity to use it on the dozens of femmes who'd be knocking on her door. *I might as well toss this out*, Slate thought, fingering the long pink sex toy. *What the fuck—just go for it.* Without a second's thought, she slid the dildo into her mouth, slowly, as if she were giving her own cock a hot and heavy blow, then withdrew it and pushed it inside her throbbing snatch. She'd only tried this once before—a few months ago—and couldn't get it in, but that night she'd been drunk on four bad Chi Chi's margaritas and had been dry as a bone. This time the cock slid in easily, the wide head spreading Slate's vagina, filling her. *Long, slow, excrutiating, blinding screw.* Slate moaned, envisioning her butch caller from this evening—she had Amy's eyes and Emily's smile and Ellen's hair and Demi's body and Tracy Chapman's lips and Slate's own strong hands and...a sweat-stained UPS uniform.

Pleasure mounted in Slate's body, the dildo sliding easily in and out. God, she'd never even let Lucy touch her like this. But she was in control now, fucking herself, allowing herself to fantasize like she'd never had. Tonight's caller had opened some door for her, had let the real Slate come out and play. *Long, slow, excrutiating, blinding screw.* Slate got up and kneeled on the bed, then pushed the cock inside her as far as it would go, its base pressing into the mattress. She rocked her torso back and forth, then slid her body up and down the pecker. "Fuck me, bitch. Pound me, you whore," she called out, fingering her wet, swollen clit, tongue-kissing her imaginary lover. Oh, god, this was good. Oh, for fuck's sake. She grabbed the bottom of the dildo with both hands, abandoning her clit, pumping and pumping until she thought she'd explode. *Long, slow, excrutiating, blinding screw.* All the women she'd never allowed herself to touch or love came flooding in her mind as a torturously powerful orgasm rolled in and out of her from a place she'd pushed down far too long, waves of warmth and come and heat and tears pouring from her body. And by the time the lyrics "You and me, babe, how about it?" shot out from the TV speakers, she had collapsed into her pillow, tears streaking her chiseled face. She was spent.

But shame and fear lurked just beneath the surface of Slate's pleasure.

"Jesus, Shirley, you didn't bring the extra battery pack?" were the last words she heard before falling into a deep sleep.

The cold morning rain fell steadily against a darkening sky. Slate pulled the cords to the hood of her red windbreaker tighter as she finished the last quarter of her two-mile run to work, which she'd been doing every day, rain or shine, for the past seven years. It was good for her; the adrenaline rush helped to keep her calm, focused. (Just imagine what she'd be like without it.) But today Slate's mind was going a mile a minute. Every person she passed, she wondered, *Could that be her?* She knew she must be going loco, since she'd even sized up an old woman with a walker and a 15-year-old skate rat.

As Slate started her cooldown walk, she was just entering the UW Hospital parking lot, which was nearly as big as a football field. She glanced at her watch: 7:35 A.M. She'd have plenty of time to dry off and change clothes—and do a few minutes of snoop work—before her 8 o'clock shift.

Still sweating over her mystery caller, Slate relaxed against the chain-link fence and scoped out the parking lot. A dozen or so uniform-clad employees were climbing out of their cars or putting the final touches on their makeup or hair in their rearview mirrors. Slate spotted a couple of nurses from pediatrics rushing—first one, then the other a minute later—from a beat-up Tercel with newspapers over their hot-combed heads. "Who do those Bobsey Twin lezzies think they're fooling?" Slate snickered out loud.

She glanced over her right shoulder and saw Lorraine from hematology barreling up in her Durango. Lorraine and Slate had squabbled over that little blonde bartender Tammy at the Crystal Corner a few years ago, but that was water under the bridge, right? *Who knows with these crazy dykes and this screwed-up town*, Slate thought.

The rain was really coming down now, so Slate decide to jump ship and head inside. Besides, she'd want to have enough time to spruce up, just in case any hottie patients came in today. She'd never cross the line—she was always strictly professional—but she had a bad case of BHC (butch hair complex) and *had* to make sure she looked slick all the time.

Inside the physical therapy changing room, Slate opened her locker and grabbed her hospital blues, then saluted the photo of Flo Jo she'd taped inside the door, a ritual she'd been practicing for a while now. Drops of water trailed down her cheeks as she pulled off her windbreaker and tied it to the door handle to dry out. She stripped down to her bra (which she didn't really need but wore for show at the hospital) and panties (which, again, if she'd had her druthers, would be low-riding boxers).

"Nice abs," came a low voice, almost a growl, from the other side of the lockers.

Slate whipped her head around faster than a riled rattlesnake. "Who's that?" she said, quivering just a bit—in several places.

"Although I know some exercises that could build them up even more."

That was her, that sure as fuck was her! Slate would give that wench her comeuppance, that was certain. "Listen, you bitch," Slate called out as she darted around the corner in hot pursuit. But instead of catching the mystery woman, she clipped the shoulder of little blue-haired Elaine Rudin, her 65-year-old supervisor, who was just six months away from retirement.

"Whoa, Shirley! You know I've only got a few years left in me. Make 'em easy, huh?" Elaine mock-dusted herself off, then grinned.

"Sorry, it's just..." Slate was out of breath and a little bewildered.

Elaine looked Slate straight in the eyes. She'd always been frank and fair with Slate but never overly friendly. She was all perfumed and fluffed up, definitely old school, probably with a couple of grown children and a half dozen grandkids. "Listen," Elaine said. "If I find out any one of these little pussies called and harassed you last night, I'm puttin' them on my permanent shit list. No one messes with us P.T. bulldykes."

Slate eyes grew wide. Who knew?

"You're a good egg, kid—and your show is a riot. Just watch your back. And Slate..."

"Yeah?" Slate peeped, still stunned.

"For Christ's sake, put some clothes on."

Slate quickly got dressed, fixed her hair, then headed for the P.T. desk, where she'd take a look at her schedule for the day. She loved physical therapy, enjoyed the satisfaction of making parts work again as a whole, like repairing a watch or an engine but with breath and blood and spirit. And she relished ordering around her coworkers; she was a Leo, after all. *That's where I really shine*, she often thought.

"Hey, Sandy," Slate addressed the new receptionist, then picked up and scanned the printout of her appointments. *Good, no one until 9:30*, Slate thought. *I'll have plenty of time to scope out that cafeteria bulldagger.* Just then she heard that familiar off-key whistle and looked up to see one of her fellow physical therapists—what was her name? Onette? Odessa? Oh, for the love of Mary, she had her Walkman on again. Hadn't Slate told her a million times it was against hospital rules?

"Hey, what's the matter with you?" Slate called out, but it was no use; the woman was in her own world, swaying to the music in her ears, her long braids swinging across her broad shoulders.

That's it, thought Slate. *One more violation and that bitch is out on her ass.* She approached the woman from behind and placed a firm hand on her shoulder, swinging her around. Her name tag read ONYX DUNLAP.

"What's your damage?" Onyx asked, her full lips stuck in a scowl, the mocha skin of her prominent forehead creasing.

"Listen, Onyx"—and Slate pronounced it "Oh-nix"—"haven't you heard a word I've said? No Walkmans on the job. This is your final warning. Got it, swee' pea?"

"That's 'Ah-nix.' 'Ah' as in 'Open up and say ah.' " As Onyx took off her headphones, Slate made out the final chords of "Come to My Window." Lord, she was Slate's caller! It was all coming together now: all those altercations over Onyx's tardiness, her blatant distrust of authority, not to mention that voice. Well, Slate would teach her a lesson.

Onyx leaned against the P.T. desk, one hand on her hip. "I don't understand why Ron and Jackie can listen to music when they're not on duty yet and no one calls them on it. You're not even my supervisor."

"They're orderlies! Who cares what they do?" Slate frowned. "It's *you* that's making P.T.s look bad."

"And we all know looks are all that matter to you." Onyx came in real close to Slate, just a few inches separating them. "I think you take some sort of twisted pleasure in riding my ass." Damn, she was a handsome woman, with an even handsomer ass. "I've had enough of your holier-than-thou bullshit, Shirley." And sassy to boot.

"I think it's time for a little chat, Goldilocks," Slate said as she slung an arm around Onyx's muscular back and led her into a P.T. patient room around the corner. The room was dark inside, the lights set low for patients to relax on the roller beds and heating pads.

"Sit." Slate pointed to a chair, then shut and locked the door behind her.

"Make me," Onyx said, all business.

Slate pushed Onyx up against the wall, pinning her shoulders firmly. "So, you think you can just waltz into my world and shatter everything I've worked for for the past seven years?"

"Cut the crap, Shirl. You think I don't notice you checking me out all the time?" Onyx's breath was warm and laced with cinnamon. "I'm not blind, sugar. If we're gonna get it on, let's get it on. I'll show you who's boss—at least in bed."

"How long have you been cooking up this little scheme, huh? You think you're tougher than me? You think you can top me?"

"Listen, woman, I'm tired as fuck of this two-stepping we do every day. There's only one way to settle this." And with that Onyx grabbed the back of Slate's shorn head and pulled her into her warm, inviting mouth. Slate resisted at first, but that lasted all of three seconds, as Onyx's thick tongue explored Slate's gaping mouth, releasing a shudder from her cunt. *Long, slow, excrutiating, blinding screw.*

"This isn't right," Slate breathed, pulling back a little.

"How 'bout this? Is this right?" Onyx slid her hand down Slate's thin cotton pants, easing her long fingers through Slate's neatly trimmed thatch, into her slick, juicy cavern. "Holy shit, Old Faithful's tellin' me it is."

"Bring it on," Slate barely whispered.

It'd now been ten months, five days, and 15 hours since Slate had been with any woman, and her body was on fire, her blood nearly boiling with the heat rising from Onyx's rock-hard body. Shame succumbed to pheromones and sweat.

"I think we need to get a bit more comfortable," Onyx said almost tenderly, pushing Slate onto one of the roller beds in the corner. "This ought to do it."

Slate lay on her back, her eyes focusing on the tiny bumps of plaster in the ceiling, her body stiff. *This can't be happening*, she thought, but then she remembered all the times she'd mentally undressed Onyx, ran her eyes over her firm 30-somethin' ass, those pumped brown biceps, those sumptuous tits. But she hadn't even thought Onyx was a lez, just a little rough around the edges. For all her bravado, Slate's gaydar was wacked; half the time she couldn't tell a dyke from a doughnut.

Onyx climbed on top of Slate, and Slate's eyes bugged at what she felt riding her thigh. Damn, the bitch was packing—at work too! Slate was impressed, although fear flooded her arteries. Onyx definitely deserved a guest spot—maybe even a permanent cohosting job—on *Butch Talk*. But they'd have to discuss that later, because right now Onyx was pulling up Slate's shirt over her small titties, swooping in on her left nipple with that heavenly mouth. Slate's mind went blank as a blackboard, her thoughts overpowered by the warm, wet snake circling her breast, Onyx's braids tickling Slate's washboard stomach.

Words weren't necessary—Onyx's silky, frenetic tongue was more than enough—though Slate usually loved yelling shit in bed:

I'm gonna fuck your brains out. I'm gonna come all over your greedy snatch. You feel that, bitch? Slate liked it rough, but what could she say to Onyx now? If she uttered what she was thinking, it'd be the end of her. She fought to silence the kittenish words begging for escape: *Oh, baby, you're so good. Fuck me, Onyx. Screw the life out of me, sweetheart.* Yeah, right.

Onyx's lips were soft, her manner gentle, but her tongue and mouth were fierce, centering on the space between Slate's breasts, then quickly traveling down her abs to the space between her navel and the drawstring to her hospital pants. Warm, wet, wonderful. Onyx seized upon one end of the cord with her teeth and pulled. Then she grabbed both sides of Slate's pants and eased them down to her knees. She was quick but methodical, the way the mailman or garbage collector is. Slate was still in her panties—oh, god, did they have to be the ones with the tiny tulips?—and Onyx nuzzled into the warmth of Slate's crotch, burying her face into the wet cotton. She tongued the fabric, searching out Slate's clit, then locating and attacking it with her mouth. The combination of the fabric's softness and Onyx's hungry tongue lapping at Slate's hard clit undid her. "Oh, fuck me," she mumbled—but of course she'd meant that figuratively…right?

"My pleasure, darling," Onyx chuckled, but before Slate could protest, Onyx had risen to her knees and whipped out her thick blue cock, holding it in her calloused hand like a guy at a urinal. She pulled down Slate's panties, then slid in the strap-on, Slate's pussy gushing more lubrication than a Texas oil well.

Onyx flattened her palms on either side of Slate's shoulders, her hands pressing into the brown vinyl of the narrow roller bed. Her deep cocoa eyes locked with Slate's as she pumped Slate good and hard, faster than a sewing machine needle, pleasure and dull pain throbbing in Slate's snatch. The wide head slid in and out of Slate's hole, teasing the entrance, then diving in for more. Slate bucked her hips to meet the cock, both women in perfect rhythm. She gripped the edge of the roller bed as she felt the tip of an orgasm rising like a buried iceberg—a small crest on the surface disguising an unbelievable phenomenon below. *So this is why Lucy could never get enough*, Slate thought, and a tear trickled out of the corner of her eye: one part sadness, one part unbelievably engorged cunt.

"Oh, baby, you're something else," Onyx whispered, then added, "Who's your daddy now?"

But Slate stayed silent, sensation washing over her entire body.

"I said, 'Who's your daddy?' "

"You are," Slate mumbled, eyes closed, Onyx still sliding in and out of her.

"What's that? I couldn't hear you."

"You are," Slate repeated, her senses overcome with the rising heat and funk of hot, athletic sex.

"Louder."

She'd had enough of this torture. "Pound me, you dirty whore," Slate finally bellowed, summoning her fantasy fuck from last night, but Onyx would have none of that. She stopped mid-thrust and slapped Slate across the cheek, then grabbed her shoulders and shook her.

"I get enough shit from you on the floor—you think I need this crap too?" asked Onyx, her eyes drilling into Slate. "Man alive, I thought you'd be different half naked."

The sting of Onyx's hand left a faint red shadow on Slate's cheek, and a few more tears streamed down her iron jaw, but there was no way in hell she'd wipe them up in front of Onyx.

Onyx stood up and removed her dildo, then pulled up her pants and tied her drawstring. "Here, take this home and practice," she said as she dropped the wet strap-on onto Slate's bare stomach. "You can call me when you're ready to give me some respect."

"Respect? Is that how you treated me last night during my show?"

"Show? Girl, I don't know what you're talking about."

"Wait, where are you going?" Slate managed to get out.

"On break." And with that, Onyx stormed out, leaving Slate all undone, tinged with regret, on the sticky vinyl.

"Shirley Dixon, please report to the cafeteria stock room. Shirley Dixon to the cafeteria stock room," came a no-nonsense, gritty voice through the overhead system, glasses and dishes softly clinking in the background.

Whaddya know, it was Slate's mystery caller.

"Oh, shit," said Slate, burying her sweaty, flushed face in her hands. "Round two."

8

Plaid Skirt, White Shirt, Blue Socks, Blue Shoes Ellen Golden

The museum is just down the street from the school. It is a big museum, very old, very famous. There are paintings and statues and high stained-glass windows that turn the light into sapphire-blue squares on the polished limestone floors. The girls are wearing blue too: blue jackets, blue kneesocks, blue stripes through the gray and red plaid of their skirts. This year, for the first time, the girls wear blue rubber-soled shoes. Up until now, only hard-soled shoes have been allowed, but the rules were relaxed and so some of the girls are now squeaking against the stone floor by sliding sideways and soon all of them are doing it and then there's laughter, high and stifled, until one of the nuns turns around and glares and it stops.

This year, fifth grade, the trip to the museum is to see the friezes. The girls twitter like a flight of birds down the wide gorgeous corridors. A. and H. lag behind. The Two Musketeers—that's what Sister Bernadette, who sells the blue plastic rosaries in the school store that's really a closet off the auditorium, calls them. They have spent the year after school sitting on the bed in H.'s brother's room throwing toilet-paper balls out the air shaft window, or leaping from tabletop to tabletop in the living room playing Don't Touch the Floor, or ringing doorbells and running as fast as they can down the street and around the corner, then piling onto each other to peer around and see if anyone came out to see who was calling.

Now they're alone in the huge statue court—the rest of the class has disappeared around a corner. They are laughing and breathing hard from something H. said, holding their hands over each other's mouths to keep from making noise. Their breath in the close air between them smells like peppermint gum, which is strictly forbidden. The statues are on pedestals all around them, tall naked women carved out of marble, breasts with marble areolas and the curve of hips swelling into behinds and the twin butterfly wings of stone shoulder blades beneath rivers of flowing stone hair.

A. is waiting at the bus stop, on the east side. She has her books in a backpack that's strapped on her shoulders, and she's unsnapped her plaid tie from around her neck and stuffed it in the pocket of her blazer, which also has her bus pass in it. She's holding a copy of a magazine with pictures from *Pretty Baby* in it, the movie that's just come out. When the bus comes it's almost empty and she walks to the back and sits down in the last row, the one with the seats all the way across. She sits next to the window, so she can put her shoes up on the side of the seat in front of her and watch the sidewalk as the bus goes across town.

She's already read the magazine, but she opens it up again as the bus starts to move. She stares at the pictures again. Brooke Shields is naked, almost, long and skinny with red lipstick and long blonde streaks in the hair that falls over her back. She and H. have talked a lot about Brooke Shields because they're all exactly the same age, 12 years old. Sometimes they argue when they're looking at the pictures, tracing the lines of Brooke's face and body with their fingers to illustrate their points. A. looks up, smooths her plaid skirt down over her knees so no one on the bus can see her legs, then puts the magazine away, stuffs it into her backpack next to her math text-book. The bus pulls away from the corner of 85th Street and Fifth Avenue and turns right, heading into the park.

When the bus gets to the West Side the sidewalks are crowded, suddenly, and A. watches the people from her seat by the window. There are boys from the collegiate school in their gray pants and blue jackets, pushing each other, and there are doormen standing in the lobbies of the buildings, and men in business suits walking with briefcases at the end of their extended arms. A. glances at them briefly then looks away.

When the bus reaches the corner of 81st Street and Columbus Avenue, it comes to a full stop for the light and there's a woman walking there on the sidewalk going west. She's wearing a brown T-shirt, this woman, a very tight brown T-shirt that is pasted onto her body, over her breasts and then tucked into her jeans, which are also tight and light blue, wrapped around her like they're holding each one of her cheeks in the palm of their hands, and the woman has long, wavy brown hair down her back, and coffee-colored skin, and she has on tall platform shoes that make her hips swivel in a circle as she walks. A. stares at the woman, at her breasts in the brown T-shirt and at her stomach where the shirt tucks into the top of her jeans, and before A. can stop, she thinks of what it would feel like to reach out and run the palm of her hand over the woman's breasts. It's like a tidal pull, this feeling, strong and sharp. A. knots her hands in her pockets, twisting her plaid tie into a ball, and makes herself look away, her hair skimming the collar of her white shirt, black and shiny and bright as rain.

H.'s parents are away in Europe. The apartment echoes. H. lives on Fifth Avenue in the upper Nineties, and the apartment has many rooms, leading into and out of one another, wood and stone under-foot, doors ajar. There are never any lights on during the day, which gives the rooms an underwater feel, with the shadows of the leaves outside rippling on the walls and the sound of the traffic below like the sea. A. and H. sit on the bed in her parents' room. It's after school, mid-year—they have five more months to go before they graduate from eighth grade.

"The only way to get good is to practice," H. is saying. They've been talking about sex, which A. doesn't know anything about. "You never want anyone to know that you've never done it before, so you have to practice."

"Really?" A. says. She and H. are sitting side by side, but now H. lies down on her back and runs her hands through her hair, which is crinkly and long and very streaky blonde. They've taken their jackets off and their shoes, so they're wearing just their skirts and their white shirts and their blue kneesocks, pulled up just under their knees.

"Being experienced is very important," H. says. "Otherwise you're just going to look like a fool."

They are silent for a moment, staring at the walls.

"So have you ever kissed anyone?" A. asks.

"Have you?" H. says.

"I asked you first," A. says. She's lying down on the bed now too, because it's more comfortable that way. They're side by side, but it's a big bed—A. can stretch her arms all the way out without brushing against H., which she knows because she just tried it.

"I don't want to say," H. says. "It's private."

They ponder this for a while longer.

"But then what if you kiss someone and it's no good? What if you don't know what you're doing and so nothing happens and it doesn't work out?" A. says. She's certain she's speaking in riddles enough so that H. won't be able to tell what's she's talking about, not exactly, but close enough so that maybe she'll understand a little bit.

"I think what happens then is that it's over," H. says. She sounds very definite about it. "There's no way to tell beforehand, so that's what happens—it's like it never happened, and nobody ever knows."

"Oh," A. says. Out of the corner of her eye, she can see H. running her hands through her long hair. H. sees her watching and rolls onto her stomach, her plaid skirt riding all the way up to the top of her legs. H. looks up over her shoulder and smiles at A., and goes on brushing her hair.

So then it is every afternoon. A bit of arm wrestling, then a bit of full-body wrestling, then running up and down the stairs in A.'s house pretending to be Jesus and Mary Magdalene, then around 4:30, before A.'s mother gets home from work, practicing.

"Like this?" A. says.

"Harder," H. says.

A. has her lips on H.'s forearm, and she's trying to give H. a hickey. They are sitting on the floor in the living room, which is on the second floor of A.'s three-story house.

"Here, let me do you," H. says. She takes A.'s arm in her hand and runs her fingers along the tiny hairs that run like bright blades on A.'s skin. Her fingertips feel like feathers, or a waterfall, on A.'s arm, dancing and very alive. H. traces her lips lightly along where her fingers have been, traces up toward A.'s elbow, where the soft silky skin is delicate, translucent, pristinely untouched, and then kisses her there, right in the crook of her elbow, with a sudden, pressing heat. The kiss is hard, honing in, pressure and pressure and then just when A. doesn't think she can stand it anymore she feels her whole arm relax and give itself over to H.'s mouth, to the insistent heated sensation of her lips and flickering tongue. She feels like her whole body has disappeared except for the hot point where H.'s mouth is.

"There!" H. says, sitting back. A red circular mark, like a bruise only fainter, is on the inside of A.'s elbow. They both look at it with intense interest.

"That didn't hurt at all," A. says. She feels like her voice is coming from someplace very far away.

"I don't think you kiss hard enough," H. says.

"Maybe not," A. agrees.

They sit for a moment in silence, thinking their own thoughts. Then A. says, "So maybe we should practice something else now."

"Like what?" H. says.

"I don't know," A. says. Then she says, "Wait, I know what." And she turns so she's facing H., still sitting cross-legged on the floor. She takes the plaid tie off from underneath the collar of her shirt, and then unsnaps the first two buttons of her shirt. Then she pulls her shirt out from the waistband of her plaid skirt so that it is outside her skirt, and unsnaps it three more buttons, so that most of it is open but the part over her bellybutton is still closed. The shirt does not gape open very much; it hangs pretty much together even though it is unbuttoned, but still A.'s bra is visible, and a little bit of her stomach.

"I thought it was my turn," H. says.

"It is," A. says. So then H. does just what A. has done, and then they're sitting facing each other cross-legged on the living room floor, with their legs tucked underneath their skirts and their blouses undone.

"Are you ready?" A. says. H. nods. Her eyes are closed.

A. reaches over and tucks her right hand very slightly inside H.'s shirt. H. takes a deep breath. With her fingertips, A. touches H.'s breastbone, right above the little white strip that connects the two cups of H.'s bra. Then, very slowly and hesitantly, she slides her fingertips over to the left and traces the swell of H.'s breast. She pauses, petrified all of a sudden, but H. nods, her eyes still tightly closed and her pulse beating beneath the skin of her throat. So A. runs her fingers along the line where H.'s bra meets her skin, tentatively, tenderly. H. is shivering and breathing faster, short shallow breaths, and A. watches her for a second and then dips her hand inside the bra and touches all of H.'s breast, around the sides and underneath and across the top and then finally right on center, thinking about the warm feeling that H.'s mouth had made on her arm, wishing she could lean over and put her lips right on the hard center where her hand is. She thinks of how that would feel, to kiss H. right there, flickering her tongue over the top of H.'s breast like H. did on her arm.

Downstairs, the door slams.

The girls spring apart. A. feels unholy, not like Jesus or Mary Magdalene at all. But her mother just walks right past them on her way upstairs.

And then it happens. A. has her mouth on H.'s shoulder—they are lying on the living room floor, as always—and H. turns toward her just for a second and accidentally brushes her lips against A.'s lips, and then A. is kissing her, really kissing her, pushing her tongue past H.'s teeth into the warm expanse of her mouth, which is salty and sweet at the same time. H. kisses back, with a fever that takes A. totally by surprise, and then she presses her breastbone hard— hard—into the hollow beneath A.'s ribs.

The carpet beneath them smells like wool and their shirts are stained with ink and sweat and their blue jackets are on the coat rack downstairs and the traffic outside the window stops and starts and a horn blares and there are footfalls on the pavement and the sound of a dog barking. The bark snaps A. out of her reverie, and she sits up and stares at H., her eyes wide and serious, but H. has burst out laughing and won't stop, laughing and laughing, her bright long hair like a river of fire on her shoulders and back. Tomorrow, at school, they will sit through a long catechism about the sins of the flesh, and H. will catch A.'s eye and burst out laughing again, but for right now, for right now, this is what there is.

9

Betty and Veronica Jane Futcher

My sister and I were both in love with Emma. Her easy mastery of any sport she tried, her wise brown eyes and ready smile, the cool distance she kept from the other summer kids held us in a state of longing each August, when our family rented one of her father's seaside cottages on the Maine coast.

Emma lived in the village year-round, in a rambling white clapboard farmhouse on the high ground above the beach, with a gnarled apple tree in the side yard and a red garage that had once been the carriage house and hay barn. Some of the summer kids said she was stuck-up and spoiled, because she was an only child and her father gave her an entire room in the bathhouse for all her rafts and skimmers and snorkeling gear.

"She's not a snob," we'd say, thrilled that for some unknown reason Emma seemed to prefer my sister and me to the summer kids her own age from Philadelphia's Main Line and swanky suburbs in St. Louis and Cincinnati. "You're jealous because she won't let you read her comics."

I think I'd wanted to touch Emma since I was ten, when I first inhaled Noxema on her shoulders as she and my sister and I lay on her bed eating her homemade white cake with pale blue icing and reading comics. Emma had the world's largest collection, an entire walk-in closet stacked with crisp, unthumbed copies of *Little Lulu*, *Superman*, *Donald Duck*, and *Mickey Mouse*. As we got older, our love of talking animals gave way to an obsession with Betty and Veronica and later with *True Romance*. I always imagined I was one of those square-jawed young men in sports jackets who fought for the love of the narrow-waisted, sensitive girls with crystal teardrops glistening on their cheeks.

The first evening when we arrived each summer, Emma would come over with her father to Kitty Wake or Gray Gull or Pine Cottage and stand in the doorway, hands tucked in the pockets of her faded jeans, hair in pigtails, boyish but somehow glamorously feminine in her blue-and-white striped T-shirt, while our fathers, friends since boyhood, planned their annual sail to the Isles of Shoals and traded theories on the true author of Shakespeare's works.

"Emma," we'd say shyly, for she was three years older than me and a year older than my sister, "will you canoe with us on the marsh this year? Wanna walk to the tidepools on Godfrey's Ledge in low tide?"

"Sure," she'd say, and she'd disappear and return from the car with a stack of fresh comics for us. She loaned them on one condition— and this was her only rule—that we return them to her in perfect condition, without any tears or smudges or creases. It was an awesome responsibility, because we were naturally messy children for whom neatness was as elusive as the peaks of Everest.

We never got enough of Emma, because she was always hurrying off in the mornings to play tennis and later golf at the Abenakee Club, which we didn't belong to. We longed for those rare afternoons we spent lounging on her bed reading comics or out on the marsh paddling her canoe through secluded canals.

The summer of '62, when I was 15 and Emma was 18, Emma's father came down alone to Gray Gull the first night of our vacation.

His eyes were red from reading briefs, and his shoulders were more stooped than we'd ever seen them.

"Emma's not here," he said in his dry Maine accent, when he saw me still looking toward the door.

"Not here?" My sister's lip curled, and she glared at my mother, as if it were her fault.

"She's a waitress at the Wentworth Hotel in Portsmouth this summer," he explained. "Wouldn't go to Europe with the group from school or cycle across Canada with her cousins. Living in the women's dorm making $1.50 an hour."

"Jeez," I said, depressed.

"Shit." My sister had started using bad language, even though nice girls didn't say "shit" in front of grown-ups in 1962.

Emma called me at Gray Gull the third day we were there. "I can get Thursday afternoon off. If you can get up here, we can do something together. Don't tell anyone." Since my mother and father and sister were all watching as I spoke to Emma, that was hard to do.

"Um..."

"Just try, OK?"

"Sure," I said, staring down at the police emergency number taped to the telephone.

"What'd she say?" my sister asked eagerly.

I reddened. "Said she works every day except Mondays."

"Is she coming down here? Can we see her?"

I hadn't planned to lie to my sister. But I wanted Emma to myself. So on Thursday, when my father said he was driving to Portsmouth to buy a new anchor line for the dory, I feigned indifference, knowing if I said I'd go, my sister would want to come too. Just as he was pulling out of the driveway, I jumped in the car.

"Drop me at the Wentworth," I said, as if I went to the big old hotel all the time.

He glanced at me oddly. "The Wentworth?"

"Emma has the afternoon off," I said, forcing the emotion from my voice, "and we're going to..." I paused. What were we going to do? "Take a walk"

When I saw Emma, lying on the bed of her tiny, bare room at the Wentworth in her pink waitress uniform, I almost threw up. The crisp cotton dress came just to her knees; a white apron was tied around her hips, and her hair was twisted up in a sort of a bun.

"Hey," she smiled, pushing a long strand of hair from her eyes.

I swallowed.

She stood up. "I wanted to change before you got here, but I'm exhausted." She was blushing. "This uniform is embarrassing."

"No," I said. "It's...You look good." She was Patricia Neal in *HUD* and Helen Hunt in *The Man Who Hated the Dog*, although that movie, whatever it was called, hadn't been made yet. She was someone from my dreams.

We walked along the water, the huge white wooden hotel looming over us like a scene from a hand-painted postcard. It seemed weird for an amazing athlete like Emma to be here, when she could be winning silver butter dishes and gold charms and loving cups for tennis and golf at home or traveling through Europe or riding a bike through the Canadian Rockies. "Why are you working here?" I asked.

"To get away," she said, staring out at the sea.

"What about tennis?" I tugged on her apron. "Don't you miss it?"

She shrugged. "I play because my mother makes me. She thinks if I go to the club every day it'll make me normal." She smiled at me so sweetly I nearly fainted. "I'd much rather fish or paddle around in a canoe with you. I want to have my own boat someday."

"To fish?" She didn't answer. High above us, on the cliffs, a guy in a white shirt and a black bow tie was waving. She didn't wave back.

"Your uniform is cool," I said.

"I look like a maid." She curtsied to me. "Our specials today are lobster thermidor, steak au poivre, and prime rib with French beans and baked potato," she mimicked.

"You have to memorize all the dishes?"

"Big deal." Emma always got straight A's.

"Have you ever dropped a plate on somebody's lap? You've got to be coordinated to be a waitress."

Emma chewed her lip, then suddenly, without warning, took my hand. "I've missed you so much. I'm sorry I didn't write you this year."

I swallowed. The softness of her hand made feathers in my stomach. "You were busy, I guess."

"I saved all your letters," she said, stopping by the sea wall, where some painted lobster buoys were drying in the sun and the air smelled of seaweed and salt. "I read them over and over."

"Did you?" My eyes were fixed on the white napkin poking out from a pocket just above her breast. We had come to a small beach, back behind the hotel, more like a tidal inlet than the open sea, with high, green marsh grass and a feeling of privacy.

Emma pulled a little comb from the back of her head, and her long brown hair tumbled down. I don't know how, but somehow I reached out and stroked it without Emma seeing my hands shake.

"I'm fucked up, you know," she said, her brown eyes locking on mine, hand tightening around my fingers.

"Me too," I said, so close I could smell the almond of the Jergens lotion she'd rubbed on her hands.

"I'm more screwed up," she said, her lips touching mine. Then it *is* true, I thought, my arm going around her waist. She is crazy. She does love me. "My mother is an alcoholic."

"Your mother?" It was hard to think with Emma so close.

"Don't take your hand away," she said.

My fingers froze. "I've never seen your mother drunk."

"You've seen her with her cocktails passed out in the living room."

"She was sleeping," I said.

"You're cute," she smiled. "Let's not talk about it." Emma pulled me into her arms, as if she were one of the dream girls in *True Romance* comics.

I glanced at the marsh grass next to the path. "We could sit down or something."

She looked at her dress. "It's my only clean uniform."

"It makes you look—"

"Ridiculous," she said.

"Beautiful," I said.

"Let's go to my room." She stared up at the huge white hotel. "My roommate went to Ogunquit with her boyfriend. She won't be back till 5."

"Your room?" I couldn't breathe.

"It would be fun, don't you think? To lie down in bed?"

I was blushing. She was so much more experienced. Anyone would have been more experienced than me.

We walked up through the marsh, around the guest parking lot filled with black Cadillacs and Lincoln Town Cars, around to the funky, white-clapboard employee dorm where suddenly there were tons of girls, sitting on the steps, smoking Marlboros and Kools, all wearing little pink-and-white uniforms with handkerchiefs in the pocket and their hair in buns.

"Hi, Emma." A tall guy with his dark hair slicked back, wearing black pants and a white shirt with a black bow tie, stopped in front of us.

"Hey, Paul," she smiled, but she didn't stop. "He's French Canadian," she whispered as we started up the steps of her dorm. "His family runs a lobster pound in Biddeford Pool."

"Cool," I said, wishing my family owned a lobster pound. "My father's parents were from Canada," I said on the dusty staircase up to her room.

"They're not French. They're WASPs."

"I guess," I said.

We hiked up two more flights of dark, musty stairs. On the top floor, down a long hall, Emma opened the door to Room 702 with a key from her pocket. Two twin beds were separated by a sliver of bare floor and a tiny night stand with an unshaded lamp.

"Should I…." She looked at me. "Undress?"

I looked away, embarrassed. "Let's just hold each other."

We lay on top of the scratchy green wool military blanket, not touching. Emma's Jergens lotion smelled heavenly.

"I'm in love with you, you know," she said.

I swallowed as her lips inched closer to mine. And then somehow we were kissing, little soft kisses, like guppies in a tank or minnows nibbling in a pond. Suddenly, just like in the comics, a diamond tear glistened on her cheek. "I've really missed you," she said. "I don't know why I took this waitress job."

"It's a guy, isn't it?" I said, watching a small black spider drop down from the ceiling.

"A guy?" She looked puzzled.

"That's why you're here. Because you love Paul or something." Her knee was between mine, and she was unzipping my Bermuda shorts, the red plaid ones that were hand-me-downs from my sister.

She shook her head solemnly. "I had to escape. I couldn't take another summer at home."

She was touching my white cotton underpants, and I was untying her apron. It was almost like being out in her canoe or floating on a canvas raft beyond the breakers. "I thought you loved my sister more than me," I said.

"Not like this." She placed my hands on the top button of her uniform, close to her breasts. My fingers traced the pale, worn buttons. I could see a lacy bra, and no slip, under the thin fabric.

"I wish your mother wasn't an alcoholic," I said.

"Me too."

Everything was spinning and wet. The sight of her strong, bare shoulders made my legs ache. "You feel good," I said.

"I've never done this before." Her eyes suddenly grew shy.

"I thought…"

"Not with a girl."

That meant she'd done it with boys, but I didn't care. I held her tight so I could convince myself this wasn't a dream.

"Hey." She looked at her watch. "If I could get the whole day off tomorrow, could you come back?"

I blinked. "It's hard," I said. "I can't drive. My father didn't understand why he couldn't have lunch with us."

She thought for a minute. "I'll come home next weekend and you can spend the night at my house. We'll make mad, passionate love."

"Wow," I said, terrified.

"Do you want to?"

"Sure," I said. "Can we read some *Archie and Veronica*s first?"

As she leaned back to laugh, a bell shrieked through the dorm. "Oh, Christ," she said. "Dinner set-up is early on Wednesdays. I've got to go." She stood up and straightened her uniform.

"It's wrinkled," I said.

"I don't care." She twisted her hair back into a bun.

"They'll think you've been sleeping in it."

"Good." She winked at me. She was so much more daring, so much more of a rebel than I was.

We held hands walking down the stairs. "Say hello to your parents."

"When will you call me?" I asked, keeping my eyes on the curve of her waist, trying to imprint her image onto my retinas. "When can you tell me for sure about spending the night?"

"I'll know Friday morning. We'll tell your mother I've got a new shipment of *Little Lulu*s I need help sorting." She held me close, right there in front of the waiters and bus boys and waitresses all arriving for their shift, wiped a tear from her cheek, hurried toward the service door of the dining room, then blew me a kiss as she disappeared inside.

I didn't get to spend the night with Emma. She got pregnant by the French Canadian. She was ready to elope and sail to Newfoundland in her father's fishing trawler when her mother found out and arranged an abortion in Boston. Emma didn't come back the next summer, and when we went to visit her parents, the comics were all gone from her walk-in closet. She started college that fall.

10

The Cafeteria Lady Paula Neves

I first saw her in the commons slinging mashed potatoes and applesauce onto young scholars' plates. She had a flick of the wrist that immediately excited me.

I felt like she would be the one. She reminded me of all the ones who had come before: Clary, Anabel, Mrs. Stefanko. They were the cafeteria ladies, and they'd had a special place in my heart since I was old enough to know I liked mashed potatoes over creamed corn. I liked them 'cause they were the only people at school who were nice to me. And they always gave me a little extra something.

Her name was Janice. I found it out later from my friend Sue, the first "family" I'd ever met on campus.

"Yeah, that's Janice. She umps softball, and she's trying out for crew. I think she's also pre-med."

"An achiever, huh?" I pried.

"Yeah. She smokes a lot, though. Robin used to date her." Robin was, of course, Sue's current flame.

One evening I finally got up the nerve to talk to her.

"Mashed potatoes," I said. She barely looked at me as she dolloped half a scoop on my plate. "Thanks. How generous."

She looked up, her mouth and eyes narrowed in annoyance, as if to say, "What an asshole," so I didn't press on. I took my tiny scoop and sat down at a table in the back where I had the best angle of her. It was crowded, so I could gaze fairly undetected.

I think it was her arms that really impressed me. As she moved in the short-sleeve gravy-stained blue smock, I saw her muscles contract and relax as she reached, scooped, and dolloped. Reached, scooped, dolloped. The rhythm hypnotized me. I'd always blissed out watching people work with their hands, whether it was a mason troweling a cement patch of sidewalk or my mother ironing. There was power and security in strong hands and arms. Janice's were strong and veined at her wrists, and, as I had noticed while up at the counter, covered in soft, downy blonde hair.

"I don't get you," said Sue later as we walked along College Avenue. "Why do you like girls who look like Popeye?"

"She doesn't look like Popeye," I protested. "She's just strong looking and unusual. I like that. Why is that so bad?"

"If you like women, then go for women who look like women," she said. I'd heard it before. It was the new tag line among my crowd.

"Women come in all shapes and sizes. Besides, what do you care who I'm interested in?"

"Hmph." She said nothing more as I stepped onto the L bus to go back to my dorm.

On Saturday, Sue, Robin, and I went on a picnic in Bucceleah Park. It wasn't much of a picnic, since all we had been able to afford at the supermarket were salads. We munched and threw lettuce to the ducks.

"Are you going to Vonda's Halloween party?" asked Robin. Her long, curly black hair kept falling into her face, sometimes blowing into her mouth as she ate. It drove me crazy.

"Of course," I said. "Everybody's going, right?" Vonda, with a "V" as she liked to say at meetings, so people wouldn't confuse it with Wanda, I suppose, was one of the copresidents of CQ2. It was supposed to stand for "College Queers," with the 2 for "too"—to include every other sexual identity, but it came off sounding more like a cologne, which was about as much depth as we had anyway. Vonda was one of the "2s" because she openly and proudly identified as a "bisexual iconoclast."

Whatever. Most people didn't care anyway, beyond the tidbits about everyone that lubricated the gossip mill. Most people didn't care about much, really, except eventually getting laid. I was no exception.

"Yep, everyone'll be there," said Sue. "It's going to be the rave of the ages."

"Rave? What are you talking about, girl? All people are gonna do is sit around, cruise, and get drunk," said Robin, popping a cherry tomato in her mouth.

I wasn't too excited. For all my time spent at school, I had yet to get hammered at any social functions.

We got up to throw out our plastic salad containers and began to walk down the hill toward the lake. As we neared the open field across the parking lot, we came upon a baseball game in progress.

"Hey, let's stop," said Robin.

We stood on the sidelines watching peewees toss, swing, hit barely in bounds, and stumble to base, their little legs too small to contain their exuberance. I laughed, remembering what a jock I'd been as a kid, before my mother ended my sandlot career by sticking me in Portuguese school in the evenings "so I wouldn't lose my culture," as she put it. I thought of Janice and how she would look in her black shorts and short-sleeved umpire's uniform, making calls with those arms of hers, and towering above these kids. For some reason, it put me in a bad mood. "Let's go," I said abruptly.

"Why?" asked Sue. "They're so cute."

"Yeah, well, so am I, but I don't see anybody standing around staring at me. I'll see you later."

"What the hell is her problem?" I heard Robin say as I started up the path. I smiled a little, realizing how ridiculous that had sounded, but kept on toward the bus stop. My life could have been the basis for *Bus Stop*, it revolved around them so.

I went to dinner late that evening—exactly 15 minutes before the commons closed. There wasn't even anyone behind the counter at that point, so I helped myself to the dregs of mixed vegetables and meatloaf. Sure enough, Janice was there wiping down tables. I sat down a few unwiped tables away so that she would work her way up to me. She hadn't seen me because she'd been looking down, industriously wiping, her dirty blonde hair hanging down, curtaining her face from admirers. She wasn't the sort of girl who elicited admirers. She was around 5 foot 7 and somewhat stocky, with most of the bulk in her arms and back. From that description you'd imagine she was unattractive, but something about the way she moved struck me. It was fluid, almost graceful, as if she could make her body go in ways and places that confounded and yet delighted the eye.

But maybe I was imagining things. Maybe I just wanted to be pressed against another female body, and anybody would do after my long adolescent wait. Maybe.

She finally came to my table. It seemed like she still hadn't noticed me, so intent was she on wiping. "Hey," I said. She looked up, startled. She really hadn't noticed me.

"Oh, hi," she mumbled.

"I'll have some fries with that," I said as she wiped up a particularly large splat of ketchup.

"Huh?" She didn't think it was too funny.

"My name's Paloma," I said to head off any more asinine comments that might come out of my mouth.

"Paloma? What kind of name is that?"

"You know, Paloma, like Paloma Picasso. It's Spanish for "dove," but actually I'm Portuguese, and my full name is Paloma Pereira. Most people just call me P or PP, though that's kind of a dangerous name to take into certain clubs, isn't it—people think I'm into golden showers or something." I laughed. "Do you go to any clubs?" I don't know what possessed me to tell her what I just had. Paloma is indeed my name—my middle name—and I usually never reveal it to anyone because it sounds so stupid. My first name is Dina.

"I don't go to clubs," she said, ignoring the name game. "Don't have time. I've got to study too much, and I have to get back to work now." She turned away and headed for the kitchen.

In my dorm room that night, tucked inside the comforts of blankets that smelled like home, I decided that people who were interested could come to me from now on. It just wasn't worth it. And waiting, though frustrating, was probably a good idea. I turned off the light, remembering the CQ2 meeting the next night. Good, I would try out my new resolution then.

Vonda with a V was in full tilt. The meeting room was packed with a dozen new bodies, mostly boys, who'd heard either about the group or the upcoming party. Vonda must have made the V sign with her fingers about a dozen times in her introductory remarks and welcome speech. Having heard her spiel before, I kept to the back. Someone behind me, who obviously hadn't heard a word she'd said from the beginning, whispered to his companion, "Why does she keep making the peace sign? Was she raised by hippies?" I laughed. Privately, Robin, Sue, and I often referred to Vonda as "Peace."

My giggles shushed the corner crowd I was in, and Vonda leaned sideways to stare through her little black glasses, her bottle-black hair angling off her head. "Are you OK, Dina?"

I'd been hidden back there, but the identification turned heads. Several people parted, and I saw Robin and Sue look up at me from a table where most of the girls sat. There beside them was Janice, my cafeteria crush. She was talking to the woman next to her—I think her name was Clare—and didn't turn around. I eased back into the crowd. As Vonda resumed her chat, I studied Janice. It pissed me off that she was talking to Clare. Clare supposedly worked at the college as a security guard, though how she was up to that task I didn't know, since she looked about a hundred years old. Then again, she probably sat in a chair all day checking ID badges.

"So the party's at my house at 1155 Busch Street—Busch Street, how appropriate, right? Ha ha ha. And you can all come starting around 8, OK? Remember, if you have any questions, my phone's not turned on yet, so call the CQ2 hotline and leave a message for me—that's Vonda with a V. Directions to my house are at the CQ2 office. Hope to see you all there." With that and a smile, Vonda ended the meeting. I hung back, letting everyone stream ahead, and slowly made my way to the exit. Robin grabbed my arm. "Hey, D, hold up. We didn't see you come in. A bunch of us are going to Patty's for food. Wanna come?" Her hazel eyes fixed on me.

"Uh, I don't think so, Robin. I've got cramps."

"I've got aspirin, come on. If they don't work, I'll do some Reiki on you in the bathroom."

"I don't know."

But before I could hedge any longer, Sue came up, bringing Janice and Clare with her. "I think you two know each other," she said, looking from me to Janice.

"Yeah, hi, Paloma, right? How you doing?" said Janice, extending her hand.

Sue and Robin shot me inquisitive looks. I smirked, feeling my face heat up a little.

"Yeah, hi," I said, clearing my throat. *What's with the formality?* I wondered, taking her hand.

"Well, you guys wanna go to Patty's?" said Sue.

"Sure, but I can't drink," said Clare, pushing up her John Denver-style wire-rim glasses. "I'm on duty tonight."

"We can't drink either. We're all underage. Well, I don't know about you," I said, looking at Janice. She smiled and turned back to Clare.

Patty's, the proverbial campus pub, was especially noisy and smoke-filled on Thursday nights, as I'd expected. People liked to start their weekend early. The five of us sat at a table right in the middle of the place, the only one large enough to accommodate our group. The table and seats were generously splashed with beer suds. A limp $2 tip lay soaking under a half-empty mug.

"Nice place," I muttered, feeling my jeans get wet as soon as I sat down. I sat at one end, with Robin to my right. Sue sat at the other with Clare and Janice on either side of her. It was so noisy, I couldn't hear what they were saying, though Janice looked intently at Clare as she talked. Sue occasionally interjected with something and once looked up at me laughing. The only person I could really hear was Robin. She was singing along to the Smashing Pumpkins song the bar band was trying to cover.

"How are your cramps?" she yelled.

"They hurt. Aspirin didn't help." I rubbed my temples with my fingers. It wasn't the cramps that really hurt. I didn't even have my period.

"Come on, I'll Reiki them."

"That's OK," I said. I thought she'd been joking.

"No really, I've been practicing it, and I want to see how it works."

"Here?"

"Sure, why not? It doesn't take long."

I was skeptical, but I needed to pee anyway. "Yeah, OK." As we rose, the others looked up, but the only one who spoke was Sue, who asked Robin if we could send the waiter to the table on our way to the bathroom. Janice and Clare resumed their conversation.

I peed, then waited while Robin washed and dried her hands. People came in and out, barely looking at us.

"OK, where does it hurt?" she asked, placing one hand at the small of my back and the other around the button fly of my jeans.

"Here?"

"Yeah, sort of," I said, then unthinking, "but doesn't this work better right on the skin?"

She shoved one hand into my jeans and the other under my shirt. "Like this?" she asked.

"Uh, yeah."

"Well, actually, it works better just above the skin where you can concentrate the energy." She looked straight at me and smiled. She didn't move her hands. People kept coming in and out.

I saw what she meant, though—I was starting to feel a little warm. Her hand was just above my pubic hair, and I hadn't worn underwear. She seemed to register this.

"Uh, I think I'm feeling better," I said.

"Thought so. Come over later and I'll do it properly," She leaned toward me a little, pushing the tips of her fingers deeper into the top of my pubic hair, then slowly withdrew, dragging her nails lightly on the way up. "See ya out there."

I was still standing in my surprised and shocked stance, leaning back slightly, my hands raised, one foot on tiptoe, with a wide-eyed glaze, when Janice walked in.

"Uh, *Karate Kid*, right?

"Yeah, right," I said dropping back against the wall. Janice checked her hair, making sure the strands were properly messed.

"You know, your friends are real nice. I told them I was looking for another job, and they set me up with Clare."

"Oh, really? What does Clare do?" I was still confused.

"Part-time security over at the dorms."

"Interesting."

"Yeah, can't be a cafeteria lady all my life," she laughed.

"Yeah, can you imagine?"

I couldn't look at Robin when I sat back down, though I wanted to. I couldn't look at Sue either, because I thought it was written all over my face, whatever it was—I wasn't quite sure myself. I must have really looked distressed, though, because Sue eventually did say, "Are you all right?"

"Ah, no. I'm kind of out of it today. I think I'm going to head back. I'll see you guys. Thanks." I put on my jacket and moved away, hearing Janice yelling as I pushed through the crowd, "Do you want me and Clare to walk with you? We're going that way."

I didn't see my friends for a week, avoiding the commons, blaming it, when Sue called, on studying or having to visit my mom for the weekend. "Um, all right," said Sue. "But you are still going to Vonda's next weekend, right?"

"Yeah, sure," I said, not at all certain I was going. But curiosity got the best of me, and on the following Saturday, I put on my pirate costume: a billowy white shirt, black spandex tights, and the black velvet thigh-high boots with fringe my mother had bought me for Christmas one year, for what purpose I never knew. I had never worn them until now. I wrapped a red bandana around my head, put hoops in my ears, and opened an extra button on the shirt. Had to look good. I threw on the long coat I'd bought at the thrift store a few days earlier, and hopped the bus to College Avenue and Vonda's.

Vonda answered the door dressed like the good witch of one of the directions. She twirled her little sparkly wand over me before I came in. "OK, you're blessed now," she said. I gave her the peace sign.

The party was in full swing; I'd arrived at the perfect moment. It was so packed, I couldn't recognize anyone. The boys all looked like girls, and the girls all looked like variations of Xena. Thankfully, I was the only pirate.

Vonda circulated among her guests, chatting, waving her wand, passing out drinks. Somehow a beer got into my hand. Then another. I looked around the cleared living room floor for a place to sit or lean and watch. Robin and Sue were nowhere to be seen, but it was so dark and crowded, I wouldn't have recognized them anyway. I downed most of my second beer, then, thinking what the hell, started to dance. I was in disguise, and the beer had warmed me up, so I danced and didn't feel like a fool. For all her quirks, Vonda at least had good taste in party music, mixing up a lot of old and new dance stuff. I felt the bass pounding, closed my eyes, and slipped into a trance as the beat overtook me. I was doing a pretty good grinding thing to Amber's "Sexual" when I felt a poke in the ribs and jumped.

"Can I see some ID for that?" a cop with a fake mustache and wire-rim glasses pointed at the beer. Figures Clare would be imaginative enough to wear her campus cop uniform to a Halloween party. "Yeah, sure, officer," I said, blowing her off and moving into the crowd. I came out on the other side and leaned against the wall, pissed. I had really liked that song.

In a few minutes, she was in my face again. "You keep doing that, I'm going to have to take you into custody," she said.

"Yeah, sure. Go ahead," I mocked. But before I knew what was happening, she snapped real handcuffs on me and shoved me in front of her. My beer bottle dropped and shattered on the floor. Suddenly my anger was tinged with confusion and panic as it dawned on me that maybe this really was a police bust of a noisy underage drinking party. *Oh, shit*, I thought, as she pushed me through a door. I stumbled into a room and at first saw nothing; it was dim, just like the rest of the house. I bumped hard into some kind of furniture, then stepped clear and began to see that there was some light: candles here and there in the room.

She kicked the door shut. *Oh, shit, Clare is going to attack me*, I thought. *Oh, god.* Then I heard laughter. A little table lamp snapped on, and Robin ripped off the mustache and took off the cop's hat, her curly black hair tumbling out.

"Who did you think?" she asked to the (I'm sure) priceless look on my face. She slid off the glasses and placed them carefully on the table.

"Not you," I managed.

"Surprise, surprise." She slid her hand behind my neck up into my hair and kissed me, her tongue just grazing mine. I felt a pounding in the center of my body, hard and hot, as much from her as from fear and relief. But I didn't stop. I raised my still-cuffed hands up to her chin and kissed her back, not too gently either. I had leaned into her so much that she fell back onto the bed. I lost my balance too, and as I fell my hands naturally tried to come apart but pressed up painfully against the cuffs. After a few moments of rolling around, her hair in my face, I asked. "Can you unlock these?"

"Say please," she said, straddling me. She started unbuttoning her blue starched top.

"Aren't you afraid someone's going to come in?" I asked. Actually, I didn't care.

"Why?"

Although I had plenty of questions, I couldn't ask them because the next thing I knew, all she was wearing was the unbuttoned top and the holster.

"Please?"

"Thought you liked rough stuff," she teased. "Like that big Janice. She was so happy about lending me her new uniform too."

Robin leaned over the bed and me, reaching into the discarded blue-striped pants for the key. She found it and then hesitantly, as if she wasn't sure whether I'd bolt or not, unlocked the cuffs.

"Thank you," I said. I rubbed my wrists, opened and closed my hands, then deliberately spread my palms against her flat belly, flicking her navel ring with my thumbs as I did so. It sparkled a little, even in the dim light.

"I'll let you play with the other ones too. She twirled and tugged on the small hoop on her left nipple.

"What other ones?" I asked, as she pulled on and rolled her puckering nipples between her fingers a bit harder for my benefit. "I only see one other one." My voice cracked a little from the pounding I felt in my chest and the sensation that all the liquid was draining from my mouth and rushing over my throat down to my belly, into my legs and toes.

"You'll have to find it," she said, leaning over and rocking a bit so that her breasts hung in my face. I touched the tip of my tongue to the cool curve of the tiny gold loop, then bit down on it and pulled a little, then a little more.

Vaguely it crossed my mind that this little scene would cause problems for me later, but later would be the time to worry about it. All I wanted to do now was find the other trinket Robin had hidden for me.

"Where could it be?" I whispered, licking her neck and burying my face in her hair as she pulled off my costume.

After we dropped my boots over the side of the bed, she took my hand and guided it into the other dark curls that would drive me crazy. "I'll give you a hint," she smiled. I laughed.

This was better than an extra serving of mashed potatoes any time.

11

High Pressure E.D. Kaufman

While she was sleeping I slipped out of bed, still naked, and pulled her turnouts from her work bag.

She had brought the bag home from work that morning because she'd been working CR—classified relief, otherwise known as over-time—at a different station. She'd worked four days straight, and my hormones were riding high, needing release. I was still in bed, masturbating, when she'd first walked in. I smiled at her and threw back the covers so she could see me rubbing myself, clutching my breast and squeezing.

"Oh, sweetie, you look so good, but I was up all night at a fire and I'm wasted." She collapsed beside me on our bed, sighing, "Ah, the marshmallow," and fell asleep in her black station uniform with the white buttons.

I loved our bed. We both did. Right then, though, I hated it for being too comfortable. But she was so tired. My poor honey had worked so hard.

So I waited.

Until I got sick of waiting.

It was after letting her sleep for six hours that I crawled out of bed naked and got her turnouts. At first I was just curious. I pulled the heavy pants with the wide red suspenders up over my naked body and walked to the full-length mirror. My pierced nipples pushed forward between the red suspenders. I pinched a nipple, hard, until it turned purple. I slid my hands under the straps at the shoulders and lifted the pants so that they rubbed up against me between my legs, wiping the wetness. I inhaled deeply, the fresh suggestion of sex mingling with smoky remnants of heat and sweat in a burning building.

I pulled on the turnout boots and walked back to the bedroom. I put on her helmet and hit the alarm clock buzzer so it went off loudly; a cruel thing to do, but so is leaving your girlfriend high and dry for four days. I knew hearing an alarm would make her adrenaline kick in.

She flung her body out of bed and looked around the shaded room, confused and half asleep.

"Looking for these?" I asked, standing in the open doorway with sunlight at my back, snapping the straps of the suspenders so that they bounced back and jiggled my breasts.

"That was so not nice. False fire alarms are a punishable offense," she said, rubbing her eyes with the backs of her wrists.

"So spank me. Tie me down with a hose and spank me. Or do something else with the hose."

She gave me a long look and ran her fingers through her hair. She seemed a little disoriented, so I waited in the doorway, leaning my head to the side against the frame so my neck curved open onto my shoulder, smooth and exposed. Only the king-size bed separated us.

"Take off my turnouts."

I couldn't tell if she was really annoyed or not, but I decided to push it anyway.

"No. You take your turnouts off me."

"Fine. I will."

"Catch me first."

She jumped over the bed and caught my waist with both arms as I headed out of the room. She pulled me roughly onto the mattress, knocking the helmet off. Something hard and pointy struck the side of my leg as she landed on top of me.

"Ooh, what's that?"

She pulled a metal tool from a pocket in the turnout pants. It looked like a hook.

"It's for opening hydrants." She held it up, and it glinted in the rays of sunlight entering the room. "See?" She lowered it and rested it on my neck. "It's a very important tool. I use it all the time."

She used it to slide the red straps off my shoulders. I giggled.

"Shh! No laughing. Fire safety is serious business. Impersonating a firefighter is also a punishable offense. I'm going to have to remove this gear."

She yanked the pants down with the hook until they bunched up against the boots. Then she grabbed hold of each boot at the sides and yanked them off too, pulling them, pants and all, away in one quick motion. She was moving with such calculation and force that I felt jumpy, nervous. She didn't usually act like this, but of course I'd never woken her from a nap after a four-day stint on the job while wearing her work clothes.

I wondered if she truly was annoyed that I'd messed with her gear. I lay still, not quite sure what would happen next.

She inched back up the bed and trailed the cold, hard tool over my neck and through my long dark hair that lay splayed around my head. The hook grazed my skin, imprinting it the way a fingernail leaves a red mark.

She traced my lips with it slowly. It smelled of grease and rust. My nervousness turned to excitement. I wanted to suck the tool, feel it with my tongue. I wanted to warm it and make it slick. I arched my neck back and parted my lips.

She dipped the hook in, and I watched her eyes grow wide as I circled my tongue over the silver curve. The taste was sharp and sour. The lines of soot over her brow and around her neck ran down her skin in gray streaks as beads of sweat came up on her forehead. She unbuttoned her uniform and pulled off the shirt. Underneath were just her white tank undershirt and bra. Her nipples, always so huge, were erect, pressing the outlines of her silver piercings through the bra and white cotton tank. Her calloused fingertips traced up and down my breasts and ribs, touching the places that made me quiver. I watched the muscles of her arms flex and constrict as she moved. With one hand, she pulled her pants down. She straddled my thigh and rubbed on me, breathing faster, making my leg damp.

"Lube." She didn't ask for it, she just said the word, like an order.

I reached behind my pillow and pulled it out. I'd follow any order she gave me at that point, and she knew it, even though we'd never been like this before.

She swiveled and straddled my head so that I saw her ass and cunt clearly exposed. Her asshole was puckered dark purple, her cunt shining pink with moisture. I craned forward against the weight of her straddling me to smell her and touch the tip of my tongue to the hood of her clit. She tasted like peaches. Her hips angled for easier access.

I heard the top of the lube snap open and then the wet smack of liquid dripping out and being rubbed onto something. I assumed it was her fist until I felt the hook again, cold and hard against my cunt.

"Don't worry. It's the handle. I'm a trained professional."

"You're not going to—"

"Shh. I know I can get this open if I just try."

I knew, or thought, she would stop if I asked her to, but I wasn't sure what she was going to do with the hydrant hook, and I wasn't sure I wanted to stop her either. I thought of how wide the tool's handle was, how unyielding. No, I didn't want her to stop.

She circled the hook once, then twice around my cunt, as if thinking about it, and then forced entry, sliding in fast and hard. I moaned, and the space around me went darker. It was too big, too hard, but so good. Her teeth clamped down on my clit, nibbling just enough to hurt well as she maneuvered the handle of the hook in and out of me. Her fist wrapped around the handle, pushing it in as far as it would go, banging against my cunt, twisting it inside me as she pumped.

"Harder—so good," I panted, dropping my knees wide open.

"Yes. Harder."

I felt for the lube and dumped it over my hand until it was sloppy wet. I pushed one finger into her ass, squeezing it through the tight opening, and thrust two inside her cunt. Her hips clashed down onto my hand, pushing the fingers further in. I sucked her clit, wanting to drink and swallow from it.

The tool bucked in and out of my body, cranking sounds from my mouth I'd never uttered before. Her hand moved with the tool like it was a weathered, skilled extension of her, grown there with hard work and long hours, like she'd been practicing to use it this way. She moaned, and I wondered if she could feel me with it. My hips rocked steadily faster.

"Slow down."

"I'm going to come," I whined, arching away from her.

"No. Not so soon."

"I'm gonna come. I can't stop it. I can't stop it."

She slowed her movements to a torturous tease.

"Who's in charge here?" she demanded.

She knew I liked it when she made me wait. She coaxed the feeling wide and desperate. It built in me until I couldn't wait anymore. It became an intense flame licking out to singe my fingers and toes like paper held too close to fire, then igniting.

"Oh, fuck," she moaned. Her hip shuddered against me, and her cunt convulsed around my finger in orgasm.

As I came, I held my breath, and an image sprang to mind—a giant red hydrant, stuck and rusted. She cranked at it with the hook, grunting and sweating until the jet spray of water released, shooting high up into the air, raining down hard and cool on a hot, fast fire.

12

Katie took the uniforms out of the closet. She would never wear them again, and Maryann could use them. Katie had only glanced at them once since the accident, after she and Erin had broken up, when she was packing to move out.

Maryann had held them up, her expression the only question: pack them or not? Katie had responded with a curt nod, then turned away from the blue that had so defined her life. She had limped to the kitchen to help Allen, Maryann's husband and her former partner. The glasses and forks were safer.

I should have just given them to Maryann then, Katie thought. But she knew that she wasn't ready for that kind of practicality, to simply banish the blue uniform from her life. *How our past claims us*, she thought, fingering the cloth. *Or haunts us,* she added, removing the sergeant's stripes—Maryann could earn her own. Katie knew that Maryann would take off the badge, the insignia, the stripes, and return the pieces that made the uniform Katie's instead of generic blue cloth.

Maryann and Allen had two kids, and their cops' salary didn't go very far. As Maryann said, between the perps on the street and the kids at home, everything gets dirty more quickly than the laundry can keep up—her explanation for why she sometimes wore a blue shirt with a tomato stain not quite washed out.

Yesterday, the time had just come to let go of the uniforms. Katie had called and talked to Allen. Maryann would have asked her how she was, if she was sure, but Allen understood that she was talking to him to avoid those questions, and he had simply said thanks and that they would be by this evening to pick them up.

It had been a year since the accident, four months since she had last seen Erin, six months since their painful breakup. *Time to move on*, Katie imagined her therapist saying, although Kathleen would never say any such thing. Sometimes it felt better to have an external voice guiding her, as if the decision were less her responsibility.

"Erin just loved the uniform; she never loved you," Maryann had spat out when Katie told her what had happened.

Katie had agreed at the time, felt the comfort of another voice saying the bitter things she was feeling. But it was more complicated than that. Erin had loved who Katie was in the uniform. Erin, living in an academic world, surrounded by books and papers, violence contained to arguments about obscure Virginia Woolf essays, had found in Katie a compelling—and erotic—other.

Katie, working-class Katie, a high school diploma, the police academy, her accomplishments on the force, had piqued the interest of Erin with her Ph.D.

"I've never dated a woman with a gun before," Erin had laughed nervously on their first night out.

"Do you even know any women with guns?" Katie had asked. Erin had silently shaken her head no. That was when Katie decided that she wanted Erin, to have her for the night—a few months at most. She saw no future beyond that.

Erin may have wanted the uniform and the toughness and strength it implied, but Katie also wanted Erin's world of books and classes and the intelligence and belonging. No, it wasn't as simple as Erin just wanting Katie's uniform.

They had met when Erin's car was stolen. Katie and Allen had taken the report. A few days later Katie spotted a car fitting the description that Erin had given—a five-year-old gray Saab. Katie could have just called it in, but she had a hunch that Erin was a dyke—and Katie liked to follow her hunches. When she got off duty, she called Erin up and asked if she wanted to drive by what might be her car.

It was her car, but not in the best shape. Katie had waited with her for the tow truck, playing—no, not really playing, but being—the tough cop, helping Erin through the foreign land of theft and damage.

But it was Erin who called a few days later to let Katie know what had happened to her car, that it could be fixed but would be in the shop for a week. Then she added an invitation to coffee. And after coffee, it was Erin who suggested taking Katie out to dinner—to thank her for finding her car, she said.

Katie had both been amused and intrigued by Erin's covering herself—just a thank-you dinner, as if there was no sexual interest between them, the glances they had exchanged over coffee, the way Erin had let Katie help her into her jacket, her hands lingering on Erin's shoulders.

Erin's car was still being repaired, so Katie drove. Over dinner she had been content to let Erin keep her middle-class reserve in place. A few veiled references to sex, the mention of an ex-lover, and silence where talk of a current lover would fit.

But when they left the restaurant, Katie had reached out and taken Erin's hand in hers. A simple act, but it had made the physical explicit instead of implicit. They were no longer just two women having dinner together. After letting Erin into her truck Katie had again claimed Erin's hand with hers. Letting go to shift, then again taking it, the possession becoming such a given that Erin started reaching for Katie's hand instead of waiting for Katie.

"I had an enjoyable evening," Erin said as Katie parked in front of her house, letting her hand linger in Katie's. "Much more enjoyable than I would have thought."

Katie marked that it was both a compliment and an insult. Her reply was to wrap her free hand around the back of Erin's neck, pull her close and kiss her. She knew she couldn't possess Erin with words, all those years with books had given Erin the edge there, but Katie could take her physically, have her in a place where words didn't matter.

Erin allowed the kiss for a moment, then stiffened. Pulling away, she said, "I don't know where this can lead...."

"This isn't a marriage proposal," Katie had answered. "I just want to fuck you." Not giving Erin a chance to reply, she kissed her again. For a moment Erin remained stiff but then allowed the kiss and finally returned it. She had told Katie they had no future, and having fulfilled that responsibility, Erin seemed willing to let desire lead her.

Katie had played—no, again it wasn't playing, but an aspect of who she was, a part of her that Erin was attracted to—the aggressor, the one who only waited for the door to be closed before taking Erin in her arms, kissing her, undressing her, leaving Erin's clothes in a heap right on her doorstep. Katie wanted to prove that there was a place where their worlds could intersect—besides the random moment of a stolen car.

It had been a night of fucking, Katie repeatedly taking Erin, the kind of hard, physical sex that blotted out thinking and any idea of the future. Katie knew it was more than a desire for sex—but also for possession and control—that guided her. It gave their sex a hard, passionate edge.

Erin had at first just used her tongue, until Katie took her hand and guided it into her, pushing deeply inside. She smeared her juices down Erin's wrist to her elbow, holding fast to Erin's slick wrist with one hand as she used her other hand to guide Erin's head back between her legs and keep it there.

Then Katie pinned Erin down on her stomach, holding her as Erin made a token protest of squirming away. Katie languidly ran her fingers down Erin's back, over her ass, then between her legs, teasing her wet opening. Katie stretched herself so that one of her breasts was on the pillow next to Erin's head.

"Take my nipple in your mouth," Katie whispered in her ear. "Show me with your mouth on my nipple what you want me to do to your clit." Erin eagerly lifted her head to obey, but Katie arched back, just enough to keep her breast out of Erin's reach. Erin shifted closer, but Katie again moved just barely out of reach.

"You must not want it very much," Katie said, her fingers still slowly stroking the rim of Erin's cunt. "You're awfully damn wet for a girl who's not interested."

Erin muttered a "damn it" and writhed closer, struggling against Katie's pinning weight. For her efforts, Katie thrust her breast forward, letting Erin finally wrap her lips around it.

Katie rewarded her by plunging two fingers into her cunt. Erin kept her face to Katie's breast for the first few thrusts, but the third time Katie's fingers went deep, she let go of it with a loud groan, her hips arching into Katie's hand.

Katie pulled out but didn't go in again. "Thought you wanted it, babe," she whispered teasingly into Erin's ear. "Suck my nipple like you mean it or you don't get any."

Erin let out another groan, but this one had an edge of frustration. She roughly twisted under Katie, again clamping her lips around Katie's nipple, then sucking as much of the breast as she could into her mouth. Erin sucked hard on Katie's breast, her tongue rolling Katie's nipple against the roof of her mouth. Katie let her continue just long enough to make her point.

Then she rolled directly on top of Erin, sliding down to better reach between Erin's legs.

"You've been a good girl, and good girls get good fuckings," Katie said as she started to again plunge her fingers into Erin. She wrapped her other arm around Erin's waist, using one finger to gently brush her clit as Katie continued her hard fucking with the other hand. She kept the pressure on Erin's clit gentle, almost a tease, until Erin pushed herself onto Katie's fingers, her moans and motion begging for more. Katie gave it to her, rubbing her clit between two fingers. Erin came and came hard, a long shuddering orgasm that left them both drenched in sweat. They made love several times that night, always with that same edge of tease and power that kept it unexpected and hot.

But the night gave way to the clarity of morning, the two of them having breakfast in Erin's kitchen. The silence between them was dense and awkward, as if, with the physical spent, there was no connection between them. Was it just sex; just a quick fuck? Katie wondered if she should just decline the food, say her good-bye, and leave it at that. She had thought making Erin want her, making her allow Katie's hands and mouth between her legs, would be enough. But now in the clear light of day, Katie knew she wanted something more. Later, much later, she admitted that she wanted Erin to love her. But at that moment, all she knew was that she didn't want to be just some one-night fling, the fantasy of a woman in uniform that lasted only until the morning.

Almost at random, Katie had asked Erin about her breakfast cereals, ones that Katie had never seen on the shelves of her grocery store or on TV commercials.

"I get them at the food co-op," Erin had told her. "Healthy and all that jazz."

"So are they really better than Cheerios?" Katie asked.

Erin gave a soft laugh, then admitted, "Probably not, but I live in the rarefied world of academics. Appearances count. I can be open about being lesbian but closeted about eating Frosted Flakes."

Then they both laughed, and some barrier came down. Katie had always been curious about other people, other lives, and the right to ask questions was part of what attracted her to being a cop. Erin, too, shared that searching curiosity. The questions, and the willingness to be open and honest in answering them, had taken them through a long, lingering breakfast.

Katie had then offered to drive Erin around to any errands she needed to run. They had gone to the food co-op, then to the university to pick up some books, Erin letting Katie glimpse into her life.

A few days later Katie had taken Erin to pick up her car, then, in unspoken agreement, followed her home. This time Erin took the lead, as if having to prove she could give as well as take. Wordlessly, she led Katie to the bedroom and slowly undressed in front of her, almost a striptease. Then she knelt in front of Katie, roughly pulling her pants down and began licking and sucking until Katie had no choice but to fall back onto the bed and let Erin spread her legs all the way open to finish what she had started.

When she caught her breath, Katie threw off her remaining clothes and got on top of Erin. She didn't waste time on foreplay, her fingers finding where they wanted to go, Erin's slick cunt welcoming them. Katie quickly followed her fingers with her mouth, her tongue finding a hard, erect clit waiting for it. Erin let out a murmur of surprise when Katie slid one of her fingers into her ass, but she didn't ask Katie to stop. Katie liked the feeling of being inside her as she came, riding the arching hips, the spasm that tightened around her fingers, as if Erin was getting so much pleasure she didn't want to let Katie's fingers go.

As Katie was getting ready to leave that morning, they made plans to get together for the weekend.

Somehow, promising that there were no promises made it easy to be together. To Maryann, Katie just said, "Oh, it's a fun affair, maybe some book learning will rub off on me." Katie didn't know what Erin said, probably something equally dismissive, such as "She's good in bed and gets my tickets fixed."

The sex changed from the burning intensity of the first few encounters to an exploration, learning each other's bodies and pleasures. Katie discovered licking and kissing the soft underside of Erin's breasts, kissing her nipples to full erectness, then caressing and tonguing her entire breast was how to get Erin wet and hot. Just as Erin learned to adjust the pressure of her fingers inside Katie, the spread of her legs that signaled she wanted it deep and hard, or the slight pulling back when she wanted less intensity, a softer touch.

Weeks, then months passed, and they were still together, still exploring each other and enjoying the exploration. Their friends started treating them as a couple instead of just an affair.

It was Erin who first said "I love you," then softened it by adding, "This must be a lesbian record—we've been sleeping together for four months now and haven't moved in or declared that we're soul mates." Katie glimpsed the fear and vulnerability behind the words, Erin afraid that she was asking too much, saying words Katie would never say to her. They had just made love, Erin coming to a shuddering climax.

On hearing those words, Katie realized how she too was scared. Her response had been to stay away from the words, to kiss Erin, her mouth, neck, cheeks, more than she normally did after their lovemaking. Then she had guided Erin's hand between her legs, keeping her hand on top of Erin's as Erin touched her.

Katie found her own way to the words, the next day, while they were driving. She kept her eyes on the road, too scared to look at Erin as she said, "You know I love you, don't you?" Then a quick glance at Erin's face because she couldn't *not* look, then back to the road again because she couldn't keep looking.

Erin had responded by resting her hand on Katie's thigh, the top of her inner thigh, a place that proclaimed them lovers, before answering, "I know. I was just wondering how long it would take you to notice."

A month later they moved in together.

Three years later Katie pulled a child out of a burning car. She did-
n't save the other child or the mother because the car exploded as
she was coming back for them.

She had two clear images from that moment. The car, its hood
crumpled into a light post, the trunk replaced by the front end of
the speeding car that had rammed it. The woman was slumped
over the steering wheel, the rear door open. Katie had wrenched
it free to pull out one child. The other girl was still sitting there,
looking at Katie running to her. The second image was the sudden
shroud of orange and red that obliterated the child, the mother,
and the car.

After that there were no clear memories. Heat, pain, a world that
she couldn't focus on, a roaring that never seemed to clear, fire,
sirens, people talking, nothing distinct or strong enough to break
through the searing pain. One voice close to her saying, "Cut it off,
just cut the belt…" and the pain of feeling something like her skin
being pulled off, the uniform burned to her skin. After that, there
were no memories.

The ambulance, the emergency room, the first few days in the
hospital, Katie knew nothing of them other than the stories she was
told. Her mother and father were there, her two brothers, their
wives, a rotation of people as if they felt that someone should be
with her at all times.

At first she was too drugged and in pain to comprehend what had
happened. But slowly Katie learned to focus again, to listen. She
knew the extent of her injuries from one of Maryann and Allen's visits. Maryann talked, almost a constant stream of babble, but it was
Allen, silent Allen, the tears streaming down his cheeks, that told
Katie how badly hurt she was.

"Will I walk again?" Katie had slurred out, the drugs making the
words so hard to say.

"Babe, of course you're going to walk again," Maryann assured her.

But Allen didn't stop crying.

Erin was there, usually reading or marking papers, which annoyed Katie's family, her father saying, "Miss Professor makes it clear she doesn't have time for us." His unspoken, "or you" hung in the air, as he had intended.

Katie didn't have the energy to defend Erin. It mattered that she came, that she cared enough to pile the papers together and haul them along to sit with Katie. As when they had met, they didn't talk about the future but just let it happen.

"Do you think you could have saved your relationship if you had talked about your injuries?" Kathleen had once asked Katie.

"No," Katie had replied, not wanting to look at a road not taken and that now never could. "No, Erin loved the person I was in that uniform. Take off the uniform, and it stripped me of who I was." How could she keep loving someone she didn't know?

When Katie came home from the hospital, she was too numb, too much still in pain to understand the fault line that now was part of their relationship. All Katie could do was concentrate on herself. She couldn't tell Erin who she was or who she would be, because she didn't know.

She didn't know if she would walk again, how visible the scars would be when they finally healed, what kind of person she could become with the woman in uniform gone.

Katie hated the dependency, the harried look in Erin's eyes as she tried to manage both the life she had and the needs of taking care of someone…injured. Neither Katie nor Erin would say *crippled, disabled*.

Katie forced herself to learn to walk again, a limping shuffle made possible only with a cane. The muscles in her left leg had been badly damaged by the flames, the strength she had so taken for granted gone forever.

The scars remained visible, the left side of her face disfigured. The grafts had helped, changed the lumped flesh into a smooth, shiny surface, but it was a new face that Katie looked at every day in the mirror.

Katie got a medal for her bravery and a disability check for her pain.

She didn't see the distance growing between herself and Erin; she could barely stand to look at herself in the mirror. They rarely talked, only about what was necessary. Usually, Katie later admitted, about what her own needs were, medications she needed to have picked up, arrangements for her to get to physical therapy, things she wanted from the grocery store, what they were going to have for supper that evening. Katie's family helped, but often their offers were like favors, not something to count on day to day.

"I think I just wore her down and wore her out. How could she love me when I resented her for being whole? Guess she got out while she could," Katie had told Kathleen.

"Do you think it would have made any difference if she had been honest, told you that she was leaving?" Kathleen had asked.

"No," Katie finally replied. " I don't think it would have made me hate her less, just respect her more."

Erin had taken another lover, one of her fellow teachers. She didn't tell Katie but let the evidence accumulate until even Katie, blinded by the mirror, couldn't avoid seeing it—the unexplained lateness, the calls from the same woman always asking for Erin and never giving her name, the tepid way Erin told Katie she loved her, a facade of words.

They hadn't made love since the accident. Erin made excuses; too tired, too busy. Katie tried to believe her reasons. After all, she was often the tired one, not in the mood, and it wasn't fair that she demand that Erin perform just because she wanted it.

Then the strange woman, whose voice Katie recognized, came to the door. "I'm going to tell you this because Erin is too much of a coward to do it." And she told Katie that it was over, that Erin no longer loved Katie, and that it wasn't fair for Katie to keep Erin chained to…this life.

Erin came home only long enough to mutter "I'm sorry" over and over again as she hastily packed some clothes.

Katie wasn't proud of herself at the end, alternately begging Erin to come back, to not take love along with everything else that she had lost, and screaming at her to get the fuck out of her life.

A month later Katie, helped by Maryann and Allen and her family, moved out of the place she and Erin had bought together. She couldn't afford to keep it by herself, and every room, the walls, the doors, that long mirror in the bathroom, held too many memories.

The last time she had seen Erin was at the act of sale for the house.

There was a knock on the door, Maryann and Allen, breaking into Katie's thoughts.

She draped the uniforms over her shoulder, picked up her cane, and hobbled across the living room.

They entered, Maryann as usual talking from the start, the latest kitten/kid story, the weather. Katie could tell Maryann was on alert, her words speeded up from their standard 70 miles an hour to 90.

Allen kissed her on the cheek. Katie had noticed that he alternated cheeks, the good one and the scarred one, as if there were no difference. Katie handed Maryann the uniforms. Maryann started to say something, then stopped. Instead she hugged Katie, and then they were gone.

Katie hobbled around the apartment, some loss in her coalescing. The problem with the numbness subsiding, she had told Kathleen, is that it lets in the pain . She had thought she was ready to let go of those uniforms—and maybe she was ready, and maybe it didn't matter whether it was now or ten years from now—but taking those uniforms out of her closet and giving them away would always be a palpable moment of loss.

The bare walls of her apartment offered no comfort. She hadn't wanted to put up the pictures she had bought with Erin, or shelve the books that so often had been gifts from Erin. They stayed in boxes, and the walls remained blank.

Suddenly, loneliness became a stabbing pain, and Katie couldn't stare at the walls anymore. She grabbed the keys to her truck and stumbled to the door, moving with too much haste to keep balance, having to stop and right herself at the door frame.

The truck, one that her father, a mechanic, had arranged for her to get in a trade—she could drive an automatic but not a standard—at least offered the distraction of motion. The streets, the other cars, all demanded her attention. Katie drove aimlessly for several hours, but even that space of time only diffused her loneliness, changing the sharp pain to an ache that seemed to have found a piece of her soul and wouldn't let go.

She glanced at her watch and found it was almost 9 P.M. *Maybe I should stop and eat something*, she thought. She didn't really feel hungry, but she hadn't had much lunch, and nothing since then, so she knew she should eat. She also knew that stopping somewhere to eat, the concentration on the menu, watching the people around her, would be another distraction. There was a restaurant that had recently opened right across the street from the lesbian bar that she used to go to. *Two distractions in one neighborhood*, Katie thought. After eating, if she still couldn't stand the idea of returning to her place, she could have a few beers.

She cruised by the restaurant, then went around the block before coming by again. *Not too many cars out front, so it shouldn't be too crowded*, Katie thought as she parked. The old Katie would have welcomed a crowded restaurant, wanted to see all the people there. But now Katie was unsure of herself, her welcome, and was afraid of the staring and the pity.

Katie was immediately greeted when she came in and just as

quickly led to a table, the young waitress leaving her hobbling behind.

Someday your gait will be slow too, Katie wanted to say to her. *Age or accident, you'll be left behind by young women in a hurry.*

Maybe this wasn't a good idea, Katie thought. *Maybe I should be at home with the honesty of my bare walls—bare walls for a bare life.* But the waitress returned with her drink order, and Katie looked over the menu. It was one of those eclectic places, everything from a basic hamburger to tofu-and-sun-dried-tomato pizza.

"Katie, would you like to join us?"

She turned to the voice. It was Caroline, one of Erin's friends from the university. Katie quickly scanned the faces at her table. She recognized Vivian, Caroline's partner, but no one else.

Caroline got up and came over to Katie's table. "Come on, it's safe," she said softly in a voice only she and Katie could hear.

Katie had always liked Caroline, had found her much more welcoming and friendly than most of Erin's other colleagues. They'd had a chance to talk during one Christmas party, and Katie found out that Caroline was the first one in her family to go to college, and that Vivian, who owned a flower shop, didn't even have a college degree. After that conversation Katie had sort of taken them on as role models for what she and Erin could be. Caroline had also been the only one of the people she had met through Erin who had called her even after they'd broken up.

But Katie hadn't returned the calls, taking out her anger and hurt at everything surrounding Erin and the life they'd had.

"Promise?" Katie asked in just as soft a voice.

"Erin and I were never close. I liked you better," Caroline said matter of factly. "And I hate what's-her-name, so I can't promise that they won't walk in the door, but I can promise they won't sit at our table."

Katie nodded, realizing that should Erin and what's-her-name enter, she'd prefer to be sitting with Caroline and her friends than at a table by herself. Caroline picked up her menu and her soda, and Katie followed her back to her table.

About eight other women sat at the table; Katie gathered that they had all been at some lecture that evening and had come from there. She was relieved to discover they all weren't from the university, but some, as she now liked to think of it, were "real people with real jobs." Caroline simply introduced Katie as a friend, leaving it to Katie to decide how much of her history she wanted to have join them at the table.

"What do you do?" the woman next to her asked.

Katie had learned to hate that question, thinking of it as "What uniform do you wear—cop, academic, lawyer, salesgirl—that I can use to define you?" She answered, "I used to be a police officer, but now I collect a disability check. So I no longer do, I just be."

The woman nodded vaguely—as if, not getting the answer she expected, she could think of nothing more to say. But the conversation drifted to other subjects, movies, books, topics that Katie could safely venture into. Sometimes she spoke, other times she was silent, but other than that first awkward question, she felt she had gotten lucky and found the level of distraction she needed.

The evening wore on, and Caroline and Vivian left, but Katie was content to stay and let the conversation swirl around her. Finally the restaurant was closing, and several of the women suggested that they move on to the bar and keep the party going.

The three women who suggested the bar got up and headed out, and the rest of the women, like a herd, followed them, leaving Katie behind, struggling with her cane and slow gait.

The divide that hadn't been apparent at the table now opened up—Katie couldn't keep up with them, and they weren't going to wait.

One of the women stopped and turned around. She had probably left something at the table, Katie thought. She had been at the opposite end from Katie and they hadn't spoken.

But the woman seemed to be waiting for her. Katie felt a flush of embarrassment at this stranger and her unasked-for kindness.

As she approached the woman, Katie said, "I don't need pity." She regretted the words the second she said them, realizing that her anger wasn't so much at this woman but at her disability and a world that had no place for her limp and her scars.

"Just as well—I'm fresh out. Had to use it all on those Ph.D.s who never learned basic courtesy," the woman answered.

"Sorry," Katie mumbled. "I should probably just go on home."

"You can't yet. I never accept apologies without proof that they're really meant. Buy me a beer, and I'll believe you."

"A beer?" Katie asked, trying to match the woman's friendly bantering. "Aren't you with the white wine crowd?"

"Does this look like a white wine body?" the woman asked with a laugh.

The woman was heavy, one of the people Erin would have referred to as "shoot me if I get that fat," but Katie liked her smile and her laugh, and appreciated the grace and compassion the woman had returned for her churlishness.

"Sorry, hang out with academics, and their effeteness rubs off," Katie said, allowing the woman to hold the door for her.

"By the way, not that one can manage a truly proper introduction standing on a street corner, but my name is Molly."

"Hi, Molly, I'm Katie." Then the light changed, and they crossed the street.

The bar had the usual blast of music, making conversation hard. Molly let Katie buy her a beer, but then she bought the second round. Katie had wondered if she hadn't hooked up with some lush who would con a disabled person into buying her drinks. Erin had proved so false that now Katie always wondered what lurked beneath a smiling face. But in this small exchange Molly seemed to be offering the camaraderie of buying each other drinks without actually spending more money than they would have otherwise.

Halfway through the second beer, Katie realized how tired she was. It had been a long evening for her, as truncated as her life had become: driving, dinner, and a few beers, all in one night, was more than she had managed since the accident.

Katie thought about asking Molly for her phone number. The old Katie would have. The old Katie probably would have asked her to dance, asked her to spend the night, been able to find someone who would keep her from going back to her empty apartment with its bare walls.

But the new Katie couldn't even ask her for her phone number. Instead she settled for tapping Molly on the shoulder, then thanking her for the second round and nodding a good-bye.

I have too much time to think, Katie thought as she sat in the truck. *It was just a phone number, a "let's go see a movie sometime" phone number. But who would want to even see a movie with a crippled, scarred woman? Molly may have been fat, but she didn't look that needy. Clearly everyone in the group liked her; they all chatted and laughed with her. She had a great smile and beautiful eyes and.... Am I so desperate for friends that I'm making a chance meeting with a kind stranger into something more than it was?* Katie started the truck and drove away. *Stop thinking and just drive.*

When she got home she immediately opened another beer and drank it down. With that, sleep came and took away the blank walls.

"You could still get her phone number," Kathleen pointed out later that week. "Caroline probably knows her, call her and ask."

"You really think that if I was too much of a wimp to ask for her number after she'd just bought me a beer that I'm going to announce to all her friends that I'm desperate enough to beg them for the number? Besides, she didn't ask for my number either."

"So she has to ask first?"

"Makes sense, don't you think? Better to assume that no one is going to be interested in an ugly, crippled woman unless she proves otherwise."

Kathleen just nodded and left it at that.

And that was where Katie left it too, until a chance encounter in the grocery parking lot.

"Tell me I'm not wrong. You look like the kind of sensible woman who carries jumper cables." The words brought a set of hands to help her load the groceries from the basket into the back of the truck.

"Thanks," Katie said, turning to look at Molly. It had been almost a month since that night in the bar. "Yes, I have jumper cables. My dad's a mechanic, so my usual Christmas gift is some new auto thing."

"Jump me and I'll buy the next six beers," Molly said.

The old Katie would have replied, "I'll jump you for free, but starting the car will cost six beers." The new Katie just said, "Where are you parked?"

"That beat-up red Honda over there." Molly pointed.

Katie pulled her truck around so it was hood to hood with the Honda. It took her a few moments of fumbling—and realizing that she was going to need Molly's help—before she could get the cables set up. The last time she had jumped a car she'd had two free hands, strong legs, and perfect balance. But they managed, and her fumbling was rewarded by Molly's smile of relief when her car started.

"Thanks," Molly said. "You've managed to save my life—or at least my career. I was delegated to pick up the nibbles for the board of directors' meeting. Hence being at the grocery store in the middle of the afternoon. Now, not only will I make it almost in time, but the ice will be only slightly melted."

"Glad to be of service, ma'am," Katie replied, ducking her head in a mock bow.

"A white knight in a green truck." But Molly was obviously in a hurry. She got in her car, and with only a final quick wave, she was gone.

Katie went back to her truck, reminding herself that she had frozen groceries that needed to be kept cool. *A lonely white knight in a not-so-new green truck*, she thought as she pulled out.

But later that evening the phone rang. "Hi. I survived my board meeting. Now I can be a decent person and thank you properly. Oh, this is Molly, by the way. You know, jumper cables in the parking lot? For all I know, I was the fifth damsel in distress you saved today."

"You were the only one," Katie answered. "It was a slow day."

"You probably did 20 and are only saying that to make me feel special. Since, thanks to you, I still have not only a job, but a happy board of directors, I thought it only fair that I repay you by taking you out to dinner."

"Dinner?" Katie repeated slowly.

"Yeah, food, eating, necessary for all living things."

"Dinner. Of course. Really the only reason I keep those jumper cables around. I might starve if it weren't for grateful jumped women."

Is it a date or just a thank-you? Katie wondered as she put the phone down. Better to assume the latter. It wasn't as if Molly had gone out of her way to see Katie again. But still, she felt a happiness and lightness that she hadn't felt in a long time. *How could one phone call make me so giddy?* It wasn't just the dinner but that Molly had assumed that Katie could help her. Before the accident it seemed all her friends called for favors: Could she start their car, give them a ride, help them move, install the new air conditioner? Erin would sometimes get annoyed at yet another phone call, but Katie really didn't mind. She liked being able to help people, to know she could make a difference.

Now no one called. Katie was the cripple who couldn't do anything, couldn't rescue damsels in distress. Today Molly had been in distress and asked Katie to rescue her. Some part of her didn't dare hope that Molly's invitation was anything more than a thank-you. But since the accident, Katie had lost friends. Some of them, like

Maryann and Allen, even Caroline and Vivian, had stayed. But some either didn't know how to deal with Katie out of uniform and no longer strong, or didn't want to bother.

It had been hard to meet new people, make new friends. Part of the difficulty was just that she had less energy, part that she no longer had things like work or soccer or any of those other outlets to meet people. Some was that it was hard for Katie to believe people might have any interest in befriending someone like her—like who she was now. The old Katie was fun and useful, could tell a great joke, fix the perfect barbecue, impress the girls by taking them on a date to the shooting range. But the new Katie? Who was she and what could she offer?

The dinner was enjoyable, and Katie found it easy to talk to Molly, but they parted with a handshake and a murmur of "This was fun. Let's do it again."

"Still didn't get her phone number?" Kathleen asked later that week.

"Not officially," Katie admitted, "though I did catch it off the caller ID. But I can't call her."

"Why not?" Kathleen asked.

Katie just looked at her for a moment. *Because I'm a crippled freak living on the government dole*, she wanted to scream. Katie finally stammered out, "Because...I just can't."

"You told me that before the accident you used to be assertive, calling up people, that you led the way in your relationship with Erin," Kathleen said.

"I'm not that person anymore," Katie cut in.

"Ah, presto-change-o, take off the uniform and the naked Katie becomes a wimp, unable to manage a simple phone call?"

"No," Katie retorted, "just aware of the realities."

"Katie, the uniform didn't make you who you were, you made you who you were," Kathleen said in that maddeningly calm way of hers.

Katie couldn't think of a reply, and the hour ended. She sat in her truck afterward, her thoughts jumbling around Kathleen's words. "I didn't make myself a cripple, I didn't make myself scarred and ugly," she said, staring at her windshield.

But I can make myself someone who picks up the phone and calls another woman. I can make myself do something besides stare at the blank walls that only reflect my anger and loneliness back at me.

Katie drove home. She didn't call Molly that night. She started to several times but never managed to dial all the numbers before her fears caught up with her.

The next evening she didn't give herself time to prowl around the phone but instead just picked it up and dialed. Molly answered on the third ring.

"Uh, hi, this is Katie," she stumbled. "Uh, jumper cables, dinner, beer?"

"How could I forget a combination like that?" Molly replied. "I was thinking about you the other day—and not just because my car was acting up. Are you an adventurous diner?"

"I eat raw oysters. Does that qualify?"

"That's not a bad start...."

When she hung up, Katie wasn't sure whether she had asked Molly out to dinner or if Molly had asked her, but they were going out for sushi the following evening.

The week after that it was Vietnamese. And the next week, Indian.

"Is this a date or a friend?" Maryann asked when she noticed at Katie was usually not in on Friday evenings.

"Just a friend," Katie answered. "We like to eat ethnic food."

That night, in the Chinese restaurant Katie watched Molly as she perused the menu. *Are we dating or just friends?* she asked herself. The old Katie would have passed Molly by, not been interested in a woman who was overweight, not conventionally attractive.

But the new Katie appreciated how Molly matched her steps to

Katie's slow gait, how she picked inexpensive restaurants without Katie having to mention that she didn't have much money, the way she offered to help without taking over and making Katie feel useless.

The new Katie enjoyed the way Molly listened, occasionally asking questions, sometimes just letting the silence invite a response. She and Erin had pushed each other—who could be wittier, always searching for something interesting or funny to tell about their days, a kidding one-upmanship about who knew more, Erin trumping Katie about books, but Katie mocking her about not knowing the streets. Katie didn't feel she needed to be smart or brave with Molly. She could just be…Katie. She suddenly realized that just as she was fumbling with a body that had changed, she was also struggling with who the new Katie was. Molly had no preconceived ideas of her, didn't see her as the butch cop or the aggressive lover or any of the other things she had been.

As she watched Molly, Katie began to feel desire build. Not just the random desire of wanting sex, but desire for this particular woman.

But she said nothing, did nothing, needed the friendship of someone who accepted the new Katie too much to risk it.

As the weeks passed, though, Katie realized she was falling dangerously in love with Molly. It was hard not to want to reach out and hold her hand, but the hand on the cane always reminded her that she might not be wanted. The old Katie could have risked it, would have taken a chance on desire.

But I'm not the old Katie. I won't ever be her again, she thought as she stared into the mirror, into the scarred face that stared back at her. The new Katie had lost so much that she couldn't risk losing anything more.

That night she and Molly again met for dinner. And again Katie felt the agony of wanting more than she thought she could ever have. They met once a week, a few phone calls in between, calls that had come to matter too much: a ring turning into disappointment when it wasn't Molly. There were times when Katie thought she should just back away, not be available for dinner, let the machine pick up when the phone rang, turn away for the rebuff that she feared she was headed for. Erin, who had promised to love her forever, hadn't. Even the women who had formerly looked at her with beckoning eyes now averted them, making sure Katie knew their lust had only been for the woman in the blue uniform, not the Katie who could no longer wear that uniform.

"I'm so glad that my weeks end with you," Molly said as she joined Katie at the table. "This has been one hell of a week, funding cuts, berserk clients, including one that we had to call the police on. Then to add that extra dollop of ego destruction, I'm sitting quietly, finally having my lunch, when the five other lesbians at the office start reading the personals out loud and describing all the words that fat women use to hide their weight. *Zaftig, Rubenesque, big country girl, voluptuous*, they're going on, with me sitting there. Like it's perfectly OK to tell fat women how ugly we are to our face."

"You're not ugly," Katie said.

"Thanks. But you're a friend, you're biased. You should see the women sidle away from me at lesbian bars, afraid I might ask them to dance—like they might get my fat cooties."

"You're far from ugly," Katie repeated. "And they don't exactly come running in my direction when they notice the scars and the limp."

"Maybe we should hit them from both sides—me from the front and you from the rear—and we could watch them jump out the window," Molly said, then added, "You're a very attractive woman, Katie. Any woman that runs from you is crazy."

"You think these scars are pretty?"

"No, they're not, but you are."

Katie looked at Molly for a moment, then looked away. Suddenly she realized that if Erin were standing here asking her to come back and she could choose between the two of them, she would take Molly. She would take Molly with her kindness and humor and compassion over Erin with her gym-toned body and hot-shot academic credentials. It was a surprisingly easy choice.

A bit of the old Katie came back—or maybe just part of who she was becoming. She reached across the table and took Molly's hand in hers. "You're one of the most beautiful women I've ever known."

Molly just smiled a radiant smile that made her even more beautiful as she entwined her fingers with Katie's.

Katie could barely remember the food they ate, what else they talked about, only that the desire she had so long tried to keep repressed suddenly sprang free. She could look at Molly and imagine slowly taking her clothes off, touching her breasts. Katie didn't have to hide her desire as she stared at Molly's cleavage. Passing the salt or pepper became a chance to brush their hands together. It felt like a miracle that Molly returned her desire, that she looked at Katie as if she were undressing her.

"This isn't a romantic parking lot," Molly said as they left the restaurant. "Too well-lit and too many potholes. I presume you know that I want to kiss you."

Katie laughed, a bubbling laugh of joy, then said, "I'm glad to see your desire isn't compromising your standards."

They let their desire build as they drove to Molly's apartment, with Molly's hand lingering on Katie's thigh, a claim and a promise.

As Molly closed and locked the door behind them, she said, "You know, I wanted you the first time I saw you."

"The first time? Really?" Katie asked, surprised, remembering that first awkward, angry encounter.

"Yeah, there was something both strong and vulnerable about you." Molly put her arms around Katie, pulling her close. "Smart, no pretensions, gets me every time."

"Not so smart—it took me a little longer to want you." She returned Molly's embrace, but didn't kiss her yet, suddenly shy. *Oh, hell,* Katie thought, *I've never made love with this crippled body. What if I lose my balance or flop down on top of her?* This shyness and uncertainty was new to her; she had made so many compromises with a body that could no longer perform as she wanted it to. This would be yet another one. "Uh...so what do we do now?"

"Scared?" Molly said softly, as if reading Katie's thoughts.

"I guess," Katie admitted. "First time I've...made love since the accident."

"Then we need to change that. You don't strike me as the celibate type. Hot babe, ardent lover, cunning linguist, but not celibate."

"I don't think celibacy is an option with you around," Katie said, letting Molly's confidence buoy her.

It became so easy, the flow of passion. Letting Molly undress her, revealing all her scars, didn't become the obstacle Katie had feared it would be. Instead, Molly explored Katie, taking her time, letting her hands slowly travel down Katie's back, lingering in the small of her back before sliding down to cup her ass teasingly, then moving to caress her thighs. Katie closed her eyes, reveling in the warm stroking of Molly's hands until she could stand it no longer. She wanted more than a gentle exploration.

She wrapped her arms around Molly, their kiss exploding immediately from a touching of lips into a probing and sucking of tongues. They kissed and kissed again, letting their kisses punctuate the no longer careful journey of their hands.

Katie slid her hand to Molly's nipples and felt them become hard and erect under her touch. Her large breasts filled Katie's hands, her fingers stretching to encompass their heft. Then Katie wanted more than the nipples. As she ran her hand down Molly's stomach, she thought *voluptuous* was the only word to describe the feel of the flesh beneath her hands. Molly let out a gasp as Katie's fingers circled around her hair.

Suddenly Katie felt a kind of power that she couldn't remember since the accident. She wasn't crippled, scarred Katie anymore—

she was someone wanted and capable of wanting and pleasing and giving. She led Molly to the bed, spread her across it, even held her down when Molly tried to be fair and equal and hold Katie the way Katie was holding her.

But Katie wanted the power, to make Molly gasp and groan and shudder as Katie touched her. She slid her fingers into Molly's wetness, then let her tongue follow, licking and sucking and thinking, *This woman wants me, wants me so much that she's dripping down her thighs, her clit is huge and filling my mouth.* Katie felt a ravenous hunger, a need to touch and be touched like this. She took nourishment each time her tongue glided over Molly's clit, from Molly's heavy breathing and shuddering gasps, from the way Molly's rocking hips matched the rhythm of Katie's thrusting fingers and how she started chanting, "Oh, Katie, oh, babe, yes, yes" as her pleasure mounted. Her words dissolved into a gasping cry as her hips arched into an orgasm. Katie continued to lick and suck, reveling in her languid murmurs of "Oh, yes, it still feels good, so good," until Molly finally said, "Can't take any more," then added, "I'll die of pleasure if you don't stop."

It was an astonishing affirmation, the strength of their desire. They made love again and again. Katie reveled not only in her power to so arouse Molly, but also in how much Molly wanted her, the ardor with which she made love to Katie.

She had been quietly lying in Katie's arms, recovering, when she suddenly rolled Katie on her back and growled, "I want you. Damn, do I want you!" Her actions proved her words, her hands and mouth concentrating on Katie's breasts, first just the tip of her tongue flicking over Katie's nipples, teasing them. Katie discovered that Molly could be an exquisite tease, dallying with her breasts, a lick with her tongue, then softly blowing on them, making them almost painfully erect before she finally covered them with the warmth of her mouth.

"But I'm not finished with your breasts," Molly said, answering the increasingly insistent writhing of Katie's hips. Her tongue became a soft caress of Katie's nipple as if she could linger there all night.

"Please," Katie said.

"Please, what?" Molly answered, blowing across the newly wet spot.

"Please me," Katie demanded.

"I love women who beg," Molly answered, "but they have to beg explicitly."

"Fuck me," Katie begged. "Fuck me hard, fuck me every way you can."

Molly did, with her tongue and her mouth and her hands. And her voice and her laugh and her desire.

Katie's body responded, rejoiced in how deeply she felt what Molly was doing to her and the discovery that she hadn't lost desire and passion but instead found a place where they could reach in and touch her soul.

It became the kind of weekend that Katie thought she had lost forever. They stayed at Molly's place, making love, and between making love, talking or just lying next to one another.

"We spent all weekend fucking," Katie told Kathleen. "And I'm going there tonight. And was there last night."

"You look very happy," was Kathleen's comment.

"I am very happy."

It was odd, Katie thought that night, lying next to Molly, their legs entwined, her thigh gently nestled against the wet place between Molly's legs, how fate had brought them together. The two of them, the cripple and the fat girl, the undesirables, had found such profound desire in each other. Katie felt no clinging or neediness in their being together; she didn't feel she had "settled" for Molly. There was a wonderful emotional connection between them but there was also an incandescent sexual tug. This evening Katie had simply walked through the door, taken Molly in her arms, and they had fucked right there in the middle of the living room. It wasn't the first time they had so easily just fallen into each other. It surfaced in other brief moments, Katie licking Molly's fingers as they cooked, Molly unbuttoning Katie's shirt as she left for work, kissing both her lips and her breasts good-bye.

The stripping of clothes was one kind of nakedness, but the stripping of all those talismans of self, job, income, the physical, a body that never betrayed you, brought Katie to a place where her soul was naked. They touched each other in that place.

Two months later Katie moved in with Molly. "I'm living over there anyway, I might as well," she told Maryann.

"And here I thought it was because Molly's a wonderful person and you're damned lucky to get her," Maryann responded, as she helped Allen pack the kitchen utensils.

"That too," Katie admitted. She had been pleased at how well Molly and Maryann and Allen got along. The four of them had a friendliness and camaraderie that hadn't existed when she was with Erin.

That fall Katie started college, a scary and hard decision for her to make. No one in her family had gone beyond high school. Molly had encouraged her without pushing her, helping Katie with the foreign world of admissions testing and applications. Katie wanted to find some new place for herself, something to replace the blue uniform that had defined her days. She wasn't even sure where she would go with it. At times she considered being a social worker like Molly, or perhaps a lawyer, finding a different place in the justice system.

"Those are grad degrees, babe," Molly had said. "For now, just learn what you want to learn and have a good time."

"Good time? It's hard enough learning that studying and beer drinking don't actually go together."

It was all part of the new Katie finding a new life.

At the end of the semester, walking across campus with Molly, she had run into Erin. It was sudden, no warning—just a turn of the corner and her past was there.

Erin was with…that woman. Katie didn't even know her name.

"What are you doing here?" the woman exclaimed, almost as if Katie had violated some division of territory.

"I'm going to class," Katie calmly replied.

"Katie, how are you? I've been meaning to…" Erin trailed off.

"I'm fine," Katie replied. "This is my partner, Molly Brannigan."

"I know Molly," the woman said.

"The lesbian community here is too small for us not to know everyone," Molly said. "Hi, Dora, how's the tenure battle going?"

"Still fighting the old farts. How are you, Molly? Have you saved the world yet?"

"No, still working on it."

"Glad someone is. I'll just never understand preferring unwed mothers to libraries full of books."

"Something about living life instead of just reading about it," Molly replied.

"I see you haven't given up your habit of taking in strays," Dora said.

Erin had only enough grace to look abashed, not enough to counter her lover's statement or to even break the mounting silence with banalities about the weather.

"Oh, me and my honesty—seems to have gotten me in trouble again," Dora inserted into the silence her comment had caused.

"You confuse honesty with opinion," Molly retorted, "and with cruelty."

Katie could feel Molly's fury; she didn't even need to look at her to know. Dora's remark had sparked anger in her, but only a quick flash. Katie looked between the two of them, Dora with a slightly smug look on her face, as if she knew she'd been outrageous and knew she could get away with it. Erin was looking at the ground, her discomfort etched from the slump of her shoulders to the awkward way her hands played with the strap on her purse.

There's nothing you can do to me that you haven't already done, Katie thought. *And you have no power over me.*

"We all have our abilities and our disabilities," Katie said. With that, she took Molly's hand and walked away. Dora's brand of cruelty and Erin's waffling and guilt were greater disabilities than her crippled legs or Molly's weight.

"Couldn't do any better...." drifted after them.

Molly started to turn and fight, her anger still not abated. But Katie held her hand firmly, and they kept walking.

"Odd, but I have to agree with them. I couldn't do better than be with you."

"Would you...would you really have chosen me if you hadn't had the accident?" Molly asked softly.

"I don't know," Katie said. "But it would have been my loss. Maybe without the accident I'd still be so caught up in appearances and the externals: job, prestige, all that. All I can tell you is that from where I am now, the idea of still being with Erin, living that life we led, and missing out on you, is abhorrent to me."

"Abhorrent? Just abhorrent? OK, I suppose that will have to do," Molly teased.

"So, oh best lover of mine, when we get home, shall we do it under the kitchen table or spread out across the living room floor?"

"Oh, hell, let's be really kinky and do it in bed."

Katie paused for a moment, then leaned over to kiss Molly. She knew she could spend the rest of her life kissing this woman, this woman who loved her as no other woman had.

They settled for the bed, leaving the kitchen table for another day and the living room floor until after spring cleaning.

13

Falling Away Linnea Due

Glorious light flashes through the darkness and then runs off fast as a yellow dog, as if the sun carries too many burdens in this weary age to climb up over the hill and howl away the night. Over and over the sun struggles into the sky, then sinks away behind a brow of gloom until I begin to lose heart that I'll ever again bask in her warmth or glimpse dappled light twinkling through skeins of pale-green leaves. Then I comprehend that in my extremity I have taken the sun's measure when I should have looked to myself: It is I lingering cold in the gloom, tumbling fast down that darkened hill, unable to crest the summit. I strive for a reason, think of none, and open my eyes. Then snap them shut, trying not to shout. Too many are doing that for me to add to the clamor: Opening my eyes has unstopped my ears, and I don't like what I hear.

I reach a hand to my head. Nor do I like what I touch. As I finger the crusted, matted hair, I recollect Lucas walking ahead through a hellish field the likes of which no body should have to see, the trees half shot up, twisted branches on top of dead men, dead men on top of dead horses. Drifting across it, a snowfall of letters. Letters written in handwriting so beautiful or cramped or angular or near-illiterate primer printing. Photos of wives and children and mothers and fathers on top of the horses and men and trees. Men lie there reading still; reading the words of a loved one as they wait to die. I see myself skirting a cairn of stones someone has erected, but after that, there is nothing in this broken head for me to find. No shot, no cannon, no yelling horde of half-starved men, no explanation for this dried blood and stabbing pain.

Where is Lucas? My one real friend here, a baker. Imagine, a man who combines simple ingredients to create the miracle of sustenance is reduced to subtracting lives as if he were a banker toting up a debit sheet. For Lucas is a very good shot, and he has saved me on more than one occasion. He would say I had saved him, but he is a better shot than he is a liar.

The sun is warm on my face and it wakens a powerful thirst. So powerful I forget the pain that almost made me faint. I open my eyes and see naught but leaves swimming through a blue sea inverted over my head. The clouds are puffy as cotton and I hope they don't come down to be sullied by us, the grand destroyers. A cloud is a sacred event, like bread, though it takes a bigger man than Lucas to bake a cloud. I have to remember to tell him. I want to close my eyes but I don't. Too much darkness can't do me good. I have to swing my head to retch and this time I can't help but yell.

Comes then an angel. Who speaks. Pats my brow. Wipes my mouth. This time the darkness gallops at me, and good or bad, I must succumb. All I can see in the brief moment between the light and the shadow are worried eyes and a mouth too tight for the wearer. I have a powerful thirst. I say as much. And then I fall away.

I hope to tell him that he will be gone from here as quickly as I can get him on his feet. I've seen the panic that comes into their eyes when they wake up to see the surgeon and hear the screams. But he faints before I can make him understand. At least I have put him where he can see the sun when he awakes again.

His friend came twice already. I wonder if he knows. In this hospital no one knows but me. Perhaps this man is a friend for life, and so he can be trusted. I wish I knew this as well as the other, for then I could talk to him.

I must keep the surgeon away. This is not hard because there are so many who are critical, and he is in the area of the lightly wounded, reserved for those who will not need a surgeon's saw. Ira, the only other here, spends time behind the curtain with the dying. He tries to make them comfortable, give them water, talk to them if they are conscious. He has promised so many that he will find parents, sweethearts, brothers. I asked him once what he will do when the war is over, and he said he will take a year to travel, to fulfill what pledges he can. I envy him. His life seems simple and good.

I linger by the side of this young soldier with the head wound until duty forces me onward. There are just the three of us, and the surgeon is half-drunk, his apron covered with blood, his wild eyes as red as the cloth. A line of men awaits his horrific carpentry. Ira comes out from behind the curtain to administer whiskey, to the men, not the doctor. The surgeon administers that to himself.

When I come to again, the pain is less, probably because the light is fading in the sky. A man with a slight limp hobbles by, carrying an oil lamp. Men scream as much as they did earlier. Perhaps it never ends; perhaps they just keep screaming.

I wonder if I dreamed the nurse. There has been no alarm, so I have passed undiscovered. The uniform is my savior. No one looks close; people see only what they expect. It is my shield and my sword; if it kills me it does not matter because I was dead before I donned it.

It still stuns me that Robert was killed in the first few minutes of battle. We heard so quickly, from the man who returned home because his brain was addled. Mother said we could not believe him, but I saw he told the truth and I left.

I am Robert's younger brother. None saw reason to doubt. I have come to avenge his death. Their weary eyes filled with resignation, and one said revenge was solace only for the weak. It pained me to test their patience, but I knew they would ignore me if they thought I was hotheaded.

It has been both harder and easier than I thought. My courage, apart from fighting boredom, is rarely tested. We do nothing for long stretches but play cards and write letters. Lucas has no one to write either. His fiancee died soon after he enlisted, struck down by sickness. It seems to me that the war has brought contagion to all of us. So many have cramps, so many spend their time hunkered over a hole. Sometimes I think it is the hardtack, sometimes the salt pork. Once Lucas found some flour and made frybread. That plugged us for a spell, but then the cramps returned.

I have not dreamed the nurse. Here she is, wiping my brow, giving me water. My thirst is less, and I realize she has been by my side before. Her hand under my neck is familiar, my head a weight she has lifted already. Her fingers part my hair and she explores gently. She asks how old I am. I subtract four years from my age. She is grave and tells me to go home. I do not tell her I am avenging my brother.

Her eyes are crystalline, shiny and brown, with great depth and reflection; I can see the flutter of the wick and under that a caring that is at once marvelous and puzzling. When she takes my hand, I nearly rip it away, then realize that will never do. I tell myself I am sorely tested.

Your friend Lucas was here three times. I told him you can go soon.

I make her say it again for I can hardly believe it. Lucas is alive, I shall leave with four limbs and a functioning brain. Her hand feels so warm in mine. I wish I could stay and look into her eyes at the dancing pins of light.

I ask why she is here.

She wanted to better her station, she says. I wonder what she did before. A teacher. Yes, she seems a teacher. But how is her station bettered? I do not ask, for that would be impolite.

My brother wanted me to get married, she says.

I know about that, though not from Robert.

Her parents are dead, she explains. They left her a small inheritance, but her brother guards the capital, says it should not be spent except as an investment in the future. He believes she should work when she is young, while she can meet people. He is unhappy because he has introduced her to several men and she has spurned them. They do not interest her. Teaching also does not interest her. She would like to go west, but perhaps she is a dreamer. She is talking too much.

Her apologies are sweet. Her eyes waltz with the light as she talks about the west, her brows rise with excitement as high as Lucas's dough. I would love to bring her there, but my uniform can only take me so far. My savior and my prison, I cannot abandon it nor can I leave as long as I wear it. My uniform has become my religion; I am like a missionary venturing into danger, protected only by my cross and my faith. Yet this religion is my own invention, one of necessity only I can understand.

She strokes my hand. As I cross a boundary of comprehension, I understand clearly that this territory is the most dangerous of all.

Three days have passed, and we have not talked since that afternoon when I felt him pull away. I am certain it had not to do with my foolish prattling. Perhaps he realized that I might know and feared exposure. Or perhaps he feared that I did not know.

There are men here with grievous injuries who still have not seen the surgeon. I feel so for them. Jed—that is the name he told me—has taken over the task of cleaning wounds and fetching water. He doles out coffee for them, even the Rebels, who weep when they smell the brew they have not seen for months. Jed's friend Lucas has come several times to help, and so have others from his unit. They seem so tight-knit that I feel lonely and bereft. I even wish for my sober brother, with his scowls and dark brow.

A man came today and sang "Home Sweet Home." Tears rolled down gray cheeks, leaving clean lines through mud and half-grown stubble. I blinked my own away. So many here are but boys, and they expect me to be the pillow on which they can rest their weary souls. Some even address me as "mother," though I am hardly older than they.

Yet this idyll, if it could be called such, when lightning splits the sky and men lie crying in their filth, must end. We are following the march and will move up closer to the front in our ambulance. Ira has elected to stay here, while the surgeon and I leave tomorrow. By the time the sun is high in the sky I will be in another place, with these wounded left behind, and the cannon booming and the guns blazing. As for Jed, he shall return to his unit. I will miss him, though we have barely talked since that first day.

I sense him watching me as we work. I am fond of him but cannot go close. If my mother were alive, I would tell her it is like hunting a rabbit. When you go near, the rabbit disappears down a burrow, but each time you look from the side of your eye, he is staring at you, nose quivering.

If Lucas and the rest know, I have seen no sign. But what effrontery, to essay such a hoax! I have stayed awake these past two nights, aghast at the boldness of it. I have heard of this, and more that I shall not speak of here, but never thought that I, Anne Gilchrist, would ever see such with my own eyes.

And heart. For it would be untrue to pretend that Jed has not touched me. I question my own fascination—am I captivated by the ploy itself or its actor? If I saw "Jed" in another circumstance, would I give him a second glance? Since he is so shy of me, I fear I shall grow no wiser. Perhaps that is best for both of us. When one hunts a rabbit, one ends up with dinner; I have no wish to make Jed my supper simply to satisfy a curiosity about myself.

Yet to my startlement, my real hope—that I should have more time with him—is granted. The surgeon and his kit must ride ahead on his fast horse, while Ira shall stay here at the base hospital. Someone must drive the wagon with me and the supplies, and who better than Jed, well enough to fetch water and change dressings? I saw the shadow cross his face when he was chosen, and I cringed inside. He sees me as danger, and perhaps I am. With his life at risk, I care not about my motives, but know them for the pale, ghostly wraiths they are, undeserving of the light of day.

The boys come to see me before we drive off at dawn. Payne and Lucas and John, each so dear. John unlettered and rough but valiant, Payne a gambler, wants to cheat and never be cheated; he taught the suttlers a lesson when they tried to overcharge us for some tobacco at the last camp. Lucas, of course, loyal and proud. He never says about Robert, whether they were friends, whether he saw Robert die. I think not. Surely he would say.

As we share coffee in our tins, I think that for these, my brothers, glory is a birthright. Even Lucas, who just wants to bake bread, who never thought he'd have to defend the Union, who says let the Rebels go, what do they bring us but shame and strife, even he answered the call to arms. They are prepared to sacrifice their mortal souls to keep a united America. For me, everything I do is muddied, like a river the horses have tromped through. Am I escaping my destiny, making big of myself? Am I a criminal (and I'm sure many would think such)? Yet why cannot I sacrifice for my country? Of the lot of us, I have the strongest views—and express them, to the annoyance of some, like German Karl, who joined for the bounty and lets us know it every hour of every day. He says some men are born to slave and it's folly to pretend other.

I know about what is prevented to me, just as freedom is prevented from the black man. I cannot achieve glory because of my birth, I am not allowed the grand gesture. Whatever gesture I can make is to family, and then it is only expected and far from grand. This is a bitter draught I have not been able to choke down. It is why I am dead even as I draw breath, my uniform a magic shroud that lets me walk among the living so long as I wear it. These thoughts carry their own danger, though less to me than to my fellows. Twice I have put Lucas in jeopardy when he has followed me into the center of the fight. This is why I have agreed to drive the nurse in the wagon; Lucas will survive the coming battles better without me, for in truth I *am* hotheaded. Playing the fool when I first arrived was easy, as I am a bit of one.

The nurse comes to say hello to us around our campfire, and the boys tease and trial me, asking when is the wedding. The words bring tears to my eyes so unexpected I scrub at my face and scold John for kicking up the damned dust. Would that I could marry her! It is a cry from my still-beating heart that does not know my brain has already surrendered. It is a cry from deep under this coat of blue, a cry I have concealed from my own consciousness yet truer than any I have ever uttered, even that with which I greeted this world. Once I felt her hand on my brow and saw into her eyes, I wanted not to leave her side. I am aware of how her eyes follow me, and how mine own are on her as she tends to the wounded in her long cape and bonnet. We seem bound by yarn intent on being knitted even as I try to break the needles. For I know this sweater is unholy and in being made, shall unmake us. It must be unraveled. I cannot let her partake of my folly.

❋   ❋   ❋

He swears at the horses, but I know it is for show. Four horses, a light load, it should go quickly. But the roads are messy from these days of rain, with the sky dark and threatening. War turns men nomads; everywhere troops are moving, so the mud is churned up to the axles, and the horses must tug and slide and tug some more. Our slipping has tossed me against his shoulder again and again, until finally I move close as if for a rock to lean on, and he allows it. I wish this ride to go on forever.

And as we travel across this drenched, scarred landscape, all gray and black-green and brown, my spirit becomes strangely animated, as if I could dance atop the sodden grass. I feel in the center of a grand paradox: It is only by being carried away by this flood of events that we are allowed to be ourselves. Jed's body tells a different story than his soul has embarked upon; were he to follow his body he'd leave the greater part of him behind. My situation is less apparent, but no more consonant. My brother's intentions for me are identical to my own in almost every way, yet he would banish me were he to learn the truth. We legislate each other without knowing the depths of the souls we judge, and thus pass rulings that make lives mockeries. Only when lives become less important than grand events can those lives be lived true, and perhaps that tells the tale, that we should always look to the grand and let the truth seek its own.

A mile from our destination a man gallops up to say we are wanted nine miles to our south. Jed questions him closely; who told him so, was he sent to find us or just a nurse, why should we believe him when the sounds of battle are so clear ahead? But he answers well and soundly, even stating my name, and Jed is forced to believe him. We must continue driving into the worsening weather. This time when Jed curses, he means it.

And he is to curse more. Barely a mile down the road, we are rocked by thunder, and the horses spook 'til Jed must stop and go steady them. He comes back soaken wet from the road, his old boots clumped with the red clay that characterizes this Virginia countryside. Another mile gone we are deep in a wood, and the road forks. Our guide had said nothing of this, and the sky is slate. Jed takes the right, for it seems to head toward the direction we want. But shortly it begins to flag, and we end up at a large mansion, deserted except for an elderly colored man with shock-white hair who wants to know our business. None here, Jed tells him shortly, and explains what we are about. The man knows where the fighting is, he says; tells us Jeb Stuart has been taking the long way around McClellan's forces, and that battles are being waged along the railroad. There's a short cut, he says, around mile four.

So we take off again, back the way we came. This time we go left, with Jed gnawing like a dog at a bone at the problem: shall we take the short way and maybe run aground, or go on the road like we were ordered to? It's getting dark when we come to the track off to the right, and Jed hesitates. The horses are nervy again, and I think he just wants to end this ride. He takes the cut, partly, he says, so we'll be in more open territory, which will calm the horses.

The old man knows his business. Once I get the lay of this valley, I see we can cut a mile or more off our route. What he couldn't have known is that Stuart's damned raiders blew the bridge across what they call Chester Creek. Some boys throw rocks at us 'til I threaten to scatter their brains 'cross the road, and they tell us Stuart's men stopped hardly an hour earlier and busted up the bridge. They say two days past we could drive the creek in such a fine carriage (ha!) but now the water's high and unruly, and the horses high as the creek. I'm in trouble for sure, taking this track when I should have stayed on the main road. Fine one I am, here to be the walking dead for however much time I can glean in this uniform—and now I'll probably get shot for disobeying orders.

We're barely on our way back when the skies break free with a bang that shies the horses again. I get down and lead them into a copse off to the side of the track. In this deluge we'd just mire ourselves and never get out. Best to let it blow past us before we continue. After I picket and grain the horses and tuck them back into the trees, I head to the driver's seat, but Anne Gilchrist just shouts out the back of the wagon. Says if I intend to sit out there in the pouring rain she'll have to as well, and she'll get out the hind end and walk around in the mud to do it too. I tell her it isn't right for a man to be in back of a wagon with a woman he isn't married to, and she asks me if I do everything by the rule book or just what I find convenient? While I'm puzzling on that, she starts to climb out over the back and so I must run and stop her, and finally haul myself in. Once there, she starts to clucking over how wet I am and wants me to take off my jacket. "No, ma'am," I tell her, and she can see I won't bend.

It's dark in the back of the wagon, shelves on either side blocking out what light might filter through the canvas. The shelves are stacked with medical necessaries for the battle up ahead, necessaries that men are probably dying in need of. I curse myself again, for listening to the old man, even for listening to the rider. If we'd just gone on the way we were going, at least we'd be where someone needed us! I wonder about Lucas and John and Payne, marching to another battle. We've made headway this week. I pray that the Rebels will see reason, and we can all go home. Not that I shall. I won't talk of that. Not to Anne Gilchrist, though she seems to want to tell me everything, of her brother and his wife and her parents and mostly of her escape, she calls it, to the war. She says that my escape is just as profound, and then she looks at me, expectant. I'm still as a stone. This is treacherous footing inside this wagon, and I must be a sure-stepper to keep us safe.

I convince him to take off his jacket only after he starts shivering uncontrollably. I tell him that as a nurse, I can't allow him to sicken himself just for modesty's sake. I even get his muddy boots and pants off, saying he'll dirty the stretcher. His legs are hairy and well-muscled; he's a hard worker, with smooth, bulging muscles. Yet I can't believe they don't know, don't see a smoother behind, a shapelier buttock. Perhaps they turn away in their tents, do their best in crowded circumstance to give as much privacy as they're able. Or perhaps the uniform is such a blinder no one looks beyond it.

And he so fits that uniform. I've never seen handsomer, with chiseled chin and heavy eyebrows, fine cheekbones and delicate lips. He's a solace for lonely eyes like mine. I could stare and stare, yet when I do, he begins to stammer and won't meet my gaze. I would give years of my life for an honest conversation.

I give him burlap to scrub away the wet, and in time he stops shivering. He insists on sitting near the back flap to guard me from the cold. And it *is* cold, with the wet beginning to seep through, and the wind buffeting the wagon back and forth on its axles 'til I fear it will fall. When I start to tremble, Jed loses sight of his own trouble and comes forward quick to rub warmth into my hands and shoulders, even holding me close to stifle my shakes. Just then a clap of thunder like a bellow from the Almighty startles us, and I cling to him as if I were a monkey cleaved to a broad tree trunk. He comforts me as the wagon rocks, our own wet cradle. He worries about the horses, saying he should by rights go out into the storm, and it is then that I catch his chin and kiss him. I just do it before I've thought it out, like a branch will suddenly trip you, and there you are on the ground before you know it.

So there we are on the ground and this time the thunder struck him. We stare at each other and then he kisses me. I've never known such sweetness. I knew not such sweetness existed in the whole wide world. Is this what my brother wanted for me? If so, I've been cruel to him, for his intentions could not have been better. It was only his target that was wrong.

How could her mouth open a universe? Kissing her is like falling into a liquid that seems to flow everywhere at once—into the realm of the angels, through the crust of the earth, into my body that I now grasp is connected by strong cords to the sky and the earth and the deep beneath the earth. I have wandered blind for life, glimpsing this only when I swam in the river with the fish at my side, when I came up for air and startled the frogs. This kiss does the same, throws me into the river where I swim and can breathe the liquid and rejoice.

And there is Robert at my side, swimming too, his head thrown back to let it all slide down his throat, his long dark hair trailing behind in the fluid, all bubbles and light. Did he feel this in his flesh? Surely this is a wondrous gift, a marvelous boon that must only be visited rarely. He looks exultant. Do I feel this because I am about to die? Then I wonder how I know.

I begin to pull away though I can bare stand it, for I figure if Anne Gilchrist is swimming, she is afloat not only with a dead man but in a lake of lies. She grasps my wrist to hold me and puts her hand under my shirt to show me she has known all along. She says she has heard of such things, has heard it whispered. I tell her decent folks aren't described by whispers, and she says back sharp that I have made my neighbors and kin St. Peter on Judgment Day. It's true it hurts me that Ma and Pa are so mightily disappointed in me, and not just 'cause I'm better at plowing than sewing. They don't like my book learning, and they think I work too hard.

When I tell Anne Gilchrist this, I conjecture that working too hard must be the devil's doing. She chuckles and admits she was afraid I had no sense of humor. "I thought," she says, "it would be my cross to bear." I stammer and stutter for I can't believe she means what I hear, but I do manage to say this is the first time I ever felt so fine with a woman, a real one, that is. She commences laughing and can't stop for so long my face flames up. When she finally gets calm of herself, she says, "My brother had such high hopes when he sent me off, and here I've succeeded in finding the one man in the Union Army I *can't* marry."

I suppose that's a knee-slapper, but I can't find the fun of it. She traces a finger down my cheek and says that separation of church and state should apply to marriage. The church says they marry soul to soul, but the state wants to pass laws on the bodies too. I snort and tell her no minister would marry us, much less the state. And how can I be two people at once? She says she feels only one and that is me. Then she kisses me again, and every inch of her flesh against mine is salvation. I am unbuttoning her dress with shaking fingers, and she is helping. She keeps kissing me as we go, and it is all I can do to not leap on her, but I know that is wrong from Robert, who is counseling me to go slow and not startle her with rough behavior. I become smooth as a fine-gaited horse; even my hands steady down. But when I see her breasts fall from that bodice I gasp, and she smiles at me, proud as she ought to be. Cream they are, soft as a kitten's belly, and they fit my palms like they were born to rest there. Looking down, she says she never saw such a perfect match: my hands, her breasts. I say she's fresh and she gets all saucy and asks do I want to see the rest of her. Well, I don't deny it, so she struggles out of the underthings she has on, with my helping at the tugging parts, and I never thought I would see a sight so beautiful on this earth. I tell Robert this can't be happening, and he says to keep my head.

A head is nothing to lose, not with Anne Gilchrist, because she has plenty to say even now. Between the words she makes sounds, and when she begins to breathe like a winded horse, with that whistle of a good race run, I can't hold off any longer. I sink somewhere beyond but more myself than I have ever been, and I know how to find where she is swimming and soon she is twisting against my chest and biting my collar bone, and her whistle joins the wind's wail until they sound near the same.

Then she wants to kiss me and we do, and we spoon with each other until we start up again, and I think in the middle of it that I am saved. The rain pounds on the canvas and starts to drip in on the bandages and the stretchers and our foreheads, as if the sky is crying tears of happiness and gratitude and grief. We cover each other with my big cape from this Brothers' War, and it is then that we sleep, with me blessed to have this night, to have swum with Anne Gilchrist on this last eve of my life.

I tried to talk with him near dawn. I told him we could go away after the war, even during it after his enlistment was over. He wouldn't hear talk of the future, said his uniform was his protection. There are other uniforms, I told him gently. There are other ways to gently weave a fiction. But he shook his head and touched me so tender and said only that he wished he could leave me what he had. And he did give me a coin, said I had to carry it with me. We left barely a quarter hour later, with him driving hell-bent for leather. He was sure we were needed, and we were.

I hardly saw him after we got to the battleground near Fair Oaks. He helped establish a surgery and found a couple walking wounded to staff it. We worked until we were wavery on our feet all the following day through the night to the next day when Jed went off to fight, having found his friend John and learning that Payne had been struck and that Lucas was missing.

The base hospital was overrun two days later by Rebel forces, and the wounded taken prisoner. Most shall surely die. Ira is gone; no one knows whether he stayed and fought for the hospital or whether he surrendered. The surgeon did perform miracles, I'm told, on another section of the front.

When I heard a ball had cut Jed down near Gaines Mill I was not surprised. I had seen it in his eyes. I kept on nursing through the whole long war, though my heart shriveled in my breast. When I returned, my brother said he thought I would find a man in the first months, and I told him I had. After that he treated me better. I put Jed's coin on a chain and I keep it close at my throat.

I wondered if Lucas had survived, but then I heard from a friend who visited Jed's hometown that a baker had come to the home of Jed's parents and told them how their daughter, who had disgraced the family by running away to be a nurse, had saved so many Union men that she was called the Angel of Mercy. He said she nursed 18 hours or more, day upon day, until no man could complain about being overworked. My friend says that after the baker left, Jed's father looked so much lighter and bragged on what a worker his daughter was, how she could outdo most men with her plowing and shearing and woodsmanship. A crack shot, the baker had said as well, but all agreed that she hadn't had a chance to practice that skill in the nursing profession. And the baker told them his daughter had a friend name of Anne Gilchrist who might be calling on them one day.

I might, I suppose. But first I go West. I tried my own speech to Jed's parents and it felt like treason to call him Sarah. Lucas is a baker indeed—he can make pride rise in unleavened bread. I have no such talent, only the love to carry on.

14

TeddyLou Hill

Five months into her active duty commitment following her ROTC-financed college degree, Lt. Sarah Parker had been assigned section commander with a maintenance squadron at a large base in Northern California. Moving from Ann Arbor, Mich., to California was strange enough; stepping from her senior year into flying a desk in the Air Force was even stranger. She was still learning her way around.

One afternoon Sarah sat in her office studying a regulation when a rap at the door interrupted her concentration. She looked up at the female sergeant standing, hands on her hips, in the doorway. The woman wore camouflaged fatigues, a Day-Glo orange vest, and glossy black combat boots. Her jet-black hair was cropped closely on the sides but stood a bit longer on top.

"Come in, sergeant," Sarah said, eyeing the woman.

The sergeant crossed the room, stopped in front of the desk and saluted. "Ma'am, Sgt. Teddy Haynes reports."

The sergeant stood about 5 foot 10, her shoulders broader than Sarah had ever seen on a woman.

Sarah returned her salute. "Have a seat." Sergeant Haynes draped herself across the chair next to the desk, almost casual in her demeanor. "What can I do for you?"

Sergeant Haynes answered with a lopsided grin, a smirk almost beaming from her brilliant green eyes. "I just got back from temporary duty and wanted to introduce myself to the new L.T. Where're you from?"

Most airmen Sarah had met seemed uncomfortable talking to her, intimidated either by her rank or position. Apparently Sergeant Haynes was unique. "Michigan," Sarah answered.

"Michigan, huh?" Sergeant Haynes's smile widened, exposing perfect white teeth. "I'm from Ohio. How do you like California so far?"

"I haven't seen much of it. What about you? Have you been stationed here long?" A tiny mole on the sergeant's chin reminded Sarah of Cindy Crawford.

"About three years," Sergeant Haynes said. "It's a great assignment. Lots to do. Good weather. You need to get out, check it out." She nodded, agreeing with herself. "You're what? Twenty-two? Twenty-three?"

Sarah sat back, amazed at the woman's aplomb. "What shop are you assigned to, Sergeant Haynes?"

"Autopilot. Black boxes, ya know?"

Sarah crossed the room to her file cabinet and thumbed through the folders until she found Sergeant Haynes's slim jacket. The sergeant shook her head and chuckled. "You think you're gonna find out all about me from a file, L.T.? I'm afraid you're gonna be disappointed. There isn't much there."

Sarah laid the file on the desk and opened it. Sergeant Haynes was right. The folder contained only some in-processing paperwork, a dorm room assignment, and a letter of commendation from the squadron commander.

When Sarah looked up to find the sergeant watching her, her face flushed. She turned away, but not before noticing the gold flecks in Sergeant Haynes's green eyes. She looked back to the file, unnerved by the sergeant's confident air and her own reaction to it.

"Twenty-two? Twenty-three?" Sergeant Haynes asked again.

Sarah gave in. "Twenty-three," she answered.

Sergeant Haynes spotted a framed diploma hanging on the wall. "University of Michigan, huh? What was your major?"

"Sociology," Sarah said, closing the folder.

"I went to college. Didn't like it much." She looked at Sarah again. "Well, gotta go." Sergeant Haynes stood and stuck out her hand. It felt warm and calloused, her grip firm.

Sarah looked down at the sergeant's hand holding hers and up again at her face, which wore an impish grin. "I'll see ya, L.T.," Sergeant Haynes said.

The first sergeant entered as the broad-shouldered woman strode from the office, then moved aside as she passed. "I see you've met our Sergeant Haynes," he chuckled after she was out of earshot. "What do you think?"

"She's definitely not shy," Sarah said. "What's her story?"

"Oh, Teddy's an interesting character. I think everyone on base knows her. She's a good kid, a hard worker. Unintimidated by rank. I've seen her walk right up to a two-star general and stick out her hand. Surprisingly, they respond to her. She's definitely got moxie."

I wouldn't call it moxie, Sarah thought, but she wasn't sure what she would call it.

After that day Sergeant Haynes stopped by the lieutenant's office at least once a week. At first Lieutenant Parker did more listening than talking as Teddy told her about places she visited on her days off and suggested places Sarah might enjoy. She invited the lieutenant to go with her on weekend excursions: whale watching, the wineries of Napa Valley, San Francisco.

Making friends had been difficult for Sarah, as she didn't feel she had much in common with the other junior officers she'd met on base. She wanted to say yes to Teddy's invitations, but the policy concerning fraternization between officers and enlisted personnel had been pounded into her head in ROTC from day one.

And then there was the way she felt when she'd catch Teddy staring at her. *She makes me feel like a kid*, Sarah thought, *even though she's only two years older*. In these moments Sarah grew flustered, blushed furiously, avoided eye contact, became tongue-tied. What was going on?

Sarah was certain Teddy knew how she made her feel. She'd look up and discover Teddy watching her, then the sergeant would smile and look away, pretending not to notice.

As the weeks passed, Sarah grew more relaxed, finding herself thinking about Teddy all the time, looking forward to her visits. Teddy made her laugh.

Then the day came when the first sergeant suggested Sarah conduct room inspections in the female dorm. "Room inspections?" she echoed.

"Right. You just go over to the dorm once a week and open a few rooms. I try to inspect each room at least once a month. Piece of cake." He handed her a master key and a copy of the inspection checklist.

The squadron maintained a separate female dorm: a small two-story building set apart from the larger coed dorms, with a kitchen, living room, and laundry room. The rooms were located along four separate hallways, and each woman had a room to herself. A nameplate on each door listed the name, rank, and duty section of the occupant.

Lieutenant Parker randomly selected rooms from each hallway, opened the doors, and checked inside. As the first sergeant had predicted, most of the rooms were clean and presentable, so the inspection went quickly. Soon she had just one hallway left.

Sarah wandered down the center aisle, stopping in front of room 210, Sgt. Teddy Haynes's room. She hesitated in front of the door, key in hand. But curiosity overwhelmed her. She opened the door, her heart pounding in her chest.

Sarah stood in the middle of the room and looked around. Light streamed through the blinds. A barbell rested against the wall at the head of the single bed. Telltale posters of the Indigo Girls and Melissa Etheridge hung on the wall next to the bed. An entertainment center covered one wall. A small TV and stereo occupied the shelves along with stacks of paperbacks and CDs.

Sarah crossed the room to the desk. A framed photograph of Teddy and another young woman, their arms draped casually around each other's shoulders, sat at one corner of the desk. Sarah spotted a large calendar nearby and glanced at the penciled entries. What she discovered made her heart beat faster: Teddy had been keeping track of the days she visited Sarah's office.

Behind her, Sarah heard a key turn in the lock. She swung around as Teddy entered the room, wearing dark sunglasses and carrying a motorcycle helmet. Teddy stopped, tossed the helmet onto a chair, and pulled off the sunglasses. Silence hung in the air.

Sarah felt like a kid caught with her hand in the cookie jar.

Teddy crossed the room and stopped in front of Sarah, towering over her as they stood toe to toe. Sarah held her breath as Teddy reached around her and laid her sunglasses on the desk, then swallowed hard and looked up at Teddy.

Teddy smiled that smile, the one with all those perfect teeth. The one that made Sarah's stomach do a little flip.

"I'm inspecting rooms," Sarah stammered. She held up the master key. "Nice room."

Teddy cocked her head to one side and looked at the lieutenant. "You finished?"

Sarah didn't answer.

"L.T., you finished inspecting?" she repeated softly.

"Oh, yeah. I'm finished. Sorry. I'm leaving," Sarah said, embarrassed and angry with herself.

"You don't have to rush off," Teddy smiled.

Sarah looked into Teddy's eyes and saw something she hadn't recognized before: desire. The look Sarah had mistaken for scrutiny had been one of longing. *She runs her eyes over me the way I want to run my hands over her*, Sarah realized with a start.

Sarah glanced at the posters, at the photograph on the desk. She knew now why Teddy made her feel confused. *How could I have been so stupid?* "No, I don't have to rush off," Sarah said. A million questions ran through her mind, but she didn't know what to say or do. *What if I'm wrong? God, I hope I'm right.* Sarah wanted Teddy, and she wanted Teddy to want her.

"L.T.? You OK?" Teddy placed her hand on the lieutenant's arm.

Sarah looked down at Teddy's hand, then glanced up, her eyes meeting the sergeant's. This time Sarah didn't turn away. Teddy's hand tightened on the lieutenant's arm. Sarah swallowed hard, her heart beating so loudly she felt certain Teddy would hear it.

Teddy leaned in and kissed her passionately.

While they were wrapped in each other's arms, time stood still, the rest of the world forgotten. Teddy covered Sarah's face and neck with kisses, her hands caressing her body. But a warning flashed through Sarah's mind: What if someone walked in? She knew what they were doing was prohibited, but she didn't care. She wanted more; she wanted Teddy. Teddy kissed Sarah's neck softly. "I want you," Sarah whispered. A soft moan escaped Teddy's lips. She picked up Sarah and carried her to the bed.

As she kissed Sarah, Teddy unbuttoned the lieutenant's uniform blouse. Sarah let it fall from her shoulders, then Teddy slid her hand under her lover's bra. Each spot Teddy's hand touched burned with desire. Teddy removed Sarah's bra and covered her breasts with her mouth, sucking each nipple until it grew hard and erect. She reached down to unzip Sarah's pants.

"Wait." Sarah moved away from the bed, studying Teddy's face as she removed the rest of her clothes. "Now you." Sarah straddled Teddy's legs and unbuttoned the fatigue shirt. The sergeant wrapped her strong arms around Sarah, kissed her neck and chest and caressed her back. Sarah pulled the T-shirt over Teddy's head, not surprised a bit that the sergeant wasn't wearing a bra. Sarah pushed Teddy onto the mattress and covered her small breasts with her hands, then moved her hands down to her belt buckle to undo her pants.

"We need to get rid of these boots," Sarah laughed, and moved so Teddy could sit up. Teddy unlaced the boots and removed them. She stood and stepped out of her trousers, then pulled off her jockey shorts to reveal perfectly trimmed pubic hair.

Teddy covered Sarah with her body, and Sarah ran her hands over Teddy's broad, muscular back. As Teddy moved down, she left behind a trail of kisses. When she began kissing the inside of Sarah's thighs, pushing her legs up, Sarah's knees fell to the side. Now Sarah was exposed for Teddy's inspection. Teddy spread Sarah's labia with her fingers and ran her tongue over Sarah's clit. Sarah's ears burned as she gasped for breath. Teddy flicked her tongue across Sarah's swollen clit, circling it slowly. She moved her hands under Sarah's butt, kneading and squeezing. The lieutenant moved her hips, straining to get even closer to Teddy, certain she would burst.

At the first waves of Sarah's orgasm, Teddy thrust her tongue deep inside. Sarah cried out and grabbed Teddy's head, pulling her closer. Teddy licked, lapped, and sucked until the waves subsided. Sarah pulled her up until Teddy again covered her.

One kiss had altered Sarah's life. She was hooked. She wanted Teddy, in her bed and in her life.

Teddy's enlistment would end in six months. After a few weeks of intense lovemaking, Sarah moved to an apartment farther away from the base so Teddy could move in with her after she separated—

but she knew she was taking a big risk. The military would hang her out to dry if they discovered an officer was sleeping with an enlisted person.

But love is blind. And maybe deaf and dumb as well.

Sarah gave Teddy a key to her apartment, and Teddy stopped by several nights a week. After they made love, Teddy would return to the base. Sarah longed for the day when they'd be able to spend all their nights together.

But soon her dream began to crumble.

Teddy took leave to go to Ohio. "I have to take care of some family business," she said. "I've had this scheduled for a couple of months."

"I understand. I'd like to go with you," Sarah said. "But I can't right now."

"It's just as well," Teddy said. "My folks don't really accept that I'm gay. It would be uncomfortable for you. And them."

A few days later Sarah drove Teddy to the airport. She stayed and watched the plane until it was just a dot on the horizon. She felt lost without Teddy and missed her already. Teddy didn't call, even though she had promised she would. It was a miserable weekend.

On Monday Sarah dragged herself into work, but all her thoughts returned to Teddy. Shortly after 1 o'clock the orderly clerk came in with distribution. He pulled one package out of the stack and laid it on her desk. "You forgot to sign this." He pointed to a line on the top sheet.

Sarah glanced at the paper, an out-processing checklist, and picked up her pen and signed her name.

"Who's leaving?" she asked, flipping through the paperwork.

"Left," he corrected. "Sergeant Haynes. She out-processed Friday."

Unable to breathe, Sarah felt like she'd been hit in the chest with a sledgehammer. The room was spinning. She looked at the paperwork in her hands but couldn't focus on the words.

"Lieutenant, are you OK?"

Sarah looked up at the sergeant, whose face revealed concern and underlying curiosity. "I'm fine. Fine," she said. But her hands shook as she handed the package back to him. "Was she separating?" she asked. "Sergeant Haynes?"

"Oh, no, ma'am. She's headed for Japan. Long tour. Sure will be quiet around here without her." He shook his head, then turned and walked out of the office.

Sarah sat at her desk blankly as a dull roar filled her head. What would she do now? She couldn't think. *Did I do something wrong? Why did she lie to me? She said she loved me. And I believed her. How could I be so wrong about that, about her?* She picked up her briefcase and hat, left her office, and inched her way out of the building, avoiding eye contact with anyone. Did they know? Did anyone suspect? Were they laughing at her?

Sarah pulled into the parking lot of her apartment building and turned off the car, then sat crying for what seemed hours. Finally she pulled herself together and decided to go inside. Before entering her apartment she pulled her mail from the box. Once inside, she flipped through it. Immediately she recognized Teddy's handwriting and stared at her name on the envelope.

Part of her didn't want to open it, but she had to know why Teddy left without saying anything. She ripped open the envelope, and the key to her apartment fell onto the carpet silently. She stared at the key for a moment, then read the letter.

Dear Sarah,

By now you know I'm gone. I know I should say I'm sorry, but I'm not. And I know I should have told you the truth, but I couldn't. You wanted me to leave the military, to stay with you. Then what? You'd get out and we'd be together forever? Right. It doesn't work that way, L.T. I like the military. I'm good at what I do. I enjoyed the hell out of the time we had together, but it

wasn't enough. We're too young to settle down. I know you don't understand this right now, but maybe someday you will. I won't forget you. Who knows, maybe someday we'll meet again.
Love,
Teddy

Sarah sat in the middle of the living room, Teddy's letter in her lap, crying until her tears tasted bitter. She felt used and betrayed.

Over the next few months Sarah's anger burned itself out, and a kind of numbness settled in. She didn't hear from Teddy. She made herself talk to people and try to get more involved in other people's lives. *If I keep myself busy*, she reasoned, *I won't have time to think about it.*

As the months passed, Teddy crossed her mind less often. Then the day came when she thought about Teddy and it didn't hurt quite as much. She didn't feel her heart tearing. She actually smiled at a memory of the two of them together—a slight smile, but a start nonetheless.

One day, however, new lieutenant processed into the squadron, and the colonel brought her into Lieutenant Parker's office. Sarah stood as they entered the room. This new lieutenant was tall and slender, her straw-colored hair cut short and brushed back.

There's something about her, Sarah thought.

"Lt. Sarah Parker, this is Lt. Rachel Sanders," the colonel said.

Sarah held out her hand.

"Call me Sandy," the new lieutenant grinned. Sarah noticed Sandy's eyes were as blue as deep water. Sandy pumped Sarah's hand eagerly, her grip strong and warm.

"Give her the grand tour and help her get settled in," the colonel said.

"Yes, sir," Sarah said. "No problem." *No problem at all*, she thought. "I'll see that she feels right at home."

Then he was gone and they were alone.

"Have you been stationed here long?" Sandy asked.

"About a year and a half," Sarah said. "It's a great assignment. Lots to do. Good weather. You need to get out, check it out. Whale watching, wine tours in Napa Valley, San Francisco."

Sandy looked into her eyes, smiling. This time Sarah didn't turn away. She felt a familiar little flip in her belly and knew everything would be OK.

15

SEAL Team Bravo Thomas S. Roche

Insertion was accomplished at 0500. Witgenstein, elected leader by her comrades, led the crawl under cover of the half-darkness as dawn cracked an egg above the stinking morass of the Florida swamp. The Mud Bath, everyone called the swamp in question— and as for the sergeant, everybody called her Witty.

At age 29 Monica Witgenstein, Master Sergeant, U.S. Marines, held a black belt in judo; she could field-strip an M-16 faster than anyone in the Western hemisphere and shoot the fruit out of Carmen Miranda's hat at 1,500 yards. Witty was the oldest among them save Eve Singer, the 30-year-old Navy lieutenant who had a hopeless crush on her.

Singer found it beautiful, the way Witty moved in the darkness, swathed in the stink of the swamp, testing each step ahead for enemy booby traps, all focus and fire as she slid through the gloom, raising a silent hand to wave on her compatriots behind her.

There was Singer herself, former Olympic swimmer and second in command; Missy Tompkins, Demolitions; Antonia Bresler, satellite uplink expert; Liz Garcia, who had busted the record for the obstacle course by a full three seconds; and pool shark Jane Palovitch, who took endless shit being called "Hell of a bitch," even though she was the most easygoing (as long as she wasn't playing pool).

They were SEAL Team Bravo of the first all-female Navy SEAL class: the Pentagon's solution to rising public pressure when the fruit salad realized that the frat boys they'd signed up to protect the sanctity of this country's borders and interests didn't want to share their toys with icky girls. Singer, Witgenstein, and the others had been picked from hundreds at the tops of their respective callings.

SEAL Team Commander Witgenstein paused in a crouch at the edge of the fetid river. There in the middle of the sluggish green water was a rusted-out old Caddy, a bright yellow beach ball duct-taped to its roof. The Caddy was about 1,500 yards downriver, inaccessible from the shore because the cover of swamp grass and cypress petered out a hundred yards down. Walking on the exposed shore would be asking to get taken out by a sniper. Retrieval of the beach ball (ostensibly a nuclear warhead from a crashed B-2) would have to be achieved by water. While they were all expert swimmers, there was only one former Olympian among them: Singer.

Witty chewed on a smokeless cheroot, the kind you order from a catalog for psycho survivalists who don't want ATF helicopters to spot them hiding in the hills with their stockpiles of AK-47s and kilos of Mother Nature. Witty took the cheroot out of her mouth, spat on the ground, and pressed the throat-mike against her jugular. Singer eyed the way she held that mike against her taut flesh. Damn, that throat was kissable.

"Target has been spotted," muttered Witgenstein. "Stay alert for enemy snipers. Retrieving by covert river assault. Singer, it's your show now."

"Aye aye, Commander," said Singer, blood pumping as she slipped off her pack and unslung her air rifle. Taking the extra dagger from her belt and putting it between her teeth, she crawled forward, belly against the ground. Singer slithered into the water like a sea snake, disappearing under the murky, slime-covered surface as the dawn sunlight lit it up. Witty chewed on her cigar, watching the trail of little ripples as Singer broke the surface every hundred feet.

"Almost there...." Witty muttered, her pulse pounding. Singer came up close to the edge of the little island, Right where the Caddy stuck into the swamp. Waterproof binocs held against her eyes, she scanned the area for enemy personnel—snipers, patrol boats—and, finding none, crawled onto the trunk of the Cadillac.

"Come on...come on, Singer..." Witty growled low in her throat, watching through her own binoculars as the lieutenant crawled from the trunk of the Cadillac onto the roof. Singer took the dagger from between her teeth and was about to sever the single strand of duct tape when Witgenstein snarled, "Jesus! Jesus!" into the throat mike. "Singer, you've got—" But by then it was too late. Floating soundlessly up on the trunk of the Caddy was the enemy in the form of Master Chief Lazarus, that smug son of a bitch—and he already had Singer's hair gripped in his hand, her head pulled back, an eight-inch commando knife at her throat while Singer's dagger dropped harmlessly into the river. Lazarus was so close to Singer that the rumble of his voice transmitted through Witty's mike— almost unintelligible but there nonetheless—a smug "fuck you" to all of them.

Sounded like "Afternoon, Lieutenant."

It was an impossible shot; the effective range of the air rifles was 1,200 yards, maximum. But Witty wasn't thinking about that—she wasn't thinking at all. She was nothing but well-oiled training and razor-sharp precision as she raised the paint gun to her shoulder and sighted the Master Chief's head.

"You should have stayed in Washington," growled Lazarus, his breath hot on Singer's neck. "Making coffee for generals who haven't seen combat and never will. Not trying to play Army with the big boys."

"Yes, Master Chief," said Singer calmly, her body twisted at an impossible angle. She felt the switchblade next to her ankle and wondered if there was some way she could get her hand down to take it out before Lazarus cut her throat.

"You looking for this?" asked Lazarus, casually reaching down with one of his long arms and plucking the switchblade from Singer's boot. Then there was the explosion, the splash of red spraying Singer as she grabbed Lazarus's wrist and twisted, bringing her hand down on his elbow and hearing him scream as she plucked the little switchblade out of his hand. She said quickly, "Yes, Master Chief, actually I was looking for that. Thanks," and then kicked him in the balls as hard as she could, businesslike and no-nonsense, taking only small satisfaction from the obscene choking sound he made as he disappeared into the filthy water.

As the paint pellets from the Master Chief's buddies exploded all around her, 30 of them hitting the Caddy at once, Singer quickly slit the duct tape holding the beach ball to the roof of the car. She grabbed the ball and dove into the river, ignoring the Master Chief's gurgling sounds as he sought desperately for a handhold on the Caddy. Singer crushed the bubbling beach ball to her chest as she swam underwater, hearing the muffled chirps of the paint pellets leaving red and green and yellow trails through the frothing water as she headed for rendezvous with SEAL Team Bravo.

Fifteen hundred yards away, Witty put another pellet in the Master Chief's forehead—impressing even herself—when he tried to crawl out of the water. She chewed on her cigar and chuckled to herself.

"That's my girl," said Witty as Singer rose from the swamp, slime-covered and dusted with red that might have been the Master Chief's blood—in a perfect world, that is.

✳   ✳   ✳

It happened later, much later, after Witty and Singer had spent an hour in the admiral's office being fitted for new assholes. The admiral wanted to talk to Witty alone for a minute or two, but then he ordered Singer into his office so the two women could sit side by side while he waved that cigar at them threateningly and yelled about the way they "went overboard, the worst thing you can do in the Navy!"

Hey, how many times could the pompous bastard expect Singer to apologize for kicking Master Chief Lazarus harder than was necessary for training purposes, or Witty to say she was sorry she had blown him away a second time while he was trying to climb out of the water? "Truth be told, sir, I didn't really expect to hit him a second time...I just figured I'd squeeze off a shot, you know, scare him a little, but I surprised even myself."

Which was not the right thing to say under the circumstances. Singer and Witgenstein had placed government property—that is to say, the Master Chief—under risk greater than was necessary to complete the exercise, and the admiral was having none of it.

Jesus, thought Singer, *it's not like the guy's really hurt—sure, broken forearm, OK, broken in two places, and a sprained ankle, but for Chrissake, SEAL trainees take those kind of lumps all the time during training exercises!*

Both Singer and Witty felt somewhat vindicated when the admiral stood for a long time staring at them, puffing on his cigar and shaking his head. Then the corners of his mouth twisted upward in a grotesque display, and finally he couldn't suppress the laughter any longer.

"You two killing machines are dismissed," he growled through his chortling. "Try not to whack anyone before reveille—is that understood?"

"Yes, sir!" they both barked.

"Your team's already scrubbed down—they're headed for chow.
You bad-asses can eat too." The admiral's nostrils flared distasteful-
ly. "But for God's sake, shower first, will you? You smell like the Mud
Bath."

"Yes, sir! Thank you, sir!" they said in unison, and hauled their
slime-covered asses out of the admiral's office, leaving trails of ran-
cid swamp water behind them.

After it happened Singer couldn't say for sure why she did it.
She'd been thinking about it since the first day of SEAL training,
even though they could get washed out in a second for what they'd
done.

But after seeing Witty—Monica—that morning, moving like a
well-oiled machine, leading the tightest-operating SEAL team that
ever graced the swamps of Florida's Camp Washington, nothing
could stop the flood of love and respect she felt for her team commander.

Then again, maybe it was just the sight of Witty, covered in slime,
stripping off her fatigues, her ropy muscles flexing under that
smooth white skin. Singer had watched Witty undress dozens of
times, of course, but she'd never *really* watched her. She couldn't
have gotten away with really watching—someone might notice, and
then there'd be hell to pay.

But this time, with all the rest of the team off getting chow, there
was nothing to stop the way Singer's eyes roved over Witty's taut-
muscled body as she stripped down to her mud-soaked skivvies and
stood there in the bunk room, looking back at Singer.

"What the hell do you think you're staring at, Lieutenant?"
snapped Witty, and Singer would have turned aside and mumbled an
excuse if it wasn't for the cocky way Witty stood with one filthy,
naked foot up on Singer's bunk, close to her pillow, her toned thigh

close to Singer's face, so close Singer could smell the sharp musk even over the rank swamp odor. Singer was sitting on her bunk, naked except for her sports bra and underpants, her bare thighs smeared with drying mud. Witty didn't need a sports bra—she just wore the tank top, which, before Singer could answer, Witty wriggled out of, pulling it over her head to reveal the firm apples of her pert little tits with their hard, mauve, grape-sized nipples.

Singer would probably have looked away even *then*, if Witty hadn't taken that filthy tank top, redolent with swamp mud and the smell of Witty's sweat—and draped it over Singer's head, pulling the fabric down into her face.

Was it the cheekiness of the gesture, or the way Witty's scent worked its magic in her body that made Singer's pussy go hot and molten? Singer felt herself getting wet fast as she took a deep breath, inhaling as much of Monica Witgenstein as she could.

That's when Singer knew she was going to make a pass at her SEAL team commander come hell or high water. Nothing could stop the torrent of hunger that was building inside her—hunger for this soldier who was doing everything but ordering her to use that mouth of hers the way it was meant to be used.

Something held Singer back, though; some sense of duty, or the knowledge that what they were about to do was, in military terms, a shit magnet. But it all became academic the instant Witty bent over her and she felt the sergeant's hot, violently hungry mouth against hers, felt Witty's tongue pressing through the thin white membrane of the discarded tank top. To do that, Witty had to bend over pretty far—the sergeant was four inches taller—and with her one combat-booted foot up on Singer's bunk, the bare flesh of her thigh rubbed against Singer's side, even brushing her left tit through the soaked cotton of her bra. Singer didn't know how her hands so easily found purchase around the slender meat of Witty's upper body, her moist palms rubbing those small, dark nipples and finding them firm with arousal. They just sort of ended up there as she fell into Witty's demanding kiss, into the rush of need that welled inside her. But it felt deliciously right to be touching Witty's breasts like that, to feel them small and tight and hard in her hand. Such an intimate gesture between comrades—so natural.

Singer could taste the salt and smell the tang of Witty's body, so unfamiliar and tantalizing; she could even taste the rank slime of the Florida swamps, so familiar and unappetizing. Witty pressed her body against Singer's, their tongues thrusting against each other until the moment Witty bit Singer's lower lip—not enough to break the skin, but enough to make the battle-hardened lieutenant gasp with pain. Then Witty pulled back, running one hand up her sweat-and-slime-streaked body till it cupped one tiny breast, pinching as her other hand gripped Singer's hair.

Singer felt the tightness of Witty's muscles, knew a wrestling match between the two of them would be a dangerous battle indeed. But wrestling wasn't what either had in mind.

Witty jerked her head toward the showers. "My guess is that we got about 15 minutes of semi-privacy before those ladies get done with their chow. I'll be in the showers. Heating up."

Then Witty turned on her heel and marched to the showers, her walk the oiled pace of a professional soldier. The grace with which she deftly hooked her panties with her thumbs and hopped out of them without breaking stride only heightened the pure militarism of those precise movements. As Witty disappeared, naked, through the door to the white-tiled latrine, Singer noticed for probably the thousandth time what a goddamn fine ass that soldier had. A pulse of anticipation and a throb of hunger shot through her as she realized that this time was different: This time she was going to *get* some of that ass.

Singer stood, noting the wet butt-print she left on her bunk— *Ten demerits right there, Jesus Christ*—and automatically smoothed it. She marveled yet again at how foul and filthy she felt. She didn't think a shower with Sgt. Monica Witgenstein was going to help one goddamn bit, but at the moment that didn't seem like a problem.

Singer stripped out of her skivvies in nothing flat.

When Singer entered the showers, Witty had all eight nozzles blasting the white tiles at top volume. Singer weaved in and out of the scalding-hot sprays as she approached Witty, who looked like a fucking Grecian goddess in all that steam. She was lathered up, her short hair foamed with white and her back dribbling suds. Witty turned as Singer approached. Her front was soaped, the outline of her body shrouded as if by a faint white exoskeleton. Clouds of steam boiled and rolled with her every movement.

"What's with all the water?" asked Singer.

Witty fixed her with a pointed stare, harder than any the Master Chief had ever given them. "We're gonna need all the noise we can get, recruit, to cover the noises you're going to make."

Singer stepped into the spray, moved closer and stared into Witty's hard eyes, saw the upward curve of her lips as their naked bodies pressed together, sliding easily against each other.

"Monica—" Singer began, but Witty stopped her with a single straight finger across her lips.

"Call me Sergeant," said Witgenstein. "It's more military that way."

And with that, the single straight finger became a hand, prying apart Singer's lips, and their lips met, hungry, devouring as Witty slammed Singer against the white tiles. With a surge of energy Witty brought her knee up between Singer's legs, and Singer felt a shudder go through her body as the hard ridge of Witty's kneecap pressed into her swollen clit. A moan escaped Singer's lips when Witty pulled back for an instant, and Witty chuckled. "I can't hear you," she singsonged softly, and kissed Singer hard again, working her knee around in a grinding circle, up and down, until each steady thrust almost lifted Singer off her feet. The hot water scalded Singer's skin, making it sting, but the pain lessened as the pleasure of Witty's thrusts brought her closer.

Now the water just felt good, damn good—as hot as hot could be without hurting, without *really* hurting, and Singer was groaning as Witty kissed her one last time and then growled "Hang on" and disappeared—down on her knees, coaxing Singer's thighs apart and pushing her back to lean harder on the white-tiled wall, as Witty's mouth molded to the contour of Singer's pussy. That tongue was pushing its way in—this time not demanding, but asking to be let in, gentle but firm, and with a shiver Singer admitted it, her swelling pussy lips parting for Witty's mouth as the sergeant drank from Singer's gushing cunt, gulping the water that ran in beads and rivulets down Singer's belly and into her shaved crotch, letting it mingle with the ripe taste of Singer's juice, flowing faster and hotter than all eight nozzles combined. Then Witty was on her clit, suckling and licking, nursing like a baby seeking the only nourishment she had ever known, until Singer was almost screaming at the intuitive dance of Witty's tongue tip on her clit. But there was only a minute of that blind, raw bliss—Singer gasping and hovering on the edge of her climax—before she felt a finger slide into her, the nail clipped close with military precision, finger curving up to tease Singer's throbbing G-spot as it stroked its way into her pussy.

"You like that?" groaned Witty hungrily, her tongue only leaving Singer's clit for an instant, not even pausing for the answer before her mouth molded again to Singer's cunt, tongue working the lieutenant's clit.

The answer from Singer was a rapturous "Oh, yeah…oh, fuck yeah" as Witty's middle finger stroked its way in and out of her pussy, and Witty let a second finger join it, bringing another moaning, squirming assent from Singer as Witty gave her the come-hither motion to beat all—and Singer could hardly say no, how could she? This was the orgasm she'd been wanting for weeks, ever since she first saw Witty standing rigid at attention that first day of SEAL training—this orgasm: twisting, writhing, and moaning on Witty's mouth, on her fingers, feeling Witty inside her, feeling Witty's tongue on her clit. And so she came hither, hard, harder than she'd ever come before, her thigh muscles spasming, her knees threatening to give out as she convulsed and moaned, her pussy contracting tight around Witty's thrusting fingers. And as she finished her hot, hard come, her body still tingling with the power and her brain feeling like the top of her head had just come off, Singer saw her whole fucking career flash before her eyes, her "operational experience" gone down the shitter because of how bad she wanted to get her pussy eaten by this sergeant from Oklahoma, and goddamn it, like it or not, she didn't give a shit. She didn't care one goddamn bit, because tomorrow morning she was going to fall out at reveille and go do her fucking job, and if that wasn't good enough for the U.S. Navy, then fuck 'em—at least she'd come hard on Monica Witgenstein's hungry tongue, and that would do nicely, thanks.

Then Witty was up, pressing naked against Singer, steadying her against the white wall as she kissed her, one more time, then twice, then a third time, their tongues mingling as the Navy orchestra began to play outside—that is, as they heard the sounds of women complaining ("They gonna make us do it again? All 'cause of that fuckin' hot shot...."), their voices carrying as they straggled past the fogged-over window, just inches from the place their team commander was having the cunt juices licked from her face by an eager, bright-eyed Lieutenant Singer.

"Tit for tat, Sergeant," said Singer as their bodies separated, and she gracefully grabbed a white cake and began to soap herself. "You saved my ass today, I'll save your ass tomorrow."

Witty was whirling around the shower room killing six nozzles—all but an adjacent pair. She took the soap out of Singer's hand and began to lather herself. "You'll have the chance, Lieutenant," said Witty. "We're back in the Mud Bath tomorrow morning."

For an instant Singer just stared. "You shitting me?"

Witty shook her head. "Admiral's orders. Reveille at 0300."

Outside the shower, the bunk room was filling with the rest of their class. Singer took a long, deep breath of hot steam as she imagined hauling her ass out of bed at that obscene hour. Then she thought about doing it with Monica Witgenstein, imagined the sight of Witty in action, imagined doing tomorrow what they'd done today: Functioning as a team, the best team in the service for another of the most grueling days anyone on earth had ever experienced. And she thought about the few minutes she and Witty might be able to steal from the Navy at the end of that day—when, tired and miserable, Singer could prove to this cocky Marine that she could do as good as she'd just been done. That's what made reveille at 0300 sound like the invitation to a friggin' party.

Singer grinned and shrugged. "Oh-three? They're letting us sleep in, eh, Commander?"

And when Witty scowled and flipped her off, Singer grumbled, "Don't tempt me, Sarge, not with the ladies at home."

Witty smirked and turned off the water.

16

Judge Benko's Decision Felicia Von Bot

Bang! Judge Benko slammed down her gavel impatiently. "Order! I said order in this court!"

"But Your Honor," pleaded several women.

BANG! "This is the Superior Court of Appealing Lesbians, not a summer festival," the judge proclaimed over a babble of voices. "Any more demonstrations and I'll confine this trial to my private chambers." Those who had swarmed up front swallowed their complaints mid-voice and retreated behind the wooden railing that separated the proceedings from the raucous crowd.

Benko turned impatiently to her law clerk. "Reno, remove all naked women from this courtroom. Now!" Always one to obey orders, Reno slipped down from behind the bench and herded out the protesting group. Several women gathered T-shirts and undergarments that had been tossed around the courtroom. One or two pieces of clothing hung from the rotating ceiling fans that only seemed to circulate the hot air in the room. Turning to a lagging woman, Reno instructed, "Now, dahling, put your pants back on. We can't have people walking around the courthouse undressed."

"I just wanted Ms. Happy's autograph," the young fan replied, as she stretched her neck around for one last glance at the defendant sitting in the witness box.

"Yes, but a tush, even a cute one like yours, is not the best place for it," Reno advised, as she helped the woman back into her jeans. Making the most of her notoriety, the defendant, Ms. Happy, blew a few kisses toward her departing admirers. With one foot leisurely dangling over the side of her chair, the buffed woman turned her heat-seeking eyes on the court stenographer, causing the stenographer's skin to resemble ice cream dipped in strawberry blush.

Watching, Judge Benko grimaced and clasped her ever-present stress ball. She glanced at the other side of the courtroom where the youthful woman who had inadvertently started this lawsuit sat in the plaintiff's chair. The only evidence of Ms. Hurt's despondent state of mind was a tightly clutched, half-empty carton of Twinkies, which had been on her lap since the beginning of the trial. Benko pondered what had brought Ms. Hurt to such a state only a year after she'd arrived in town.

Wet both behind her ears and other choice places, Ms. Hurt had befriended Sugar Muffin and Poohkie Bear, who were immersed in the cooing and ahhing phase of lesbian couplehood. The heavenly pair believed that all lesbians should be blessed with starting every single utterance with such cuddly words as "love-bug," "sweetness," and any other sugar certified by Martha Stewart. Consequently, they fixed up Ms. Hurt with every eligible lesbian who met the minimal requirements of Sisterhood.

To the dismay of her blissful patrons, Ms. Hurt rejected the courtship of countless women; it seemed she was waiting for the blemishless pulp romance version of destiny. Then, one Friday night, she met her love sponsors at a local karaoke bar. Ignoring the offered Evelyn, Ms. Hurt set her eyes on Ms. Happy instead, and the two shared a stick of gum. The proverbial juices started to flow, and they scheduled their first official date.

Anxious to prepare Ms. Hurt for her big night, Sugar Muffin and Poohkie Bear gifted their protégé with a dental dam and gel for good luck. They were ecstatic when she asked for three extra dental dams to complete a matching set. But little did they know that she promptly went home and placed them under her teacups, thinking they were environmental coasters. Only when she attempted to wash her dog with the gel did she begin to doubt her sponsors—or herself. But too timid to question her purveyors of rapture, she visited the only person to whom she could admit her ignorance—her cousin, thrice removed, twice disinherited, and once stranded in the Rockies with her butch ski instructor—Fran, who lived with Gail at the other end of town. Fran immediately set about giving her a crash course in primping, posing, and bra unsnapping.

Such testimony was disconcerting to Judge Benko. She shook her head and made a note to recommend Bra Unsnapping 101 as a mandatory course for the upcoming semester at Sappho University.

Ms. Happy was, needless to say, already a specialist in the art of undoing. After treating Ms. Hurt to an instant cappuccino at the Turkey Lurkey, the chiseled convenience queen invited her to see her massage oils in the back of her van. Within 30 seconds, Ms. Happy had slipped her hands inside of Ms. Hurt's soccer jacket, removed her new bra, unzipped her jeans and fogged the windows with a singular love bite. Ms. I-don't care-if-I'm Hurt started to palpitate in places she hadn't even known existed. Ms. Happy pinched and licked her homegrown nipples into conical Pop Tarts ready to spring out of the toaster. While thrashing her tongue against eager flesh, she thrust her hand between the virgin's legs with a masterful determination that threw Ms. Do-it-to-me Hurt's hormones into gaga-overdrive. The scent of melon musk overcame her. She grabbed the newly inflated air mattress so wildly that she poked a hole in it. The opening let out a gasp between her legs, and her flailing body lurched up to the roof. The van rocked like a burning four-wheel jukebox during an earthquake. Feel-good heat climbed the walls and ricocheted from corner to corner, jerking in a frenzied beat until...

A high-pitched giggle from the court stenographer's direction brought the judge back to today's proceedings. She wiped a few beads of perspiration from her forehead. With the courtroom finally subdued, Judge Benko gestured benevolently to the prosecutor. "Ms. Moral, please continue."

The prosecutor adjusted her wire-rimmed glasses and sauntered to the center of the courtroom. Taking delight in her own cum laude aplomb, she displayed a videocassette to the court. "Your Honor, we would like to enter this evidence of Ms. Happy's—uh—state of mind as Exhibit 24."

Ms. Happy's defense attorney jumped up from her desk. "We've already seen 23 videos today. Is this necessary?"

Benko motioned both women over to the bench. "This better be good," she warned the prosecutor. Ms. Moral pushed the cassette into the miniscreen on the judge's desk, and they gathered in behind her, each woman vying for a good view.

The athletic feline lounging across the bed was unmistakably Ms. Happy, dressed in only a sailor's cap. In concentrated butch fashion, she lay on her rippled back gazing between her own brawny thighs. The court officials leaned closer in amazement as the videocamera panned in. Using all of her gymnastic energy, Ms. Happy was delicately balancing a shot glass on her glistening vulva. Filled to the brim with liquor, the little souvenir from the Yum Yum club swayed from side to side like a sensuous belly dancer on an erotic voyage, without spilling a drop.

"Wow!" exclaimed Reno. "How do you train a vulva to do that?"

"You should see what she can do with the little pink umbrellas from a Mai Tai," answered the defense attorney. A pair of red-tipped fingertips entered the screen and reached for the glass. They came to an abrupt stop when Ms. Happy's steamy voice commanded, "No. Not with your hands."

Uncontrollable drool trickled down Reno's lower lip. She quickly grabbed her court-issued salivation kit in search of a napkin. The group of officials looked questioningly at the judge. After a moment's hesitation, she allowed, "OK. Ten-minute recess."

The defense attorney grabbed Ms. Happy's arm and dragged her out of the courtroom. The other officials immediately scattered to their individual rooms and locked the doors behind them.

"Not you, Reno," the judge said. Glancing around the courtroom, she spied the community bookmaker doing a brisk business in the far corner. "See what that bookie's up to and get her out of here."

Reno wiped the tip of her chin clean and reluctantly started prodding the bookie toward the exit. "Come on now. You know this is in violation of the Federal Dyke Code: section 23009, part XXIX, subdivision D, paragraph 7,684. No public betting on relationships." Then she nuzzled up to the bookie and whispered, "What are the odds?"

"Depends what you want to wager on. 69-to-1, Plaintiff and defendant are sentenced to a second date. 38- to-1, Ms. Happy got her bronze shine at an indoor tanning salon. 7-to-1, the judge wears boxers under her robes. Have any inside info on that, per chance?"

"No," Reno shook her head, though she had made a few attempts to peek under the judicial garments. Seeing the officials return to the courtroom, she quickly retrieved a bill from her wallet. "Five says Benko wears bikinis."

Exhibit 24 was entered into evidence. Benko gave her stress ball another squeeze under the desk. Ms. Happy's happy attorney escorted the defendant back to the witness box. She winked at her client, sure that this new evidence meant she would be labeled a freelance dyke and released from relationship custody.

Feeling Ms. Moral's intense gaze, the defense attorney commented to her, "Hey, the rules never said I have to accept only money to represent someone." After tossing a virtuous sneer in the defendant's direction, Ms. Moral defogged her eyeglasses and secured the

top button on her designer suit. Then she stationed herself res-
olutely in front of the defendant. Determined to continue her cross-
examination, she prompted, "Ms. Happy, do you consider Ms. Hurt
a friend, a friend turned lover, a lover turned friend, or was this just
a fling?"

"Objection," interrupted Ms. Happy's attorney. "The last word
implies violence."

"Sustained," agreed the Judge.

"Very well," conceded Ms. Moral. "A close acquaintance?"

"Your Honor, it's already been established that the plaintiff and
defendant live near each other."

"A roll in the hay?" the disgruntled prosecutor shot back at the tag
team of advocates.

"Sorry," Judge Benko said. "We're in town, not in the country.
That phrase is outside our jurisdiction."

The prosecutor summoned all of her preppie killer-instinct to
find the question that would knock Ms. Happy's outer child on her
keister. Trying desperately to remain distant in spite of the accused's
cologne, she confronted the defendant: "Ms. Happy, your statement
to the court says that you are an artist. But is it not a fact that you're
the assistant manager of the third shift at the Turkey Lurkey Food
Market?"

The entire balcony gasped in horror at the damaging accusation.
The grunge goddess could very well incriminate herself, leaving her
branded as a fraud. Or she might resort to silence and deprive her
fans of hearing her succulently low voice. Such reticence could lead
to tabloidian speculation from which she would never recover.

Ms. Happy flexed an arm muscle to audible admiration. "I am an
arteest," she answered, thrusting her knee through a hole in her cut-
off jeans. "I specialize in free-form relationships."

The peanut gallery started howling and throwing their phone
numbers like confetti across the courtroom, while the more subdued
members of the Sisterhood turned into a garden of embarrassed,

antsy tomatoes. Ms. Moral's milk-colored face coagulated, and she slunk back to the prosecutor's table to receive comforting pats from her six colleagues.

A wafer-thin woman hastened toward the judge's bench. "Excuse me, Madam Judge. Madam Judge." She waved *The Lesbian Dating Etiquette Guide* like a Carrie Nation pendulum. "I know the prosecutor is doing her best. But is it possible that Ms. Hurt could use more counsel?"

Ms. Hurt's big Raggedy-Ann eyes looked pleadingly at the judge. If she had any more counsel, she would certainly have a mental meltdown, provided that was not already the case. She had only wanted to know whether she and Ms. Happy were a couple. Never did she imagine that this simple question would cause a chain reaction of such proportions; the very suggestion turned out to have been a blueprint for connubial calamity.

Convinced she had found a lifetime of paradise with her lesbian-in-shining-Reeboks, Ms. Hurt had packed her bags to move in with Ms. Happy. But Ms. Hurt and her luggage had inexplicably thrown Ms. Happy into reverse mode. Quickly declaring that she still lived with her grandmother, she offered Ms. Hurt a home-cooked dinner as a consolation prize. Then she postponed it indefinitely because of an out-of-state business trip.

The ever-surveillant Sugar Muffin, a recovering chatterphile, found out that the trip was really a rendezvous with a not-so-ex ex. So, she, Poohkie Bear, and Ms. Hurt's cousin Fran immediately formed a Sapphotic task force and converged on Ms. Hurt's apartment. During the discussion, Sugar Muffin's advice became questionable when it was revealed that she knew a tad too much about the whereabouts of Ms. Happy's beauty marks. Poohkie Bear did not take this news kindly; after a grizzly stare at her girlfriend, she walked out with an intensely supportive Fran and did the girlfriend shuffle.

Judge Benko politely dismissed the offer for more counsel and called again for order in the courtroom. After a few choice slams of her gavel, she turned wearily to the prosecutor. "Ms. Moral, please, do you have any more questions?"

"Your Honor," she murmured, "no more questions."

"But— Butt—" the audience cried out.

Ignoring all ifs, ands, and bare butts, the judge asserted, "This court is adjourned!"

"But we demand to know," shouted the full house, "ARE THEY TOGETHER?"

Judge Benko adjusted her flowing black robe around her as she stood up. "You will have my recommendation in one week." With her usual poise, she walked out of the courtroom.

"Whew," Reno exclaimed, following closely behind. "They were a tough crowd in there."

"At least they didn't demand a jury trial," sighed the judge. "I'll meet you in my chambers. I need some caffeine." She walked past the Fetish Arbitration Center, rounded the corner of the Pagan Initiation Office, and stopped off at the judge's lounge for some coffee. Pressing the handle of the cappuccino machine for the third time, she heard, "It's tough these days to get enough foam when you need it."

"Pat, I thought you were in trial," she greeted Judge Caliguia.

"Oh, we don't start until 2 o'clock. In the S/M division it takes hours to get all the witnesses through the metal detector."

"I hear you have a tough case."

"Yes," the judge sighed. "Looks like bad abuse."

"Permanent damage?"

"Might be. This was a vicious bunch of women. No safe word could have stopped them. First, they tore off the woman's clothes and strapped her to a chair in the middle of a dark dungeon. And then...." The judge paused in disbelief. "They forced her to watch *Clare of the Monsoon* three times in a row. She begged for a blindfold and earplugs, but to no avail. The worst part is that I have to review the film. And I don't get to wear a blindfold or earplugs either."

"Want to borrow my stress ball?" the judge offered.

"No thanks. I have my own," Caliguia answered, as she patted a bulge on her right thigh.

"Good luck."

As Benko walked back down the hallway, she noticed that several of the courthouse personnel seemed to be afflicted by a sudden clumsiness. They continually dropped their pens on the floor, and somehow these pens always landed near the judge. Being the polite women that they were, they quickly kneeled down before the judge's robes to pick them up. "I'll get it," one sprightly purple-haired woman insisted as her pen accidentally rolled between the judge's legs.

Aware of the bets being placed about her undergarments, Benko stepped to the side, barely missing a huge magic marker that had dropped from the receptionist's desk.

"Sorry, Your Honor," the woman said with giggling eyes and a pierced nose.

Barely making her way through the minefield of dropped pens, the judge finally ducked back into her office. Perhaps it was the stress of the trial or the change in weather or the cute but transparent bailiff who had launched her gold-plated Bic across the length of the atrium. As Benko sat back in her executive vibrating chair, she suddenly felt the need to feel something in her grasp other than her *Lavender Field and Stream* magazine. A breeze, soft as a woman's whisper, touched her and lifted her thoughts out through her third story window. Away from the judge's chambers. Away from the courthouse. Away. Benko felt the caress of the shaded woods beyond, of the sensuous curves of the trail through the fir trees. They beckoned her forward into a quiet that was only broken by a faint splash in the lake ahead.

Half-submerged in the water, a nymph came forward as if she had been expecting Benko to arrive. She slowly emerged from the lake, revealing the smooth and enticing nakedness that could only belong to a woman. Her faun-like eyes smiled with longing. Her firm bosom held out the gift of natural desire. Her skin glistened in the warmth of the sun, droplets of water traveled down her body. She knelt on the grassy embankment and grazed her fingertips over her thighs, moving ever so closely to her cunt.

"Katherine," she beckoned.

Benko flushed. The sensual voice sounded both confidential and strangely exciting. As if on command, her robe fell to the ground, and she sat down near the vision. The nymph's lips ran up Benko's silky cheek and down the nape of her neck. She drew back Benko's rich brown hair and filled her mouth with deep kisses. Pushing Benko into the grass, she explored her body as if she knew better than Benko herself how to bring her pleasure. Benko moaned her delight as the woman bit her breasts, at the exciting pinch of teeth. Wet flames began to wash over her as the nymph moved insistently down between her legs. The spirit's tongue pressed into the heat, flickering with a primal rhythmic power. Every stroke filled Benko with a pulsating groan. Every lick reached into her erotic wish to be savored. She felt herself sliding into ecstasy; into a burning surge so intense that she flung herself into the fire and cried out in release.

Judge Benko was sitting in her chambers, still caressing the arms of her executive chair, when Reno stumbled in with a collage of evidence. The law clerk listed the contents: "Witness depositions— we're still waiting for one—brief from the Serial Monogamy Alliance, a couple of E-mail love poems, and a business card from a Tarot card psychologist."

Reluctantly pushing her magazine off her desk, Judge Benko took the witness statements. "You know where to put the rest," she said.

Positioned over a large trash can was a poster of a lesbian rock legend thrusting her electric guitar toward her audience. Just where her middle finger struck a twang was a conveniently sized hole.

Reno threw in the pile of offerings, saving the free massage coupon from an unnecessary fate by stuffing it in her back pocket.

"All right," the judge said, as she looked over the depositions. "Let's run down the rest of the story."

Reno immediately put down her air guitar and plopped herself in the chair opposite the judge. Over the next two weeks after their date, Ms. I'm-beginning-to Hurt had initiated daily phone calls to Ms. Happy. The conversations were filled with volumes of compliments and promises. But Ms. Give-her-the-benefit-of-the-doubt Hurt could never quite understand why they couldn't pinpoint an exact time and place for a second date; that is—and this is where the eyewitness accounts differ—until Fran caught Ms. Happy in a slow dance with Evelyn at the local bar.

"No way," claimed Sugar Muffin. "She was in the parking lot with that biology teacher."

"I saw her behind the pool table with a motorcycle mama," insisted Poohkie Bear.

Shaken by these revelations, Ms. I-have-to-know Hurt decided to confront Ms. Happy at Sugar Muffin's secondhand store the next afternoon. Finally alone together once more, Ms. Happy slowly gazed up and down Ms. Hurt's body from head to running shoes. After a long, breathful pause, she finally confessed, "My doctor told me not to have sex."

Visions of infections, STDs, terminal illness, or worse immediately popped into Ms. Hurt's sympathetic head. Sensing that her words were convincing, Ms. Happy offered her tour de force. With a perfect blend of ailing frailty and sacrificial pride, she painfully stretched her fingers and whispered, "I have carpal tunnel syndrome."

Judge Benko stood up from her desk and walked toward the window, lifting a brow of disapproval. "Amateur," she commented.

"Ms. Happy's pleading innocence under the Jock Exception," Reno said.

"I expected that. Is she in a competitive league?"

"She stole home once, sliding on a desert-dry baseline in shorts."

"Well, I guess we have to take that into consideration. Did she score?"

"Not on the field. The Burning Yonis—that's the name of the team—were wiped out 10-3," answered Reno. "But she got ten stitches in her thigh. Would've had at least 20 if they hadn't hit a keg of beer before the game."

"Hmm. When is our report before the Lesbian Board of Ethics due?"

"When President Birkenstock heard it was your case, she said she'll see us whenever you want."

The judge smiled at her old friend's accommodation. "Tell her tomorrow at 9."

Reno gathered up her books and headed for the door, knowing she was already late for her graduate seminar on Processing Fatigue Syndrome. "Don't forget Ms. Happy also wants to take advantage of the new spatial formulas."

"I'll finish them," Benko replied. The judge swung around to the bookshelf behind her and picked up a large manual titled *The Effects of Spatial Deprivation in Lesbian Relationships,* compiled by the 69th National Symposium on dimensional consensus. This newest edition updated the latitudinal—and, coincidentally, the longitudinal— needs of lesbians through a complicated method: adding height, weight, plus intake of dessert, multiplied by the area lived in, divided by the distance between cleavage, raised to the higher power of achievable orgasms in one night.

After filling two pages with mathematical equations, a disturbance outside Benko's door interrupted her calculations. Perturbed by the prolonged racket, she walked out into the hall.

"Is there something I can help you with?" Benko asked sternly. The court bookie's face took on a guilty look, and she disappeared down the corridor, leaving a streamlined woman behind to answer.

"Judge Benko?" She smiled under a mane of dark brown hair and extended her hand in salutation. "I'm Gail. I was told to drop off my statement for the Ms. Happy/Hurt case."

The judge shook her hand, a bit disconcerted by her strong but subtle touch.

Benko invited the woman into her chambers. "I see you had business with the local bookie," she said disappointedly.

"No," Gail answered with an assured voice. "I've never been to the courthouse. She was just showing me the way to your office."

"I see." Benko moved toward the window in order to scrutinize the woman more fully.

"I don't care what you wear underneath your robes. I can already tell what you look like."

The judge felt heat rise up through her body and she quickly took refuge behind her desk. "You're Fran's partner?" she asked as nonchalantly as possible.

"No. We broke up as soon as this situation started." Gail handed Benko her deposition. "I've never met Ms. Hurt or Ms. Happy. Never been to the Turkey Lurkey. Don't like cappuccino over the counter. I prefer homemade. I know how to create more froth than a double latte, the kind I want to stir all day and push my face into, licking all the sides with my tongue. I like to explore each delectable fragrance, savor the taste of each sip, every last drop until the cup's empty. Sometimes well into the night. Sometimes playing hooky on a weekday afternoon behind closed curtains. And when the liquid gushes over my hand...."

She brought her long fingers up to her lips, pushed them into her mouth like the sweet offshoots of a lollipop, and slowly brought them out again. "I'm not a gambler. I'm a risk-taker. There's a difference. Let me know if you need anything further, Katherine."

The unfamiliarity of hearing her first name spoken so intimately in these chambers left the judge staring after Gail in wet silence.

Benko gazed absentmindedly out toward the distant forest, barely able to make out the great river rushing through it. Finally, she took a short stroll around the room, taking in the numerous plaques and citations that covered the walls. With mixed remembrances, her eyes lingered haphazardly on her award for negotiating the vegetarian hostage crises, then swung to her commendation for implementing the remedial rhythmic licking program. The judge picked up Gail's statement and read its single sentence: "I'd rather go fishing." Benko let out her first chuckle since the beginning of the trial.

The following morning, the judge and Reno discussed the verdict in their case as they walked to the president's chambers. "OK, where do we stand?" Judge Benko asked.

"Ms. Hurt has been waiting for Ms. Happy to recover from her... uh... ailment. Ms. Happy says she's flattered, but considers herself a migratory dyke."

"And Evelyn? The biology teacher? And cycle mama?"

"Waiting by the phones."

"Sugar Muffin and Poohkie Bear?"

"Both gorging on other sweets."

The judge and Reno entered the chambers of the Regional Board of Lesbian Ethics. The room buzzed with hearsay about postponement of the proceedings, while everyone awaited the president's arrival. As the rest of the officials tried in vain to set a new date compatible with the softball schedule, Judge Benko impatiently looked at her watch. It was a routine case. Why was the system forever caught up in lavender tape? Finally, President Birkenstock arrived and announced that there would be no postponement. She was declaring a mistrial. They would have to start over from the beginning after the summer's dimensional symposium. "We're changing the spatial needs to include more dresses and cosmetics for the femmes. They've been lobbying for additional closet space and an official change of its name to 'clothing cubicle.'"

The president became solemn as she turned toward Judge

Benko, her longtime compatriot. For a moment everyone could see the president trying to find a civilized way of verbalizing the decision for a mistrial. After a difficult grimace, she proclaimed, "One of the officials in this case has been seen fraternizing with one of the witnesses."

Reno quickly jumped forward. "I couldn't help it. I was in the Turkey Lurkey and there she was, loading cases of pop into the cooler. Before I knew it, we were in the storeroom searching for the last Creamsicle and she put her arms around me so I wouldn't shake from the cold. She was so warm, so protective, one helluva kisser...."

"Reno," President Birkenstock interrupted her. "I wasn't referring to you." She turned again to Judge Benko. "You realize that I have to suspend you from duty?" The words came out with regret. "Maybe six months... if you have a defense," she amended hopefully.

"I'm single and available," the judge replied with an undiluted grin.

"For goodness sake, Katherine," pleaded the president. "We served together for years in the Lesbian Lower Processing Court. Your record's been impeccable up to now." She crooked her arm through Benko's and steered her over to the corner. "Listen, I know what kind of strain this work can put you under. I can book you in our private pagan resort in Newark until this blows over."

Judge Benko retrieved her rubber stress ball from her pocket. Giving it one last affectionate squeeze, she tossed it to the president. "No, thanks."

"Wait a moment, Katherine," President Birkenstock intercepted her on her way out. With a fond farewell hug, she whispered confidentially in Benko's ear, "I wagered on what exactly you wear under your robes. At least tell me what you have on. For old times' sake."

Given the opportunity to make one last gesture in these honorable halls, Judge Benko lifted the back of her robe and mooned the entire judicial staff with the cutest buns this side of virginity. Fishing rod in hand, Benko walked out the door.

"You'll have to excuse me, ladies. I have a date."

17

Dress Pinks M. Christian

The funny thing was that the day—until about 15 minutes ago—hadn't been half bad.

Rosy had gotten up at—for her—a respectable 10, and leapt into showering and primping: good shampoo, excellent conditioner, moisturizer, gentle glides of the razor along her legs, practiced sweeps of her brush to give her black hair just the right amount of lift. After, she carefully struggled into what she called her dress pinks—even though the whole outfit was just black and off-whites. Most of the time she looked at the simple black, calf-high skirt, business-high heels, taupe hose, satin blouse, and austere jacket with more than a little distaste, but this morning she felt like she was getting ready for inspection. She barely suppressed a snapped salute as she gave herself a once-over before heading out into the San Francisco fog.

That afternoon Mr. Perez had actually liked the cover and layout treatments, going as far as to say "*Bueno!* Exactly what I was looking for!" The suggestions he'd made had even helped the project and wouldn't take more than an hour, maybe two, to tweak. After the meeting downtown at the offices of *Si!* magazine, they'd all gone to dinner at Plouf's. A couple of glasses of a gentle white wine later, the handsome businessman had even hit them up to work on some designs for *Si!*'s sister mag in Argentina.

Heading back to her car, weaving just a little bit from the wine and the heady success, Rosy was beaming and congratulating herself on a job well done. As usual, however, she couldn't help wonder how much of that success came from her talent as a graphic artist and how much from the cool professionalism of her (metaphorically) three-piece business suit.

Walking down the dark streets—click, click, click on her not-too high, but certainly high enough, heels—Rosy smiled; although conventional wisdom suggested a nervous speaker imagine the audience in their underwear, Rosy turned the concept on its head—she relished the ridiculous facade of her hose, heels, and silk blouse over an old Glamour Pussy undershirt and threadbare, comfortable panties.

After all, she thought as she wandered down Dore Alley just after midnight, I'm in the business of images, so I'm naturally a canvas for a particularly effective one.

It was about that time—as she turned from the narrow alley onto the larger river of Folsom Street—that she realized she couldn't find her car.

In a blush of anger and embarrassment, she stood on the empty street and ran quickly through her memory of where she'd left the battered old Cougar. Right there. Definitely right there—she even recalled the irritatingly overflowing trash can, the *Bay Guardian* news rack, the lighting store (which nicely was still very well-lit) across the street. This was definitely the corner; all that was missing was the car.

Luckily there wasn't much inside the car to be concerned about: an old coat, an outdated Thomas Bros. map, an ashtray still overflowing from Louise's pack-a-day habit. Yet if she longed for anything, it was that damned disgusting ashtray.

Louise hadn't been the best girlfriend Rosy had had—far from it. In fact, that pack a day had been just one of a whole parade of self-centered and repulsive personal habits, but she'd been in Rosy's life for almost five years. Five years of toenail clippings in the bed, ancient dishes in the sink, moldy sandwiches in the fridge, and morning breath that could bring down light aircraft. But still, Louise had been hers and she had been Louise's—it wasn't a fancy, three-piece relationship, but it had been a smoking, fuming one.

They had melted together, flowing through many a long weekend—only crawling out of their heavily rolling orgasmic ocean when Rosy had been forced at 8 A.M. Monday morning to don her dress pinks and wander off into the real world to earn their living.

"Oh, fuck—" Rosy said, not for the car (because it was a piece of shit), not for the cigarette butts that were all that was left of Louise (because the ache was finally starting to close up), not because she had to walk home (it was only ten blocks), or that she had to get up early (she didn't), but because there was just something profoundly lonely about that ten-block walk—without anything to look forward to, without even the hollow reminder of a past love to keep her company.

"Lose your car?" said a voice nearby. "Well, that's a bitch. Stolen, I suppose."

She should have expected it: Folsom and Dore, nexus of the leather paradise for a whole generation of gay men. "Damned straight," Rosy said, turning to smile at the owner of the voice.

For someone who'd lived in the city as long as she had, she didn't claim that many fag boys as friends. Maybe it was because since she'd met Louise very shortly after moving to the city from her old home turf of Miami, and they hadn't left their little Mission flat unless they had to.

More than that, though, Rosy suspected that she had just never seen the attraction in hanging with guys. After allowing herself to love women, she didn't have time for anybody or anything else.

"Yeah, a royal one —" she agreed, then huffed out a good, deep sigh as she looked again at the empty space where the car had been parked. "Not like the thing was worth stealing."

"Had it happen to me once. A piece of shit, but it seemed everyone knew how to get in and take it for a spin. Had it ripped off half a dozen times the first two years I was here."

Looking at him, Rosy could feel a bit of the attraction—a gentle fluttering down in the pit of her stomach, and that bothered her.

He was young—almost boyish in fact, something she knew was pretty rare for a hard-core leatherman. He had ash-blonde hair cut into a severe crew that showed off both his squared and elegantly shaped skull and a very wispy mustache. He wore his own uniform well—a revelation that almost brought a giggle to Rosy's lips as she realized she was still in her severe dress pinks. He wore tight, tight, tight leather chaps, thick-heeled calf-high motorcycle boots, a muscle-contouring black vest, and even a small cap. He looked like a recruitment poster for *Drummer*, a center spread for Mach, a living totem of the spirit of Mr. San Francisco Leather.

"Well," Rosy said, shaking herself slightly, "I'd better get to a phone and call it in."

"Who knows," he said in his deep but remarkably musical voice, "maybe it just got towed. Happens all the time."

"I can only hope," she said as she started to walk away.

Half a minute later she realized she had no idea where the nearest phone was. When she turned around, she was startled—and again she felt that fluttering deep in her belly—to see him smiling broadly. "There's one over here," he said, gesturing back the other way. "Come, I'll show you."

It seemed so perfectly natural to take his arm when he offered—and together they walked off down the street. Even though she wouldn't have admitted it, on the arm of the leatherman, her day had actually begun to look up.

❆   ❆   ❆

"You don't seem freaked out—that's good!" he yelled into her ear.

Rosy shook her head, not wanting to bellow over the thumping disco. It was true, she didn't feel…well, *uncomfortable* wasn't really the right word. She felt safe, certainly, but on the other hand, she wasn't completely at ease, either. At best, she was distracted.

Looking around, she smiled again to herself. Only in San Francisco: a successful business date, a towed car (thank goodness), a short walk, and then an evening in a leather bar.

Rosy would have liked to have thought her leatherman charming, but the fact is she could barely hear him over the heavy-beating disco. It was hard, she discovered quickly, to be charming when your witty repartee couldn't be heard.

Still, Rosy was able to tell that—deep breath, deep breath, deep breath—he was (ahem) kinda, well, sorta, um…damned sexy. It was hard to accept, and in fact the first realization that she actually found him attractive rushed over her like a kind of panic. Rosy didn't have a indecisive past; she liked to say that she was a born lesbian: no clumsy proms trying to feel attracted to the boys, no waking up in the middle of a marriage to hunger for another woman's lips. To Rosy, boys were like some distant land—she knew where it was on the map, but she didn't care to visit.

Until, that is, her car got towed, and she found herself in the presence of the leatherman. Maybe that was it, she thought, mulling it over as she sipped her Coke. Was she really attracted to him or to his leather? He was almost too perfect, a dead-cow icon, a Tom of

Finland deity: gleaming leather chaps, vest with those merit badges of boy-sex S/M clubs, even the little leather cap. He was like a 33-cent stamp for hot leatherboy sex.

Seeing him made Rosy feel like she had a hot, hard leather fist up inside her. It was an unexpected and—yes, at first—shocking sensation, but the desire she felt rolling around inside her was strong enough to shove her hesitation aside. Thus she stayed, wondering about the source of that desire.

The only thing she really regretted was that her own dress pinks were so stiff and emotionless. She'd never wanted to before, but this seemed the night for first-times—she wished she had a collar on.

And as she had been thoughtfully and—yes, she had to admit it—hungrily looking at him, he'd been looking at her. The leatherman had been looking at her.

He said something. Over the pounding of the music, she couldn't make it out. She leaned forward and yelled, "What?!" at him.

That's when he'd said it. Simple enough in an everyday context, but for Rosy in her power suit and him in his incredibly sexy leather, it meant a lot more—a lot that Rosy suddenly realized, fully, she was willing to go along with: "Do you want to go to the bathroom?"

That's how Rosy, who'd never even kissed a boy, ended up being led into the dinge and tile of a SoMa S/M bar by a leatherman.

"Did I say you could kiss me?"

No, he hadn't. He hadn't said anything, not a word, not a command, since the door had closed behind them. Surprisingly, the bathroom had been empty—a fact that she didn't puzzle over until later, when she'd ascribed it to his power as the Ideal Leatherman. He could clear a room just by wanting to use it.

Even though Rosy felt a blossoming of submission within her, she was worried that she didn't have the tools to deal with what was happening. She just had Louise and half a dozen girlfriends behind her. She knew the mechanics of boy-girl sex (what there was of it), and she had a pretty good idea of what could happen to her in the tiny, moderately dirty bathroom, but that didn't mean she knew the first steps to the dance. It had seemed natural to just turn and try and kiss those strong yet soft looking lips.

Quicker than her own pounding heartbeat, he had her long brown hair in one knotted fist, pulling her head back. "Listen, slut, you're mine—you do nothing but what I tell you. Got that?"

She didn't know what to do—fear bubbled up from down deep, and—even more shockingly—anger. A part of Rosy wanted to shake him loose, gut-punch him, and walk proudly out. But another part of her…she was wet. That was it. What was getting to her? Was it his cock? Was it the possibly of a good, old-fashioned (aghast, "straight") fuck? Rosy, surprisingly, was able to look down at herself and answer, "No." So what was it, then—what was it that was making her unprofessional panties so damp?

There it was—simple and straightforward. In a little voice that sent shivers of delight and excitement through her body, she said, "Yes, Sir."

"Good, slut—very good. You're a good slut, aren't you? A hungry slut. You want it, don't you—you need it. You ache for it. Right, slut?"

"Yes, Sir—I do need it."

"Good, because you're going to get it."

One of his slender—yet very strong—hands reached up to her blouse and cupped her right breast. Before she could get ready, his fingers skillfully flicked over the swell until he found her—already hard—nipple. The squeeze was powerful, even though it was partially expected: with a gasp, Rosy gripped his strong arm and felt her knees quickly give way under the wave of pleasure spiced with pain. When her voice returned it was a high squeal: "Yes, Sir."

Again his hand found her hair, again her head was jerked back, but this time rather than his growled displeasure, his thin fingers traced the lines of her tight neck muscles. "Good—very good: Sluts should always recognize themselves."

His other hand found her breasts again. The powerful squeeze brought tears to her eyes. Again strong fingers to her aching—and throbbing—nipples. The pinch this time was even stronger, but somehow controlled: it was a precise generation of pain pushing towards pleasure...or was it the other way around? Mixed up with endorphins of all kinds, Rosy couldn't tell anything, anything at all beyond the burst of sensation—except that she wanted more.

Distantly, she heard buttons hitting tile, metal partitions. Distantly, too, she regretted the loss of the blouse—but not the cause. She arched her body forward, offering him her breasts.

He took what she pushed at him, scooping first the right and then the left free of her business-style bra. Bare to the warm air and the even hotter atmosphere of the bathroom, she groaned from their release and whatever else he was planning for their torment—and her pleasure.

His bite was quick, sudden, shocking, frightening—but, like his fingers, weren't the predatory tearing of a beast. Rather, it was as if his perfect little teeth were being used as precise instruments for the delivery of agony. Just back from the plump nibs of her nipples, he gave her a quick stinging bite before retreating just a little to slowly, ponderously, grind his jaws together. The steady progress of his bite pushed Rosy even farther from the cool tile wall she was leaning against—and increased her grip on the side of the sink she had grabbed for support. The hiss that escaped her lips was like a crack in a boiler—hot, shrill, and unstoppable.

She knew she was wet...no, Rosy was sure that the utilitarian panties under her dress pinks were soaking. She was always like that—a basely primal lover. Rosy was excited, and so her cunt was hungry.

His fingers reached down to push up—hard—her no-nonsense

black skirt. A firm pressure rocketed through her taupe pantyhose right past the pedestrian cotton of her panties. The contact blasted up through her body, a ponderous skyrocket that straightened her spine and escalated the velocity and pitch of her hiss.

A part of her that had been resting just below the surface opened its eyes, changing in an instant from groggy to ravenous.

Something tore, parting under an unstoppable force—his fingers ripping through the pantyhose. Rosy took a breath, expecting the next, waiting for it, wanting it.

As the thin veil of nylon parted, he spoke: "Good, slut—very good. You want it, don't you, slut? You want it bad. You need it, you need it like you never needed anything else in the world. You need this, slut—you need it now...don't you?"

She knew that by the rules she should have answered, opened her mouth and played the role she was supposed to. But Rosy was excited and her cunt was wet—so all that emerged from between her tight lips and clenched teeth was a notch higher on that shrill hiss. Her heart was in the right place, though; in her mind she was The Slut, his slut, his plaything, his toy. "Yes, Sir" might not have escaped her lips, but it echoed loud and clear in her mind.

In the next moment he found out how wet she was—a discovery that changed the timbre of her sounds to a bass purr. She felt his fingers expertly shove aside her damp underwear to find the slick folds of her cunt. Gentle at first, but then with more insistence, he explored her cunt: the plump lips, the tight, slick passage up inside her, the pucker of her asshole, and—deeper purr—the throbbing point of her clit.

There, he stopped—"That's you, slut, that's you right there. That's where you live. Right there, and now I've got you"—and right there he really started. He was more than a leatherman, more than her Master, he was a finger artist. The feelings rushed up through her. Not a skyrocket, no strange little metaphors this time, a simple fact kept ringing through her mind: "My Master's finger on my clit, my Master's finger on my clit." She was right in that magic spot she never realized was deep inside: Rosy the slut, Rosy the toy, Rosy the object of his powerful will.

It happened almost before she was aware it had started: a quivering, shaking body-rush of exaltation that sapped even more strength from her legs as it brought brilliant flashes of light to her eyes and a thundering pulse to her ears. As orgasms went, it was good. Not the best, but there was something else there, a kind of awakening. Not to him, but rather to Him—to her position and his power. It wasn't the sex that blasted through her but rather that she was the receiving end of his strength.

When her legs stopped shaking and she felt she wasn't going to drop down to the cool tiles in a quivering heap, she breathed in, deeply—one, two, three, four—and managed to focus on his smiling (slightly) face.

"There was never a question," he said. "Good slut."

There was something missing, something she had to do. It was part of the ceremony. She knew it was wrong to speak without being spoken to, but she had to complete the act—to place herself firmly in the world to which her leatherman belonged: "Can I suck your cock, Sir?"

"Yes, slut, you may," was his smiling response—and at some subterranean level she sense he was pleased by the eagerness and correctness of her desire.

Cool tiles this time under her knees, torn pantyhose riding up the warm, damp seam of her ass, breasts wobbling, tender nipples grazing the coarser material of her open jacket. There—in front of her, the altar of her leatherman, her leathergod: slick black chaps over too-tight jeans. A bulge of power just inches from her face. "You know what to do, slut," he said from above, thunder from on high.

Actually she hadn't a clue. Vibrators and toys, yes, but never to those other lips. But this was the new Rosy, and this was something she had to do for him—it was part of the rules. Slightly quaking fingers to his fly, a slow, steady inching down. She hoped that he'd help, give her pointers or at least free himself from the jail of his pants. No such luck, though—he stood, a leather statue, above her and didn't move, didn't say a word.

So she had to do it all. Hesitant fingers in through the metal teethed opening, a gentle dig around. Ah, contact—not too soft, not as warm as she expected. A careful pull—not too insistent— feeling the fat head slide up and then, oh yes, out. Out, out, out— her first sight of her Master's dick, her leathergod's cock.

A moment of shocked silence.

A very long moment. Longer than any moment in Rosy's life. A record-setting moment.

It ended with a smile. "It's a wonderful cock, sir," Rosy said, kissing the tip of the long dildo—tasting a little cotton lint and much plastic. "It's fantastic, Sir," she said as she opened her mouth to take the tip in.

As Rosy licked, kissed, and sucked the cock, she let the warmth of what she had discovered fill her: not that she'd been ready, willing, and able to suck a leatherman's cock; not even that she'd realized how much joy there could be in being a powerful figure's plaything, his slut; but that as with her dress pinks, the wrapping conceals as much as it enhances and reveals.

❊   ❊   ❊

Her name was Jackie. She lived in the Mission. She was a musician by choice (which was important), and a word processor out of necessity (which wasn't important). She was also Jack, and Jack was a leather...man, boy, person? Jack was leather, a gravelly tone, and firm commands. Jack was a pair of chaps, a leather vest, a white T-shirt, and a little black leather cap.

Outside, in a light drizzle, they exchanged phone numbers. Before parting—Jack on a throbbing motorcycle and Rosy by cab—they kissed: soft lips and a hesitant but electric touch of tongues. "Another time?" said Rosy.

"For sure," said Jackie.

"Be sure and bring Jack," Rosy said.

"Oh, I will—you just bring the slut."

18

Uniform Night at the Butches' Club Kate Allen

I don't know what to call her at times like this. Not by her name. Her name is for when we are playing girlfriends—for hikes and Scrabble and *Star Trek* and cooking dinner on Friday nights. Her name is for the times we make love without an exchange of power—quickly on late weeknights, leisurely on Sunday mornings. We are versatile, this woman and I. She has lived in my house for five years, and still I don't know what to call her at times like these, when the exchange of power, late in the evening, is so intense and burning that she has to concentrate, with the intensity of a shaman, to contain it. Not "Master," as common among leatherwomen as Smith or Jones. She is anything in the world but common. At times like this I simply think of her as "My Top."

She is with me when I am dressing tonight. It takes me about an hour to get ready by myself. The time is doubled when she is there. Not because she takes me while I am dressing. Far from it—I have not had her dick inside me for several days, which is always the pattern before public play. She likes me wanting. It takes longer because she likes to involve herself in every detail: from the choice of stockings to the selection of earrings. Sometimes she will dress me gently, like a doll, desire sparking between us like an electrical storm. She carefully pulls on my stockings and buckles the ankle straps on my shoes, never once touching my dripping-wet pussy. Other times she simply sits backward in a straight-back chair and watches, ordering me through several changes of clothes and accessories, often coming back to the first. No matter the actual choice of lingerie—and I have drawers full—my cunt and ass are never covered. I am always open and available to her every desire.

Tonight she has brought the outfit she will have me wear. A nurse's uniform, complete with a cap and cape that dates it by as much as 50 years, along with white stockings and a garter belt, suitable for a virgin bride. No nurse, however, ever wore white shoes with such a heel. She is dressed in the uniform of a World War II pilot, complete with bomber jacket and cap.

Regardless of how she has dressed me, the ensemble is always completed with a long, hooded cape of black velvet. The purpose of this cape is two-fold. First, the draping hood that she draws up around my face acts much like blinders, with which ignorant Victorians once tortured their horses. When I am wearing my hood there is no need for a blindfold, eliminating any chance we might be pulled over by a zealous police officer suspecting abduction. Second, the cape is our signal. We are in scene from the moment she places it around my shoulders, just before we leave the house, to the moment she removes it after we return.

After the cape there is one last touch. She brushes back the cape and lifts my skirt. Placing the hem in my hand, she kneels by my side and straps a soft leather sheath she has made especially for me around my gartered thigh. Into the sheath she slides a short dirk, which she gave to me the first time she took me to one of her parties. Antique with a beautiful carved handle, I sometimes fantasize that it has been carried between the breasts of half a dozen beautiful women who might have had the need to protect their honor.

The ride is not long. And though I've been there before, I have no idea where we are when we alight. It is a building without a name and a door without an address. I don't even know if it is rented by the night or if it's a place where these women may come at any time. These women are not our friends, not anyone we will ever invite to dinner or run into at a Christmas party. For all I know they and the building both rise from the shifting sands of the desert once every six months and then are swallowed again the next day. The feeling of mystery, the lack of permanence are essential for me to give myself in the manner which My Top demands. In this building we are in another world.

It is an invitation-only event, and a woman in black awaits inside the door to check our pass and take our coats. Before we reach her My Top halts in the hall and turns me toward her. Taking my face gently in her hands, she speaks.

"You will be the most beautiful woman in the room tonight." This is something she always says no matter where we're going or who will be there. She would say it even if we were going to the Academy Awards, and her conviction would make me believe it. "Don't let anyone touch you."

Although I've been a guest at the Butches' Club a number of times, the theme has always been leather. I've never been present on uniform night. It is a sight to behold. I find my heartbeat quickening, though before this moment I did not realize I have a uniform fetish. Around the buffet table and back as far as I can see in the dim light—they are using only candles in the sconces on the walls tonight—are women clad in crisp creases and ornamented with braid and brass. Flat-topped hats are arranged at a formal angle. Beside us two women in dress blues greet one another with a salute then move apart without exchanging a word.

As my eyes adjust to the light I see not everyone is dressed for a formal parlay. An equal number of women are dressed in battle fatigues, some stripped down to olive drab tank tops with rainbow dog tags hanging between their breasts. It is rather like being at a gathering of the Society for Creative Anachronism—officers from different eras and alliances share a smoke with Rambo types. Clergymen and medics dot the crowd, and I think I see Hawkeye Pierce. I'm reminded of last year's episode of *Voyager*, when the Borg and Klingons mixed with the French Resistance and American troops to fight Hurogeon Nazis on the holideck and no one noticed or commented. I must not be the only one who has made this connection, for the music piping through the sound system is appropriate for a nightclub of that era. Through the smoke I'm sure I see someone dressed as Seven of Nine with a butch attitude in the back corner.

The women are all butch, of course. I know that femmes only come as guests. I don't know how often or if they ever come as anything other than playthings. Like the Resistance, the Butches' Club is on a need-to-know basis and is never to be discussed by My Top or myself outside this room.

Our passage is marked with respectful acknowledgment and appreciative glances, though the former are not directed toward me. My Top, as well as being charming and sexy, has impeccable manners that perfectly match her crisp uniform. We have been stopped in greeting three times. Suddenly, out of nowhere a woman looms up behind me and, before I am able to take in her presence, slaps me heartily on the ass, leaving her hand on me after the slap.

I freeze. No reaction, not even the outrage I feel. "Let no one touch you" does not mean I should create a scene while My Top is standing not a foot from me, as if she could not take care of the problem herself. I look straight ahead with no expression on my face while she turns toward the woman who has slapped me without permission. The woman is young, dressed in Vietnam War-era fatigues. Her face is flushed, as if she's had too many beers from the bar or from the excitement of being at the Butches' Club for the first time. If it is the latter, she had better enjoy it while she can. She is not likely to be asked back.

"Don't touch," says My Top with the gentle authority a foolish woman might take for weakness. She is not one to cause a scene in public, a fact for which I am always grateful. There is nothing more wearing than going out with a butch woman who is always flying in the face of those who look too long. Nor is she a woman to be messed with. At her nod, this silly young thing would be out the door on her ass. "It's not respectful."

Instead of the gracious apology that might get her back on the guest list, the young woman grows even more flushed and blusters. "What—isn't she part of the entertainment? What's the use of having a slut here if you can't touch? Huh? What's the point? I might as well go to a straight strip joint if I want to watch some bitch on a stage!"

It is easy to see who sponsored this woman's entrance. I look around the room at the horrified faces and find the one that is the most horrified and embarrassed. She came with one of the MPs, a dark woman who looks as if she would like to sink through the floor. She has obviously decided that disassociation is the best policy in this case and makes no move to put a restraining arm on her friend. In a moment, no doubt, she will be fading into the crowd.

"You're wrong," says My Top in that gentle, dangerous tone. "About a lot of things. She isn't your bitch, she isn't your slut, she isn't yours to speak of or touch with disrespect. And if you would be happier at a strip joint, I can easily arrange for you to be driven there."

There is a bit more blustering, but no one pays attention. The crowd has simultaneously decided that the best way to handle behavior this poor is to pretend it has not happened. They turn toward one another, the food, the pool table in the same absorbed manner that My Top now shows toward me. Though her head is bent near me, she is watching the young woman in the fatigues and does not speak until she has drifted away.

"Bring us some food, please," she says to me finally, motioning toward the spread laid out next to the bar. "Be your usual charming self."

This last is a code that means she would like to watch me provoke other women to desire. There are nights when she prefers me submissive and I must move from place to place without looking in the face of the other butches. But she likes this equally—watching me turn on a woman, then coming back to her.

The selection of food is abundant, and I pick out the things I know she will like: quiche, succulent fruits, blanched vegetables with dip. Food that will last. The selection of women around the table is just as varied as the food. Officers picking up plates with gloved hands, a cop with handcuffs at her belt, a member of the Confederate Army who is all Southern charm, and the woman in the Seven of Nine outfit. She is arguing with one of the World War II clergymen. Her position is that Seven of Nine is the butchest of butch despite what they want you to believe on TV. She offers to show her big Borg implant to prove it, although we have all already gotten an idea. Those skintight suits leave nothing to the imagination.

The Confederate officer is the obvious target. I charm and flirt and offer her unlimited pleasures without actually saying the words or promising a thing. She is well versed in the dance and completely willing to be used as foreplay. When I feel I have done my job, we part with equally charming smiles and farewells, content with the moment we shared, knowing that passion need not always end in fucking.

By the three purple-felt-covered pool tables My Top is speaking with a woman I've seen before at the Butches' Club. She is tall and heavy and, like My Top, dressed as a flier. A coincidence or were phone calls exchanged? I will never know.

"Hello, Pretty Thing," says My Top, reaching one hand for the food and the other for my elbow. "This is Max. She's going to fuck you tonight. I hope you're ready."

Max is ready immediately, whether I am or not. Her zipper is down and her thick dykecock is in her hand before My Top is through saying the words. I look to My Top for instruction. Although she will allow chosen women to fuck me in her presence, they cannot give me orders. She will not pass over the reins completely.

"Get down on your hands and knees," she tells me.

I move to obey, aware that a little ring is beginning to form around us. Smelling excitement, I begin to position myself with my ass toward Max, but My Top stops me, making a little circle in the air above me with her hand, indicating that I am to turn the other way. I close my eyes for a moment before I obey. She is going to start the scene with a battle.

My Top lowers herself to her knees behind me, lifting the white skirt of my nurse's uniform to my hips. There are appreciative whistles and comments when the women in the crowd see my new, virginal garter belt. After the snap of a latex glove she draws her fingers up across my wet slit; she ends with her thumb putting soft pressure on my asshole.

On her knees in front of my face, Max has sheathed her cock in latex and moves it toward my mouth. Her hands are shaking slightly with excitement, and I can smell her cunt through her jeans.

"Suck it," says My Top, as Max moves it to my mouth. The pressure on my asshole increases, and I give a little shudder as she suddenly shoves two fingers completely inside. Max places the head of the dildo against my lips, and, as I always do, as My Top knows I will do, I turn my head.

This is the one thing she asks that I will not do. The only dick I suck is hers, and she cannot make me suck another's. We have battled over this, she and I. She has beaten me to the point of having to stop the scene herself, as I stubbornly refuse to safeword. She has ordered and punished and—worst of all—not fucked me for almost a whole month in an attempt to break me. She has even asked nicely. But I will not do it, and she cannot make me. Finally, she has decided to accept it for the compliment it is and ceased to try to force me. But she still likes to throw it in now and then to see if new lines have been drawn.

"Suck it," she says again in a low voice, and now I feel the head of her thick dykecock against my ass and know how she is going to attempt—and fail—to force me. I keep my head turned to the side.

There is a signal between the two of them, and Max takes a rough handful of my blonde hair, using it to force my head back. She attempts to open my clenched teeth with a slap, but they stay defiantly together, even though I have to blink back tears.

"Suck it," says My Top just before she shoves the head of her dick into my ass, making me moan through clenched teeth with the pain of invasion. The juice from my pussy has long since become a thing of the imagination, and my asshole burns as she begins to force her cock deeper inside. She moves one hand in front of my eyes, and I see she is holding a tube of K-Y jelly, the lid already flipped open. "Be a good girl and do what you're told," she says in my ear, leaning over me so her leather flight jacket touches my back, "and I'll put some on."

It's all I can do to shake my head no, so concentrated am I on taking the exquisite pain of her cock in my tight, dry fuck hole and twisting it to my own need. Around us women are watching intently, most without speaking, though there is the occasional moan or even a laugh as each imagines herself in one role or the other. On the top, fucking the dry hole of a disobedient bitch; on the bottom, refusing to let that part of who she is become lost in the scene. Moaning, panting through my clenched teeth as if I am about to give birth, I back myself suddenly up to My Top, taking the whole length of the cock with which she thinks she can force my submission. Moving so wildly that Max abandons any attempt to force my mouth, I begin riding her dick with my tight, dry hole, forcing it in deeper and harder than she would ever make me take it herself. This is the way I will negate her punishment—by taking it and making it mine as if it were pleasure. I cannot disguise the grunts of pain as pleasure, however, nor can I stop the tears that have begun to roll down my cheeks as I use her dick to rend my hot, nasty hole.

"Enough!" Suddenly it is her hand in my hair, pulling me back up off my hands so that my head is against her mouth. She speaks into my ear. "Don't you dare damage what's mine. If I have to pull my cock out because there's blood, I swear to god I am going to string you up and beat you back and blue for a week without ever touching your pussy!"

My mouth away from Max's cock, I am compliant. "My ass is yours," I murmur. "Use it as you wish. Stretch it, fuck it. Wet or dry."

"Oh, I'm going to," she promises, still in my ear. "I or my friends. You are a bitch who needs to be taught a lesson tonight." Still, as she releases me she is smiling, and as she pulls her dick out of my ass she says for the crowd, "Oh, my baby knows just when to say no, doesn't she? Daddy wouldn't be happy with another butch's dick in her mouth, would she?"

I shake my head no with my head down, trying to appear submissive rather than triumphant. The feel of her pulling her dry cock out of my ass was so intense that for a moment all I can concentrate on is the void and the pain, so I miss the negotiation above me. All I know is that I have been suddenly pulled to my feet and pointed toward the nearest pool table.

"Make yourself available," My Top says in an even voice, as if she were asking me to hand her the paper or put less peppers in the chili. A reasonable, everyday request. Except that this one means give yourself over into my hands, let me control your pain and pleasure for my own desire. Make me wet by the way that you spread your most intimate places for my use, whether I choose to enter you directly or through another. Show me you are mine.

She does not have to tell me she wants me face-down. I know she considers doing it from the back the nasty fuck, the way a whore presents herself, all swollen lips and open holes without a face. Just as I will not suck another woman's dick, she will not allow any other woman to fuck me face-to-face. I arrange myself bent over the table, my legs spread to open my fuck holes, my skirt still up over my hips.

I cannot believe what happens next. The crowd has followed and picked up members, now arranged in a loose half circle around the end of the pool table as they wait eagerly to see how I will next be used. Excited by the scene, several couples and small groups have broken off into butch-on-butch play. I don't really understand butch-on-butch, but it still excites me. Off to the side, the woman in the Seven of Nine outfit is shoving her big Borg implant into the eager mouth of the police officer, whose hands have been secured behind her with her own cuffs. She is much more compliant than I; Seven of Nine is fucking her mouth with long strokes that must be hitting the back of her throat. If I lift my head forward, I can see another woman bent over the next table in line in exactly the same position as I, her pants down, her legs spread. The sight makes my already dripping pussy give a sudden gush.

Then, out of the crowd like a bad dream, the Rambo girl with the bad behavior suddenly reappears. Like 90% of the crowd, she is packing. I know this because she thrusts herself between my legs and up against my ass so quickly that I can't get out of the way, and I can feel the hardness against me.

For a moment no one moves, as if they have taken a collective gasp and not yet released it. Heads are swiveling as the watchers try to locate My Top. A few butches I recognize from other visits as friends take a hesitant step forward as if considering intervention.

They never have the chance. I am tired of this woman, tired of her interruption and bad manners and determination not to learn the ways of the society that surrounds her. She pulls back for a moment, fumbling with her fly, and this is all the room that I need to flip over on my back, graceful as a dancer. One foot flat on her gut, I reach up to grab the collar of her shirt, pulling her down against me. With the other hand I find the thigh sheath and pull out the dirk. I do not put the blade against her exposed neck but move my hand to where she can see it.

"Don't touch me," I say to her through clenched teeth, barely above a whisper, my most dangerous voice. This woman might be a fool, but even she can't fail to hear the barely controlled venom and rage. "She said it and now I'm saying it. Don't touch me. Don't make me use this. No one will stop me if I start. They have a place in the woods where they bury girls like you, and they dig a new hole every time they know I'm coming. Just in case it gets out of hand…again."

All of this, of course, is spur-of-the-moment bullshit. I'm good at that. In reality, I have never used this knife for anything but paring apples, and I would never cut anyone nonconsensually unless I actually thought my life was in danger. But this young woman does not know that. She does not know it, and I can tell from the quickness of her breath and the sudden dilation of her eyes that she believes at least part of what I am saying.

We stay together, face to face for a moment with the stillness of tableaux. Then I release her collar, and as she straightens, I give her a hard thrust with my foot that sends her windmilling back into the crowd. I turn back face down without waiting to see what becomes of her. She has gone beyond the tolerance afforded a newcomer; someone will no doubt escort her to the door.

Although this has taken place in less than a minute, while still up I spotted My Top in the crowd, arms crossed, a grin on her face. She likes a feisty femme, and for a moment I wonder if the young woman was all part of the plan—another prop in the long evening in scene. I probably won't ever know that either.

"Good girl," she says in my ear, suddenly bending over me. She strokes my wet cunt with one hand as she whispers to me. "God, you're so beautiful. So sexy. What would you like for a reward, my pretty one?"

"The chance to please you," I reply, and it is not just a stock answer. That truly is my greatest desire and she knows it. This is the thing that makes it so hot between us: that true desire.

"Then I have to see it nasty, my darling. I see my dear, sweet, thoughtful Love all week long—tonight I want to watch you take it like a whore. Reach back and spread yourself for me. I want everyone to be able to see your beautiful, hot holes. It will give them incentive."

She steps back as I reach back to obey, and once I hear a collective intake of breath. I could come at this point just from being the focus of such desire.

There is movement to the side of me, and when I turn my head I see that someone has moved a small table and two chairs beside the pool table. My Top seats herself in one, placing her elbow on the table, her hand spread. The first woman, a Navy SEAL, steps up and seats herself in the other chair. They grasp hands and without a word begin to arm wrestle. It is not much of a challenge. This is something at which My Top is very, very good. The SEAL's hand is slammed to the table within a few moments, and the next woman steps up. My Top gestures for her to sit but raises a finger to indicate "just a moment." She sets her toy bag on the table beside me, unzips it, and takes out one of her favorite toys, a butt plug with both vibrating and pumping action. She slides it into my ass with a generous glob of lube and turns on the vibrator.

The next woman is sent from the table in disgrace, as is the next and the next. With each win, My Top gives one pump to the butt plug, making it grow wider and wider inside me.

By the fifth woman, however, she is growing tired. And this woman is both big and strong. The struggle is silent, but the crowd is not. Everyone, it seems, would like to watch this woman put her cock inside me. Cheering, then jeering as inch by inch My Top's hand is pressed to the table. She stands graciously, indicating with a hand my cunt, which I am still spreading open. The other butch, who appears to be a Texas Ranger, steps between my legs, spurs jangling.

There is no foreplay. She is ready and so am I. Hell, everyone in the room is ready. Her pants are unzipped before I can draw a breath, and her cock is in my cunt before I can draw another. She enters with one smooth, hard thrust that raises me to my toes and then pulls all the way out to do it again.

The feel of her thick dykecock stretching my pussy up against the vibrating butt plug forces a scream from me. I could come immediately. Instead, I try to concentrate on other things. The Gettysburg Address. Multiplication tables. My Top loves to watch me being gang-banged, but she will be very displeased if I come with any cock inside me but her own.

The wrestling begins again, but not until My Top has given the butt plug another pump, forcing another scream. I cannot watch the match. All my concentration is focused on not coming from the punishing fucking.

The next match is over. I know because suddenly the Texas Ranger withdraws, and a new woman is behind me. As I try to calm myself I hear the snap of a glove. I am well-stretched, and she shoves in four fingers easily. Working her hand into a fist takes a little more time, particularly since My Top has given the butt plug another pump. My cunt feels stretched to its limit by the time she has forced a fist and begins to pump me. It is a relief when the next woman steps up for her turn, even when I realize she is going to use my ass. She pulls the plug free without deflating it, forcing another scream. My asshole does not even have time to close completely before she has her dick inside, fucking with the same hard, savage thrusts her predecessor used on my pussy. I am starting to lose control, wondering if I will be able to save my come for My Top. The feel of the fucking switching from cunt to ass every few minutes as the women take their turns is pushing me toward the edge.

In an attempt to seek distraction I look again at the woman bent over the other pool table. The woman fucking her has knelt between her legs and is burying her fist in her cunt. The butch bottom is pounding her fists on the pool table as if she were playing a drum. My own cunt clenches in sympathy as I watch, mesmerized.

A cheer from the crowd signals changing of the guard. The thick butchdick is pulled suddenly from my ass, just in time to stop me from coming. Thank god, I think, then give another gasp when I feel the heads of a double-pronged dildo push into both holes at once.

Seeking respite from the brutal double fucking of my cunt and ass, I look again at the butch on the table in front of me. There too they are changing the guard, and I suddenly realize that the women who have been fucking me are passing directly to this woman. I feel an even more intense rush when I realize this. Watching her is obviously not the thing to do if I truly want to calm down. In fact, I am not sure if there is anything I can do to calm down at this point. The feel of a hard dykecock pumping deep in both fuck holes at once is too much to stand. I am slapping the table myself, babbling as I try to turn my head to locate My Top. I am going to come soon, and it is not going to be a come I can disguise.

There is a sudden commotion behind me, so loud and unexpected that even the woman pumping me pauses. Above the raised voices I hear one louder and clearer than the others.

"Oh, shit!" says the doorkeeper. "Cops!"

To be continued.

19

House Arrest J.L. Belrose

She's getting dressed in the predawn light, and I'm cuddled naked under a jumble of sheet and comforter, watching. This is forbidden pleasure, seeing her naked, seeing her vulnerable. I'm supposed to be sleeping. I curl my toes, giddy with naughtiness, and squint through the gray light suffusing the room from the semi-draped window behind me.

She's short, this woman I adore. Short and wide and strong, built to withstand hurricanes. Her legs are pillars, her butt cheeks pale, dimpled boulders. Her breasts, their large brown areolas tucked under, hang to her mound of belly. She's a force, this woman I love. A force you don't mess with. When she walks, all snap and polish, down a street or enters a room, people notice. They take it in, then look away. But they don't forget she's around. A force to be reckoned with.

They don't know, like I do, how soft she is, how fragile, bending naked in the gray light, rummaging through the dresser drawers, selecting her socks and underwear from my neatly folded rows. She closes the drawer that always squeaks, pushes it in slow and carefully, tries not to wake me, lets me sleep till noon. Every day till noon.

I'd roused when her weight had left the mattress, rocking me out of slumber, and had snuggled deeper into the blankets, inhaling for any scent she'd left. Drowsily I'd reminisced while she had her shower. I'd parked illegally and she'd swaggered over, that's how we'd met. Frazzled by missed appointments, sweltering under a summer sun shimmering off city pavement, I'd crinkled into tears as she wrote the ticket. "There's no sign," I'd whimpered.

She'd pushed her cap back with her pen and had pointed to a place directly above my head. That's when I'd noticed, really noticed, the cap with its shiny black visor and badge, the black tie, the sharply pressed blue cotton short-sleeved shirt, the crested epaulettes, the black leather belt with its silver buckle, the gray serge trousers creased just so, and the shiny black boots. Then I'd refocused on her face. Staring into the dark, unfathomable shades protecting her eyes, I'd seen only myself mirrored back and had yowled again. It wasn't fair. I was sweaty and late and horny and lonely and getting a ticket that would separate me from 90 hard-earned bucks.

Five days later I'd found myself in the same predicament. Again there'd been nowhere else to park. Not when rain was pissing down to ruin my hair if I parked miles away somewhere on the lot. And anyway, I only needed five minutes. The modeling agency I was threatening to sue was at that corner of the mall. They'd gouged me for photos, and the only work they'd found me was two weeks in a pet store—in a bikini with ruffles on my wrists, ruffles on my ankles, wearing a wig that was supposed to make me look like a French poodle—handing out dog food samples.

She told me later she'd thought I was strung out on something the first time, the way I'd whined and wailed and carried on, but the second time she'd figured I was just an airhead. I'd let her know how much I resented being stereotyped like that. Just because I'm a model, and blonde, not even natural, doesn't mean I'm a ditz. I'd had a good reason for being agitated that second time. I'd found an out-of-business sign on the agency's door, and they still had in their possession all the photos I'd already paid for.

Even so, distracted as I was, as she wrote that second ticket I noticed how the rain had dotted her shirt and jeweled the slick black visor on her cap. I'd gotten fixated on her hands too, the thick stubby fingers, the rectangles of nail filed down to the pink. She'd pocketed her shades, and I'd seen her eyes for the first time. Gray eyes. I'd sucked up my tears and tumbled flat into love. Her shirt, I couldn't help noticing, was dampened perfect for ironing.

She sits on the chair beside the dresser, pulls one regulation-black sock over her foot, stretches it up her calf. Peeking from my foxhole of blanket, I chew a corner of sheet as I glimpse the sparse hair of her bush, wiry and brown between her legs, the untouchable center of it buried in shadow, unreachable in the dim light to even my grop-ing, covetous eyes. She toes into the other sock, smooths it upward. Through slitted eyelids feigning sleep, I watch as she pokes her feet through the jockeys, lifts them to her knees and stands, drawing them up to fit them over her butt and belly.

I suck my corner of sheet as she struggles with the size-too-small spandex T-shirt. Her breasts, downturned nipples inverted, wobble as she works the shirt on over her shoulders. I adore her. In moments like these, *adore* is the only word that encompasses the love and respect and tenderness and awe and gratitude I feel for her as she adjusts the shirt, flattening, down over her chest. Armored now, she glances at me, reassures herself I'm sleeping, then ambles to the kitchen for her second cup of coffee.

I drag my pillow in against me, hug it, scissor my legs around it. I hadn't stalked her. Not really. Waiting for her on the corner, cruis-ing the mall for her, four days in a row, with Second Cup coffee and chocolate chip cookies in a paper bag, isn't stalking. But when she laid the charge, I didn't protest. And when she arrested me I didn't resist. "Is this a life sentence?" I'd asked when she'd escorted me handcuffed into her house, locking the door behind us. "There's time off," she'd said, "for good behavior." But I haven't earned any yet. There aren't many rules, but I somehow manage to break them.

She comes back, sipping coffee from her rainbow mug as she pads across the room. She sets the mug on the dresser, then opens the closet, lifts out a hanger, the fresh blue shirt glimmering in the morning's intensifying light. I tingle as she inspects it. A loose button, a stray thread, a crease, will be considered a serious dereliction of my duties. It passes inspection and she slips it on, buttons it, the fabric fitting snug, but not too snug, across her flattened chest.

I squirm into my pillow as she inspects the trousers. I've let them out half an inch. I'm wondering if she'll notice, if the work will please her. I float with relief as, satisfied, she steps into them, pulls them up. She leaves the fly gaped open, belly bulging, as she sits and inserts her feet into the boots I polish every night, scrubbing even the soles, every night polishing the gleaming leather, breathing in the sweet scent of her feet and polish and leather, every night.

My breasts, pressed to my pillow, ache. I bite my lip. She hasn't made many rules, but the one she enforces most stringently is the one I break most often. I'm not supposed to touch myself without first getting permission. But when she picks up her belt, slides the black leather through her hand, then threads it through the loops on her trousers, my hand burrows down between my body and the pillow, drawn to the wetness between my legs. I'm a very bad girl, touching myself without permission again. I'm incorrigible.

I nudge my clit, not daring to watch as she reaches for her tie, not trusting myself to not cry out and give the game away, knowing how she lifts her collar, lays the tie just so around her neck, knots it, adjusts for length, smooths it down. I stroke myself, barely moving, eyes closed so when she checks, as she always does before she leaves, she'll see me sleeping, smiling sweetly in my sleep, dreaming of her.

When I wake again around noon I find the ticket, one of the

special tickets she's had printed on a lavender card just for me. It's taped to the headboard. Infraction, it says in bold type. Infraction, followed by a colon, and scribbled in after the colon, Moving Violation—Masturbation Without Permission. And at the top, the date and time. I yank the covers up over my head and howl. It's not fair. I always get caught.

I work extra hard all afternoon, swirling fabric, sewing machine whirring. One of a Kind Fashions, that's my business, our living room, my studio. I have business cards too. She hands them out to special people. Unique designs for unique people, the cards say. Every creation a guaranteed original. It was her idea. "You're one of a kind," she said when she saw my sketches. "You're wasting your time parading other people's clothes. You should be designing your own."

"What kind of machine do you want?" she'd asked, and had bought me the best, the very best, the most expensive one, the one I was afraid to ask for.

But, of course, her uniform comes first. Before anything else I launder her shirt from the day before, check all the buttons, examine her trousers for any spot, press in the crease. When she comes home she lifts her cap off, hands it to me. With a soft damp cloth I wipe around the inside band, then brush the outside, polish the visor and, lastly, the badge. I don't care that it's just a private agency she works for, a company hired by the property owners to patrol their mall, the logo on the badge an eagle's wings spread beneath the motto, "Always Alert."

I wait for her boots. When she keeps them on I know it's because there's a serious matter to deal with. My latest ticket. She's troubled. "What should I do with you?" she asks me, exasperated.

"I was sleeping," I say. "Dreaming about you made me do it." I stare down at her boots, and already I'm wanting her touch, her discipline. I change my plea. "I'm guilty," I say, "guilty as charged." I should be punished.

She undoes her belt, undoes the waistband of her trousers, easing the constriction on her stomach. She strolls to the fridge, opens it and hangs there, peering inside, thinking. The jury is out. She's deliberating on whether to have a baloney sandwich, but also on my punishment. I walk up behind her, close my arms around her, my long, thin arms wrapping her girth. I bow my head, rest it on her shoulder, turn my face into her neck. "I should be spanked," I tell her, wiggling my tongue into her ear.

I watch her eat, always mesmerized by how much she enjoys her food. I nibble lettuce, a whole tomato, a carrot, a finger of cheese, and half a slice of bread to please her. I've promised to gain ten pounds to please her, and also because she sometimes holds me as if I might break, sometimes complains about my bony ass. I eat pizza now, even the crust, not just pieces off the top. Four and a half more pounds and that will be ten. Maybe then she'll spank me without complaining how my bony ass hurts her hand, hurts her more than it hurts me.

She hoists from her chair, takes her plate and mug to the sink. I follow, reaching out to run a fingertip along the hard black leather of her belt. I hesitate at the open buckle, hook my finger into the metal mouth, give it a playful tug, then back off, pouting.

"How many," she asks, "how many strokes do you deserve?" I think this over, trying to judge her mood. Sometimes she doubles it, but sometimes she halves it, and sometimes, if I'm too greedy, she changes her mind completely and denies me. "Four," I decide, playing it safe.

She pretends outrage. "Four? Only four? I suppose you think I'm going to double it. I should, you know. You're a repeat offender. I should double it every time."

I chew my lip in anticipation. I try to look worried, but not too worried. Worried enough to keep her interested, but not worried enough to make her soften. I know I won't get eight. It's too much to hope for. I've never had eight from her before. Her strong, thick hand closes over the buckle and she draws the belt free from its loops. She runs the length through her hand, flexes and snaps it. Electric current buzzes down my spine, forks into my nipples, circuits through my clit.

I would kneel and kiss her boots, but I'm not allowed to, not while she wears them. She doesn't know what I do when she does-n't see me, every night, when I polish them. It's my secret. My secret too how I sometimes touch the cool smooth edge of her belt buckle to my clit.

"Lift your skirt," she says. "Pull down your panties." I don't need to be told, but I wait for the order so I can be seen to obey. It's a balancing act, this give and take. Who's giving, who's taking? I don't analyze.

"Are you happy?" she asked me once.

"Yes," I said, "I'm happy."

I bend over the kitchen table still scattered with crumbs from her sandwich. I rest on my forearms, hands crossed, forehead placed upon the back of the uppermost hand. She fusses with my skirt, set-ting it just so up over my back. This is our ballet, this teasing, this testing. She slides her hand over my ass-cheek, on down my leg, slips back up my inner thigh, brushes my pussy, follows up along my ass crack, sweeps over to the other cheek, back to my pussy, till I'm on my toes dancing. "Stand still," she says.

Thwack. I flinch more from the noise than from the strike which is not quite hard enough to sting. She stops at four, lays the belt on the table beside my arm, then caresses my buttocks again, pausing whenever she finds a particular bone or spot she thinks needs clos-er examination. I gasp when her finger pushes into my cunt, strong and thick, circles tormentingly just inside my opening. I clench, open, clench again, trying to suck her deeper. Her thumb centers on my asshole. "Yes," I tell her as she probes, teasing my sphincter. I reach out blindly across the table, find her belt, clasp it and pull it in under me.

I whimper, want to howl, when her hand leaves me empty, leaves me aching. But then she kneels in behind me, under me, her tongue licks at me, massages forward over my clit. Her hands pinion my hips, anchor me to her mouth as I clutch the belt, biting the leather while she eats at me, lapping my girlcum as I come for her, and come and come.

I free-fall into a tranquil place as she kisses the backs of my knees, trails a warm, silky tongue up my leg, nips at my butt. She struggles to her feet, then straightens my skirt down, guides me into her arms, and holds me. But I rest only a moment before I ease away. I examine the belt until I find the place, the faint indentations my teeth have made in the leather. I get my kit.

She lowers onto a chair, pulls off her boots, as I spread my equipment on the table: my brushes, my cloths, my polish, my oil, my lamb's wool for buffing. She yawns, plods to the bedroom, the bathroom, leaving her boots for me as I begin my ministrations on the belt.

She's still awake as I lift blankets and sheet, and twine my long legs and arms into bed around her. There's something I have to tell her, but first I say, "I did up the moss-green satin today for Mrs. Dodson. It came out well. I think she'll be pleased." Mrs. Dodson is an important client, her boss's mother.

"Mmmmm," she thrums and turns onto her side, back to me, positioning herself for sleep.

"They had that same fabric in a gorgeous cobalt blue too. I'd like to get some," I tell her, talking into the darkness, edging toward my confession.

She's silent a moment, then rouses to say, "I suppose that means you want another day pass."

"No, I've got a pass left over from yesterday," I say, and snuggle up against her back, press into her warmth, connect myself down the full length of her.

She's quiet but I feel her more alert, thinking. I wait, staring out over the bulk of her shoulder, out through the gauze of curtain, out at the full-bellied moon, until she asks, "Do you need more money?"

"No," I say, then bite my lip. I've stonewalled as long as I can, my only option now is to confess, then beg for mercy. I whisper into her neck, "I need transportation."

I feel her shoulders tighten. "What's wrong with your car?"

Trying hard not to bawl, I say, "You know that tow-away zone near the fabric outlet store?"

Contributors

Kate Allen lives in Denver, with three cats and the butch of her dreams, where she divides her time between writing and much more boring work that actually pays. She is the author of the popular Alison Kaine mystery series (New Victoria Publishers). You can see more of her work at www.users.uswest.net/~kateallen.

J.L. Belrose, born in Toronto, Canada, attended the Ontario College of Art and Design, then traveled, living and working in London and Paris. She's now settled near Blue Mountain in Ontario and works with stained glass. Her fiction and poetry have appeared in multiple issues of *Lezzie Smut, Siren, Quota,* and the *Church-Wellesley Review* as well as the *Toronto Star*, the *Queer View Mirror* anthology, and the Alyson anthologies *Skin Deep* and *Pillow Talk II*. She just completed her first novel.

Cara Bruce is a senior editor at *GettingIt* (www.gettingit.com) and editor of the erotic e-zine *Venus or Vixen?* (www.venusorvixen.com). Her short stories have appeared in *The Unmade Bed* and

The Oy of Sex. She is also the editor of the bizarre erotic compilation *Viscera*.

More of *M. Christian's* work can be seen in *Best American Erotica, Best Gay Erotica, Friction, The Mammoth Book of Short Erotic Novels, Men for All Seasons, Bar Stories, Erotic New Orleans, Viscera, Desires,* and in more than 100 other books and magazines. He is the editor of the anthologies *Eros Ex Machina, Midsummer Night's Dreams, Guilty Pleasures, The Burning Pen* (Alyson), and (with Simon Sheppard) *Rough Stuff: Tales of Gay Men, Sex and Power* (Alyson). A collection of his erotic short stories, *Dirty Words*, is forthcoming (also from Alyson).

Suzanne Corson is a bookseller in the Berkeley, Calif., area. She has been published in *Feminist Bookstore News*. Suzanne and her partner, Mychaelyn, live in El Cerrito, Calif., with their furry and aquatic companions.

Lauren Dockett lives in San Francisco, a city with an underwhelming number of fast food joints. She is the coauthor of *Facing 30: Women Talk About Constructing a Real Life and Other Scary Rites of Passage*, and a freelancer for the Berkeley-based *East Bay Express*. Her book on women and depression will be out in spring 2001.

Linnea Due is the author of three novels and the nonfiction book *Joining the Tribe* as well as the editor of *Hot Ticket* and coeditor of *Dagger*. She is a writer and senior editor at an alternative newspaper in Berkeley, Calif.

Nicole Foster is the editor of the best-selling anthologies *Awakening the Virgin, Electric: Best Lesbian Erotic Fiction*, and *Skin Deep: Real-life Lesbian Sex Stories*. She lives in Los Angeles.

Jane Futcher's stories and essays have appeared in *Hot Ticket, Dyke Life, Lesbian Friendships, How We Work, Heatwave, Bushfire, Afterglow, The Next Step, Lesbian Adventure Stories*, and *Mom*. She is the author of three novels (*Crush, Dream Lover,* and *Promise Not to Tell*) and is a reporter at a newspaper in Marin County, Calif.

Ellen Golden is a detective and writer who lives near San Francisco.

Lou Hill, now retired from the military, lives with her partner, their son, and a house full of animals. Her short stories have appeared in *Early Embraces, Beginnings, Awakening the Virgin, Wilma Loves Betty, Skin Deep,* and *Hot and Bothered 2.*

E.D. Kaufman lives in Oakland, Calif., with her partner, two step-kids, two dogs, and a cat in a tiny house at the edge of a danger-ous freeway off-ramp. She is working on three novels, a book of short stories, and a survival guide for lesbian stepparents. She earned a bachelor's degree in theater from UC Berkeley and an MFA in fiction writing from Mills College.

Paula Neves lives and writes in central New Jersey. Her work has appeared in *Early Embraces, All the Ways Home, The Body of Love, The Poetry of Sex*, and numerous other publications. She loves to eat and she loves women, so those cafeteria ladies will always hold a special place in her heart.

J.M. Redmann has written four novels, all featuring New Orleans private detective Michele "Micky" Knight. The most recent of these, *Lost Daughters,* was published by W.W. Norton in summer 1999. Her third book, *The Intersection of Law & Desire,* won a Lambda Literary Award. A Mississippi native, Ms. Redmann now lives, works, and frolics in that city-in-a-swamp, New Orleans.

Thomas S. Roche's short stories have appeared in a wide variety of magazines and anthologies, including *Blue Blood, Black Sheets, Honcho, Inches, Pucker Up, Torso,* the *Best American Erotica* series, and *Best Gay Erotica 1996*. He recently completed his first novel, *Violent Angel*.

Cecilia Tan is a writer, editor, and sexuality activist. Her erotic fiction has appeared in *Penthouse* and *Ms.* magazine, in *Best American Erotica, Best Lesbian Erotica, Hot & Bothered, Herotica 3-6,* and many other places. Twenty-three of her erotic stories are collected in the book *Black Feathers,* published in 1998 by HarperCollins. And, yes, she really did play the sousaphone.

Felicia Von Bot (formerly the artist known as Von Botchinova in her remote village of Smithville) has written several short stories, including the parody "Renegades of the Coral Dawn." Though just a tad exaggerated, "Judge Benko's Decision" is based on a true story. Of course, the names and places have been changed to protect the good, the bad, the compulsives, and the fantasy-challenged.

Yolanda Wallace is not a professional writer but plays one in her spare time. She has written dozens of short stories but is still revising her version of the great American novel. She will spend her next hot Georgia summer on the lookout for a tall woman in a silver BMW.